I0760572

EAST
70

CHAOS

K. LORAINE

USA TODAY BESTSELLING AUTHORS

MEG ANNE

This book is a work of fiction. The names, characters, places, and incidents are products of the author's imagination or have been used fictitiously and are not to be construed as real. Any resemblance to persons, living or dead, actual events, locales, or organizations is entirely coincidental.

ISBN:

978-1-961742-49-9 (Paperback Edition)

978-1-961742-50-5 (Hardback Edition)

No artificial intelligence was used in the creation of this work of fiction.

Edited by Mo Sytsma of Comma Sutra Editorial

Cover Design by CReya-tive Book Design

Photographer: Wander Aguiar

Model: James R.

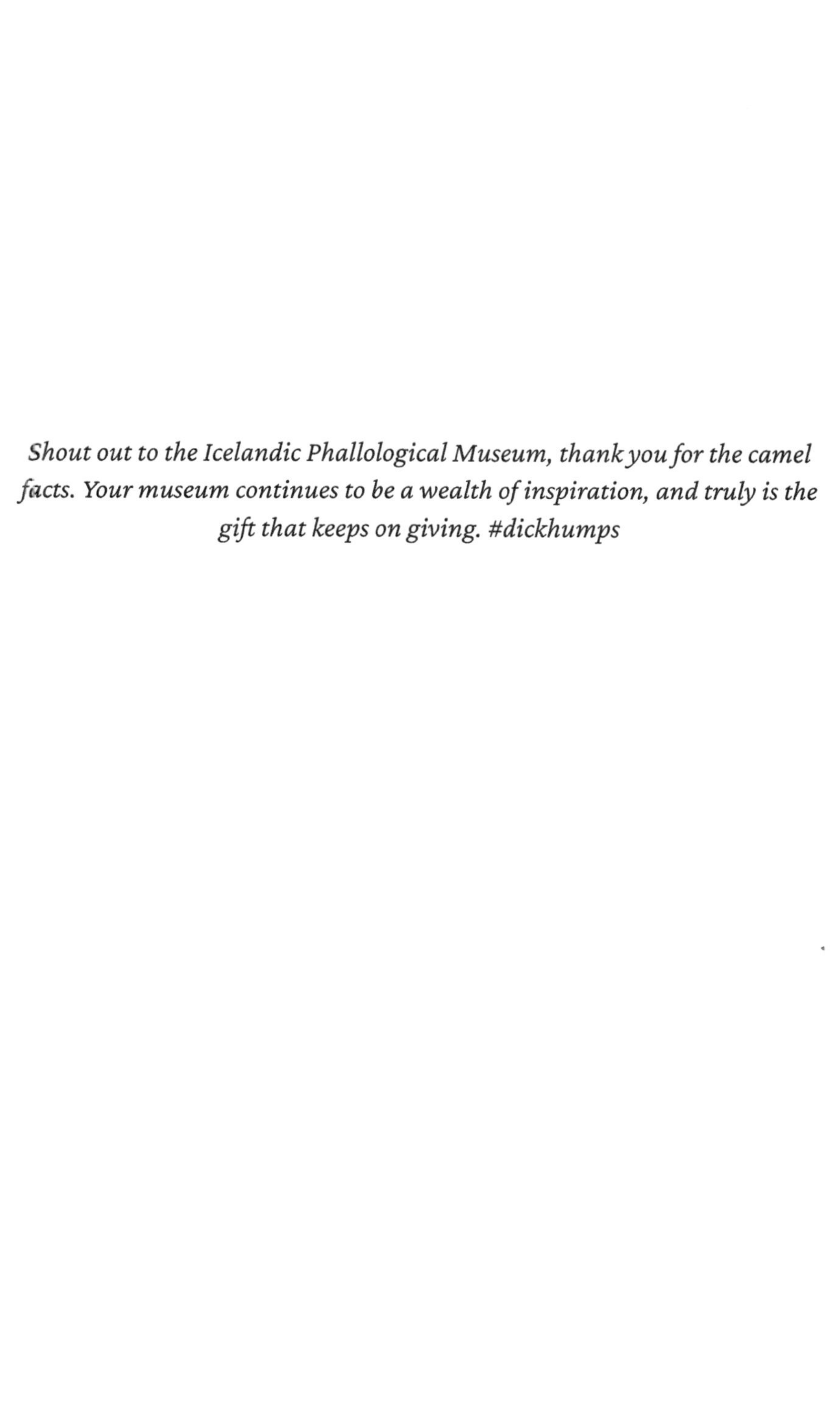

Shout out to the Icelandic Phallological Museum, thank you for the camel facts. Your museum continues to be a wealth of inspiration, and truly is the gift that keeps on giving. #dickhumps

"The world will know that free men stood against a tyrant, that few stood against many, and before this battle was over, even a god-king can bleed."

—KING LEONIDAS, 300

CHAOS

AUTHORS' NOTE

Chaos contains mature and graphic content that is not suitable for all audiences. Such content includes scenes of dubious consent, sex work, role playing, disasters and more. **Reader discretion is advised.**

As always, a detailed list of content and trigger warnings is available on our website.

OPERATION PFFN SUPER SECRET VIDEO CORRESPONDENCE: #4

Static screen blinks to life. Asher Henry appears in the camera shot, looking worse for wear. He rubs the back of his neck, sighs, and then squeezes the bridge of his nose before returning his attention to the camera.

<<static>>

Asher: *heavy sigh* So . . . here we are again. I know you weren't expecting a message from me so soon, but it's imperative we reach the archangel Gabriel as soon as possible. I've put out my bat signal, and he hasn't answered.

Asher shifts uncomfortably in his seat.

<<rustling clothes>>

Asher: As challenging as the guy can be, all of us care about what happens to him, and we really fucking need his help. So I'm really hoping his silence isn't because something bad has happened.

Asher glances away, biting down on his lower lip as a flicker of concern flashes across his face. He stares in the distance for a beat before giving himself a shake and looking back at the camera.

Asher: If anyone has eyes or ears on the Messenger, please pass on a message of our own.

Asher stares imploringly into the camera.

Asher: Gabriel, if you are receiving our messages and choosing to ignore them out of some misplaced attempt not to get involved, it's too late for that. You've been involved since day one. You know it, and so does everyone else. We need you. This is the literal end of the world. If there was any time to break the rules, this wou—

<<door slams open>>

Asher: What the fu—

Caleb: It's worse than we thought.

Caleb Gallagher, Kingston Farrell, Bentley Mercer, and Kai Nash pour into the room, surrounding Asher and shoving a piece of paper in his face.

<<sound of multiple footsteps>>
<<rustling of clothes and paper>>

Kingston: Perfect, you're already recording. We need everyone to hear this.

Asher: What am I looking at?

Ben: Th-the ch-chalice is a p-person.

Asher: What are you talking about?

Caleb: The prophecy that Pan translated. "Lucifer shall possess the chalice" . . .

Asher: Right, I'm with you now.

Caleb: Well, Pan was able to decipher more, and that's when he realized that the chalice is not an object but a person.

Asher: Possession? Again? Fucking great.

Kai: Not like that. He's after a child.

Asher: He's going to possess a child?

Kai: *frustrated growl* What part of 'not like that' are you having trouble understanding? He doesn't want to possess a child, you idjit. He wants to use one. Like a tool.

Caleb waves the piece of paper.

<<sound of rustling paper>>

Caleb: A child is the key.

Kingston: I thought we were done with this 'children as harbingers' nonsense after we dealt with War.

Asher snatches the paper from Caleb's hand.

<<sound of rustling paper>>

Asher: Give me that.

Asher stares down at the translation, brow furrowing and lips moving as he talks softly beneath his breath.

Asher: (mutters) A child. There are three already on the way. Fuck. Is it one of them?

Kai: Four.

Asher looks at Kai.

Asher: Four?

Kai: Dahlia's pregnant. We only just found out.

Kingston: Bingo!

Caleb: What the hell are you on about now?

Kingston: Well, that's three for three on the women of the Mate Games getting knocked up. Feels like we should get a prize.

Caleb: That's it. You aren't allowed to spend any more time with Remi. You're starting to sound too much like him.

Asher: Three for three? This can't be a coincidence.

Ben: I-it certainly d-doesn't s-sound good.

Kai: I don't care who he is. That bastard isn't laying a finger on my child.

Ben: M-mine either.

Kingston: Agreed. Obviously. The stakes just got even higher in my world. We need extra protection on our women. No one gets close. Not without our approval.

Asher remains quiet, gazing off into the distance.

Asher: What if it's not one of ours?

Kingston: One of our what?

Asher: Children.

Caleb: You think there's another one?

Asher shrugs, still looking thoughtful.

<<drums fingers on coffee table>>

Asher: We've already said that there's another group out there that needs to be found. What's the over/under that it's their baby?

Caleb: I don't like it, but you're not wrong. There's no way we can control that if we don't find them.

Kai stands, eyes glowing purple, expression fierce.

<<clothes rustling>>

Kai: *low growl* That's not a risk I'm willing to take. Until we know for sure, I'm treating this as a threat to my mate. In fact, I'm leaving for Faerie tonight. We need as many fae warriors protecting our women as possible.

Kingston: The pack is already patrolling the woods. I'll let them know the fae are coming.

Ben nods sharply.

Ben: N-no one threatens our f-families and l-lives.

Kingston claps him on the shoulder.

<<sound of hand hitting shoulder>>

Kingston: Spoken like a true alpha. You sure you don't want to join the pack?

Ben: N-no th-thanks. Remi and I s-sort of prefer b-being on our own. L-less people t-to answer to.

Kingston: Fair enough, but the offer's open. You're family, so you have a pack whether you want one or not.

Asher looks at Caleb and hands him the paper.

<<paper rustling>>

Asher: Tell Pan he did a great job. This is really good information, but we need more.

Caleb: Why do you think he's not in here with us right now? He's working on it. If we discover who wrote the fecking book, that will go a long way towards us getting an accurate translation.

Asher: Why does that matter? It was written, what, a couple thousand years ago?

Caleb: Knowing the author gives us context. Context will help us be more accurate with the translation. It's like with your computer writing.

Asher: Coding.

Caleb: Whatever. The language you use is specific to you and your style. Your preferences, the time in which you live. Same with whoever wrote the book.

Kingston: *clears throat*

All of the men look at Kingston expectantly.

Kingston: There's also a chance whoever wrote that 'fecking book' is still around. They could give us a literal translation if we can find them.

Caleb nods, clearly considering Kingston's words.

Caleb: If they are a demon and weren't simply a mortal possessed or influenced by one, that's very likely. Although the original Gospels were written by prophets, this certainly could have been the demonic equivalent.

Kai: What about an angel? Don't angels and demons come from the same cloth? Two sides of the same coin?

Asher: *heavy sigh* And this is why we need Gabriel.

Asher blinks and looks at the camera.

Asher: Fuck, I forgot I was recording.

Kingston: I didn't.

Kingston waves and blows a kiss.

Kingston: Hi, Mom!

Caleb: *groans* Jesus, Mary, and Joseph.

Ben: *chuckles* H-he r-really is l-like Remi.

Asher focuses on the camera again, smacking his hands on his knees.

<<sound of hands hitting knees>>

Asher: Well, I guess it's a good thing I made this video today. If you have any knowledge of Gabriel's whereabouts, please let us know. We need to talk to him. Clearly. He has more information than anyone else we've been in contact with. Time is running out, and we have a matter of days before the next Prince is released. Every second counts.

Kingston: *singing* Two minutes to midnight . . .

Asher shakes his head as Kai grabs Kingston by the neck and shoves him toward the door.

Asher: And on that note, stay safe. From the sound of things, we are going to need every ally we can get.

<<static>>

End of transmission.

CHAPTER ONE
CHAOS

Where the fuck was Sinclair? He was just supposed to be putting Merri to bed. I looked away from the flickering flame of the candle and up to the ceiling as if I could see through it and into her room a floor above.

"If that prick doesn't come down soon, we'll need to send a search party. There's no way he has enough stamina to give her more." If I wasn't mistaken, Malice sounded . . . jealous?

"This is Merri we're talking about," Grim said, as if that was all the answer Malice required. And it probably was.

Merri was the most powerful succubus any of us had ever encountered in our very long existences. If anyone could inspire Sin for another round or seven, it was certainly her.

"I'll go check on them," I grumbled, pushing out of my chair and getting to my feet.

Malice chuckled softly. "All in the name of safety, right?"

"Fuck off. I'm being responsible."

"Just make sure you don't disrupt her rest," Grim warned.

I waved him off as I left the room. Those two clearly weren't thinking along the same lines as me, but then I was a master strategist. This sort of thinking came naturally to me. It's what kept me alive when I was human, and I'd only honed the skills during my tenure as War.

Besides, whether they were in mortal danger or not, the last thing those two needed was to get locked in some sort of weird feeding cycle or something. The thought reminded me of eagles, locking their talons together as they sometimes fell to their deaths for the sake of mating. A stab of fear hit me in the chest. Sin was immortal, but Merri? What if he'd been the one to drain her?

My thoughts raced back to how Sin had looked earlier. He hadn't been feeding as far as I knew. Perhaps temptation had been too hard to resist and . . .

I took the stairs three at a time, practically flinging myself up them as I sprinted down one hallway and then the one that would lead me to her door.

"Fuck you and your stupid too-big French house, Malice," I growled. As if this was somehow his fault.

Before I was halfway to her bedroom, I was nearly doubled over by a powerful explosion of lust. I had to reach out to the wall for support as I moaned through the sensation and fought to keep control of myself. That answered my question. They'd gone for another round.

The state of my own dick made it very clear I could go again as well. Fuck, being here with her was a sort of beautiful agony, especially when she was actively feeding.

"You fucking liar!" Merri's tortured scream knocked back any lingering lust, sending me running to reach her.

"Merri!" I called, my thoughts narrowing into laser focus as I sprinted the rest of the way to her room. The door was only open a crack, but it was enough that I could clearly make out her broken whimper.

"You lied to me. You promised you wouldn't die, and you lied."

Pushing the heavy wood slab farther open, I stared at her, my fear now replaced by something more akin to concern. She was kneeling on the bed next to Sin, tears streaming down her face, one hand repeatedly smacking against his chest.

I could hear footsteps racing our way as Grim and Malice rushed to join us. They must have heard her scream. They would have felt the lust supernova, but it wouldn't have been enough to make them come looking. The sound of her terror, however, absolutely would.

"Merri," I called softly, not wanting to startle her. She didn't acknowledge me at all. She was too wrapped up in Sin.

I stepped up behind her before reaching out and tugging her naked body back into my hold. I grabbed a soft blanket from the tousled covers and covered her nudity. "It's enough, Red. Stop it now."

"I . . . I don't know what happened. He should've been fine. I didn't mean to."

"Shh, it's okay. You didn't do anything wrong," I promised, rocking her as I pressed my lips to the crown of her head. I was acting on pure instinct, hoping only to soothe the distraught succubus in my arms.

"How can you say that?" Her voice had risen to hysterical levels, and her entire body was shaking. "I killed him."

Malice's voice filtered from over my shoulder. "Not possible. We are immortal."

"He has no pulse. He's not breathing. That is about as dead as you can get." The tremble in her words was unmistakable, especially when matched with the way her body shook.

"She's in shock," I muttered, glancing back to where Grim and Malice stood in the doorway.

Malice's expression was stoic, but Grim looked as though he was evaluating something.

"A little help here?" I pressed, not entirely sure how to calm Merri down. This was about as far out of my element as I'd ever been. I didn't do gentle. I barely did kind. What the fuck did I know about comforting someone?

"Do we know what happened?" Grim asked softly, moving deeper into the room.

"Does it matter?" Malice asked, his voice carefully neutral as he padded in on Grim's heels.

"I killed him. That's what happened."

Merri had turned in my hold and buried her face against my chest. I wasn't ashamed to say I enjoyed the contact.

"No, you didn—" Grim began, but she cut him off.

"He's not breathing. That's the definition of dead, Grim. You should know that."

"You're right, I—"

But she steamrolled over him, her words practically tripping over themselves as they poured out of her. "I never should have left Blackwood. I deserve to be locked up. I'm a menace, no, a monster. How many innocent people have to die before we realize that I cannot be trusted?"

"Merri . . ." Malice tried.

"Red," I started.

"Would you shut the fuck up?" Grim snarled.

But she just took a deep breath, preparing for another round.

I shook her until she looked at me with red eyes, her cheeks stained with tears. "Listen to us," I ordered, the softness of my voice belying the steel of my words.

"He is not dead," Malice insisted.

"But his breathing . . ."

"We don't need to breathe," Malice said.

"We aren't mortal," I added, echoing his earlier sentiment.

She simply stared at me as if our words didn't make sense.

Grim sighed, taking a seat at the end of the bed. "Look at me, Merri."

She wouldn't. Her face had returned to the shelter of my chest. I made eye contact with Grim for a fleeting moment before understanding his silent request and turning her to look at him. I'd hold her there if I had to, forcing her to listen as Death spoke.

"I can still see his soul safely nestled within him. Death has not touched this place, Merri. I assure you. If you trust nothing else, at least trust that."

"He knows what he's talking about, hellcat. He *is* Death."

She worried at her bottom lip, her eyes moving over Sin's still form. "Then why?"

I shrugged. "I'm not an expert on your power, but he is. I'm sure he'll break it down for us when he wakes up."

"If he wakes up," she muttered.

"He will," I said firmly.

She still didn't look convinced. If anything, she looked resigned, but at least her tremors had subsided. "For all you know, I fucked him into a coma."

My brows lifted. That was a piece of the puzzle we hadn't had. All I'd known from the shockwave of lust was that it had resulted from Merri's orgasm, not what had been involved to get her there.

I exchanged a quick glance with Grim, wondering if perhaps Sin had managed to complete our mission. He shrugged, but I could tell he wanted to discuss this further.

"I think it's probably best if you get some sleep," Grim murmured.

"Yeah, right. Sleep is the furthest thing from my mind," she protested.

I glanced over Grim's shoulder at Malice. He jerked his chin in a nod and moved until he was standing beside us. She'd probably be angry when she woke, but she'd be better for the rest.

Malice touched his lips to her forehead a heartbeat after her soft gasp told us she realized what was happening. Then she went limp in my arms.

After laying her down with Sin and tucking her under all the blankets for good measure, I turned to my brothers.

"This can't continue. Every time this happens, she will be a wreck."

Grim paced the floor, brows drawn into a deep frown. "She should've been sated. She fed from us all beforehand."

"Maybe that's the difference?" I offered. "Down there, we were a group and split the cost equally between us, but this time Sin bore the brunt alone? Or maybe it was the intensity of the act since this time there was actual penetration"—I grimaced—"and not just mutual satisfaction?"

"What brunt? Like I said, we all fed her."

"That doesn't mean her power ceases to exist. People eat when they're full all the time."

"So she gorged herself? She has more control than that, surely."

Malice sighed and threw another log on the fire. "Look, none of us are experts here. We're all grasping at straws right now. We'll have to wait for lover boy over there to wake up. He's the only one who'll have answers for us."

He was right. Two of us had experienced unconsciousness as a result of Merri's power. That meant both needed to participate in the comparison of events if we were going to get any closer to figuring out the puzzle of keeping her strength up. Whatever happened, feeding her could not be at our own peril.

We may not be able to die, but being put out of commission when the Prince of Darkness was coming after us wasn't exactly ideal. We were supposed to keep her safe.

Well, not just safe.

I ran a hand over my face, addressing the other elephant in the room. "Do you think he was successful?"

"I guess we'll find out soon enough," Malice said, his focus distant.

"That would mean all of this would be over soon," I pointed out.

"Good. That's the goal. We'll celebrate when we find out." Grim's words and voice didn't match up. A strange tightness in his tone mimicked the tightness in my chest at the thought of not being necessary any longer.

"And then what?" I asked.

"What do you mean?"

"When she does eventually get pregnant, what happens then? Do we send her back to Lilith and go on our merry way?" I couldn't exactly imagine the four of us standing around a hospital bed while she gave birth, but the idea of just walking away didn't sit right.

"No. We protect her until the end." The vehemence in Malice's response shook me.

Of course he would be the one to have strong feelings about remaining involved. Pestilence had denied him that right the first time.

I'd never had the chance to be a father when I was alive. Which also meant I hadn't felt the pain of my child being kept from me.

Not that Merri's child would be mine necessarily.

My eyes dropped to where she slept, her expression peaceful and lax.

For the first time since this whole scheme was dropped into our collective laps, I actually thought about what Merri being with child would be like. How her body would change and thicken. What it would mean for all of us.

I didn't just imagine it. I craved it.

Fuck. She'd ruined me.

As I let my gaze linger on her sleeping form, I sent up a silent, traitorous prayer that Sin had failed this time so I would have my chance next.

CHAPTER TWO

LUCIFER

"If you want something done right, you just have to do it yourself." I stormed back into the throne room and yanked my favorite dagger free of Famine's throat. I couldn't fight the twitch of a smile on my lips as she gasped in pain. The Princes, it seemed, had continued my little game of target practice while I'd been gone. Such good boys.

"Th-thank you, my king," she rasped.

I rolled my eyes. "I didn't do it for *you*. The only thing I require from you right now is your blood. Unless you suddenly have access to the answers I seek?" I raised a brow, making it clear I knew she was still fucking useless.

"What are y-you going to d-do?"

She was so fucking annoying. If I could kill her, I would. Bloody immortal beings.

"That's none of your business, is it?"

Her lips parted, and tiny bubbles of blood spilled down her chin.

I booped her on the nose, gentling my voice in an imitation of a primary school teacher speaking to a naughty five-year-old. "I suggest you stick with silence right now, lest you get yourself in more hot water." Calling over my shoulder, I added, "Pride, bring me a chalice. I don't want to get blood on the floor."

He glanced down at the already crimson-stained stone with confusion on his face.

"*More* blood," I corrected.

The Prince of Pride approached with a gold and jewel-encrusted goblet held at the ready. My lips twitched again as my fingers encircled the stem of the ornate chalice.

"No carpenter's cup for me."

Pride cocked his head, and the confusion on his face deepened. "Why would the king of hell use a cup made for a carpenter?"

"He chose poorly?" I quoted, as if that would be explanation enough.

Pride shook his head, still not getting the movie reference. "Who did?"

I sighed gustily. "You've been locked up for too long."

Pride stiffened, his handsome face flickering with rage as his golden eyes narrowed. "And whose fault is that?"

"Don't tempt me, Pride. You may have a pretty face, but I won't hesitate to carve it off your skull and wear it like a sheet mask. Blood does wonders for the complexion, you know. Just ask Countess Báthory."

"Is she still here?"

I barely avoided rolling my eyes. Some people had no understanding of allegory or whimsy. "I didn't mean literally, you twat."

"Oh."

"For the love of me," I muttered as I stared at him for a beat and then patted him awkwardly on the shoulder. "It's okay, you're pretty. At least you have that going for you. We'll work on your social skills as soon as my apocalypse is complete."

Famine wheezed from where she was pinned, reminding me of why I'd returned to the throne room. Her fucking daughter wasn't coming when I called her in my dream. We couldn't have that. My bond with her wasn't quite strong enough yet. But it would be. I would make sure of it.

"Now, then. Wrist, groin, or throat, Sabine? You choose."

Her eyes flared with panic before a defeated sigh escaped her lips. "Throat. It's faster."

"Very good."

With a slash of my wrist, her throat opened, and blood filled the bowl of the chalice. Slower than I'd like, if I was being honest. I didn't have all day.

"What do you need her blood for?" Pride asked.

"It's a conduit. If Merri won't come to me when I call her, I will open a direct path into her dreams."

"Why didn't you just do that before?"

The look I shot him would have turned anyone else to stone. As things stood, I was surprised Pride's bowels didn't turn to water at the sight of my extreme displeasure. I was not the one to disappoint.

"I've been building a connection with her. These things take time. Temptation is an art form. Trust is a process. Until now I've been luring her with breadcrumbs, but the blood is the final piece."

Pride's face lit up with understanding. "Oh, it's the apple."

"Precisely. I knew you were more than just a pretty face."

The Prince stood a little taller and flexed his muscles. "Don't forget my body."

"Annnd you ruined it."

Merri

When Lilith had first sent me to Blackwood, I'd thought it was a prison sentence. Yes, I knew I was technically only there on a recon mission and was her Trojan horse of sorts, but at the end of the day, I was going to be locked up with a bunch of criminals.

Then I discovered the joy of finally belonging. These people might be violent supernaturals, but technically, so was I. Most of the folks here hadn't even killed anybody, though plenty of us had.

Quietly raises hand in the air.

Strangely, Blackwood was beginning to feel like a home to me. The buzz of energy from everyone, the way no one seemed to truly fear me—though there were a couple who kept their distance—the help I was getting from Dr. Masterson, all made me think perhaps there was hope for me. I mean, hell, I was sitting in the day room with twenty other creatures, and no one was dead.

I could hear Dr. Masterson's voice in my mind as I cracked open the latest romance novel I was reading.

"You said you don't trust yourself around people."

"Because I kill everyone I touch."

"Is it all people or just men?"

"Everyone."

"Why do you think you'll kill them, Merri?"

"I'm sure Lilith told you what happened."

"Not all of our actions are destined to be repeated."

I hoped she was right. She definitely had more faith in me than I did.

Plucking the bookmark from the pages it was nestled between, I started scanning the text. My lips twisted up in a salacious grin when I remembered where I'd left off.

All right, you delicious bad boy, do your absolute worst.

"This horny motherfucker is too stupid to admit how much he likes Dahlia. I swear, if I have to go through another one of his episodes with the flames and the brooding, I'm gonna bite his ankles in his sleep."

The unexpected voice distracted me almost instantly. I looked up and glanced around, searching for the little Bichon. I seemed to be the only one who could hear him, so far as I could tell, which only made his commentary more amusing.

Asshole stood at the door, head cocked to one side as he stared pointedly at Cain, his human—or whatever he was. It was true. Cain wanted Dahlia so badly he practically vibrated with unsatisfied desire.

Those burning blue irises locked on her as though he'd heard me, and even though he wasn't looking at me, I flicked my gaze back to my book. The temptation to feed on the unbridled lust simmering between them had me feeling lightheaded. It would be so easy, but I knew myself. I wasn't strong enough to stop with just a taste.

As I sank into the pages of my novel, the story swept me away, and before long I was in the middle of a passionate love scene and living for every single detail.

Caspian Hook's voice filtered faintly to my ears as he stood from the bevy of mermaids who'd been attempting to seduce him.

"No thanks. I'm a carnitarian. I don't eat fish."

As he passed me by, a wave of lust hit me hard. But it wasn't coming from him alone. Dahlia's cheeks were flushed, her lips swollen as though she'd bitten them. Cain's eyes were laser focused on her and his jaw clenched tight enough I could see the muscle twitching.

"Uh-oh. Now seems like a perfect time for me to go work my magic on that cutie in the kitchen. So what if she's a St. Bernard? I'll mount her like a pro. This ain't my first rodeo."

I almost got up to save Asshole from himself, but my focus was pulled to the wide windows at the other end of the day room. My dream man, Luc, stood there with the most beautiful smile on his face. Honestly, everything about him was exquisite, from his golden hair down to his polished shoes. This time he was wearing black trousers and a light blue button-down—rolled up to showcase his forearms, of course. The top couple of buttons were undone, exposing just enough skin to make a girl's mouth go dry. Because all the fluid in her body had shifted down between her legs. Obviously.

A soft sigh escaped me as the book fell from my fingers, completely forgotten as the personification of sex stalked toward me. It wasn't until he was halfway to me that I realized everyone else in the room was frozen.

I blinked, taking in the sexual tableau around me. To my left, a group of shifters were tangled in the beginning of an orgy, while a couple on my right had already gotten straight to business. Had I done this? Probably.

"Don't look at them, Merri. They'll be fine. Look at me." Luc's warm voice sent tingles through me. "Be here with me. I've missed you."

Luc reached out and took my hand, helping me rise from my seat. Something about him held me captive. Mesmerized. Enthralled. His touch only added to the feeling.

There was a flicker in the corner of my eye, and some unknown instinct had me turning to catch a better look at whatever it was. But Luc caught my chin between two fingers, tutting softly as he pulled my attention back to him.

"Eyes on me, Merri."

I licked my lips, and his eyes dropped to track the motion. The feral heat in his gaze made me squirm.

"Wh-what are you doing here? No one is supposed to be able to find me at Blackwood."

A slow smirk twisted his lips. "You're mine. I'll find you wherever you hide. We're made for each other, my sweet succubus."

Distantly, I realized that line was supposed to sound seductive, but something about it sent a little chill through me. I didn't really get a chance to register why before he was taking me by the hand and towing me along after him.

The room changed before we had even breached the doorway, morphing into a bedchamber complete with candles and a bearskin rug in front of a fireplace. I didn't remember this being at Blackwood. But this was a dream. Anything was possible.

"Let me love you, Merri. Give yourself to me. Don't hide from what we have."

Luc's lips pressed to the skin just under my ear as he continued to murmur sweet nothings, trails of kisses sending desire and apprehension dancing along my flesh.

"Merri."

I stiffened as Sin's voice ghosted through my mind.

"No. Stay with me, darling. Don't go away." Luc's hands gripped my arms, and he gave me a little shake.

"Merri, I'm right here."

Sin couldn't be here. He wasn't. I'd killed him.

Luc's lips crashed down on mine, violent in a way he hadn't ever been with me until now. Almost despite myself, desire twisted through me, his rough treatment echoing the way Sin had used my body earlier.

Unbidden, the sensation of Sin's hand sliding around my throat and squeezing had my breath catching. I swore I could feel his lips brushing my shoulder as he filled me from behind with hard thrusts.

My nipples hardened, my eyes went unfocused, and a whimper escaped me. Luc must've thought that was for him because he palmed my breast and bit down on my shoulder.

"So responsive to me. As I knew you would be."

"Kitten, come back to me."

This time Sin's voice was accompanied by a tickle along my neck and shoulder. I couldn't quite tell if it was the soft slide of fingers or maybe a combination of light kisses and the brush of his hair.

"Sin," I whispered.

Luc went still above me, a barely contained snarl escaping as his hold on me tightened. "What did you say?" he asked slowly.

"Come on, kitten. I'm right here. Open your eyes."

Luc's fingers dug into my arms hard enough to hurt. His face twisted into something ugly and furious. "No. No, he can't have you."

There was another phantom touch, this one growing more insistent by the second. I lifted my hands to my lips, certain without knowing why that what I was feeling was a kiss.

Sin's kiss.

Without warning, I was yanked from my dream, the echo of Luc's cursing fading in my ears as my eyes flew open to find Sin's endless brown ones staring back at me.

"Welcome back, sleeping beauty."

My breath caught in my throat at the sight of him. Reaching up, I cupped his face in my palm. "You're alive," I whispered.

He smiled, the small gesture making my heart flutter. "Told you so."

CHAPTER
THREE
SIN

Fuck. She was terrified. Merri's eyes were shining with unshed tears as she stared at me with relief so palpable my chest hurt.

She shoved my shoulder, jostling me a little as she sat up. "What the fuck was that?"

As I propped myself on my elbows, I let my smirk out to play. "One hell of an orgasm."

"One hell of an orgasm," she repeated softly to herself, shaking her head in disbelief. Then she shoved me again. "You stopped fucking breathing, you asshole."

"Thank you?" I caught her hand and tugged her against me. "Is this gonna be a thing now? I should put some clothes on if we're trying to wrestle without having sex again. You getting all aggressive and shit is not intimidating when your tits are right fucking there."

She harrumphed, and it was so damn adorable I wanted to kiss her. Something warned me that was not the right play if I wanted my dick to remain attached to my body.

"I don't know why you're so wound up. I told you I'd be fine."

Her jaw dropped. "You don't know why? You don't know why?"

she repeated, her voice rising in pitch. "I thought you were dead, numb nuts. Do you have any idea what that did to me? You promised you'd be okay," she added, her lower lip quivering as fresh tears misted her eyes.

"Hey, I'm right here. I'm fine." I pulled her across my lap and rocked my hips up into her. "See? Better than ever, actually."

Her gaze dropped from mine as she scooted backward so she was sitting on my lap rather than lining us up for round two. Damn.

"How can I trust anything you say? I watched you lie there, no pulse, no breath. You didn't even warn me that would happen."

I held up a finger. "To be fair, I didn't know it could happen. I'd never had my battery charged like that before."

Her brows scrunched together. "What the hell are you talking about?"

"You blew my circuit, baby." I could tell she still wasn't following. "What happened with your human is not what happened to me. With him, you lost control and drained him dry. Fair enough, it happens. With me, the energy your climax sent through me was so strong you basically overcharged my circuit, so my body shut down to protect itself. Like a fuse, or umm . . . what's it called? Surge thingy."

"Surge protector."

"Yeah, that. Malice makes me use them."

A wrinkle formed between her eyebrows. "Malice passed out on me too, but he wasn't . . . charged."

"Malice is still weakened from the spell."

"What spell?"

Whoops. "Uh, never mind. Long story."

She crossed her arms. "I've got time."

"Will you settle for the CliffsNotes?"

Her eyes narrowed with suspicion, but she nodded.

"Some bitch thought it would be cute to kidnap and drain us. It wasn't."

"How the hell do you kidnap the horsemen?" Merri held up a

hand and shook her head. "You know what? It doesn't matter. I'm a lot more worried about the other part."

I raised my brows, waiting for her to elaborate.

"So you've all been drained? You're all weaker than you should be, but Lilith thought it was still a good idea to leave me with you?"

Ugh. There was still so much I couldn't tell her, but I had to give her something. "Yes."

"Why would she do that?"

"Because we're still the best option. We may have been weakened, but even weak, the four fucking horsemen are like showing up to a gunfight with a bazooka."

Not even a hint of a lip twitch.

"Merri, we're immortal. We cannot die. We always regenerate or whatever. Like the Terminator. You know, 'I'll be back.' Wait, no, he didn't regen. Um . . ." I shrugged, clearly not doing a very good job explaining despite my awesome impersonation.

Merri opened her mouth to say something when it came to me.

"Like the Doctor!" I said with a snap of my fingers.

"What doctor?"

"Doctor Who."

"That's what I asked you."

"No," I said with a laugh. "Doctor Who. Like the TV show."

"I didn't realize you were such a nerd."

"Hey now. Nerds are hot. Also, he's iconic."

She finally smiled, a real, genuine one that made her eyes sparkle. "I didn't say anything about nerds not being hot. For the record." One finger trailed across my chest before she spoke again. "If you were drained—"

"You didn't—"

"I mean from the spell that got Malice. Why don't you seem like it if the others are still affected?"

Taking her hand, I brought the back of it to my lips and pressed a gentle kiss there. Fuck, what was wrong with me? This was sweet and swoony stuff, not seduction.

"I've had the opportunity to feed. It's been a slow build, but you topped me off. Chaos has been taking care of his needs as well."

"That fight club?" she guessed.

I nodded. "Mal and Grim have had fewer . . . chances."

Merri worried at her bottom lip. It was distracting enough I used my thumb to pull it free.

"I don't even want to hazard a guess what those two have to do to refuel," she murmured, her bright eyes finding mine.

"It's not pretty, if that's what you're getting at."

She shuddered. "I don't think I want to know."

The involuntary action made me incredibly aware of her position on top of me. During our conversation, her hips had migrated north, placing her right where I wanted her. All I'd need to do was give her a few well-placed rocks of my hips, and we could stop this conversation and get back to action. That's what I was built for. Not this deep emotional reflection stuff.

"Are you really sure you're okay?" she asked.

"Yes, kitten. I'm sure. You can reach between us and test that theory if you want."

She rolled her eyes. "We are not having sex again. I am still recovering from thinking I sucked your essence out of your body with my vagina."

The sarcastic delivery of those words might've worked on Chaos, who didn't understand nuance or micro-expressions like me, but I definitely picked up on it.

"If you don't trust me to tell you the truth, use your power."

"Huh?"

"Your power. You're a succubus."

"So? That doesn't make me a supernatural lie detector. I can't read minds."

"Not minds. Read my emotions."

A soft gasp escaped her. "What are you talking . . . Malice."

Ouch. Okay then. "My name is Sin."

"No. I did that with Malice. I thought he wasn't interested in helping me feed, and then he dropped his mental wall or whatever, and I was able to intentionally seek out his emotions. I could feel that he wanted me. And . . ." She blinked, seeming to remember that she was talking out loud. "I was able to ease some of the burden."

I nodded. "Lust is our bread and butter, but we can work with any human emotion. It won't fuel us, but we can still register and manipulate them."

"Manipulate?"

"You know, fan the flames of anger, or really fan the flames of anything. We're basically like a dial. We can ramp any emotion up or down."

"So I could make you afraid of me?"

"Not me, no. I have a natural immunity since we're the same. Also, you can't make someone feel something that isn't already there. You can only amp up something that is."

"And what is there with you?"

"I don't know. You tell me."

"How am I supposed to do that? Malice had to let me in."

"I mean, if you want to cheat and do it the easy way, then fine. Close your eyes and I'll let you in. I'll lower my natural guard, and you can play around inside my head a little."

She did as I told her, letting her eyes fall closed. I could feel her as she clumsily moved in my mind, attempting to lock onto something.

When she rolled her hips against me, I groaned in response as desire jackknifed inside me. "You're playing with fire."

Her eyes flashed. "Fire? Or lust?"

Oh, the little minx was testing her skills. Using what she knew.

She smirked. "Looks like I can ramp you up after all."

"Baby, you're rubbing your pretty pussy on my cock. Of course you're ramping me up. But it's not what I was talking about, and you know it."

She gave me a teasing pout and settled back on my lap. "Okay, fine. But lust was all I picked up on from you. I'm not sure how that's helpful."

"Well, you didn't sense any lingering exhaustion or anything, right?"

"No, but that's not really an emotion, is it?"

I rolled my eyes. "You're thinking too literally. You're stuck on specifics when you should be considering the bigger picture."

"All right, fine. Enlighten me. What's the bigger picture?"

"You can use this to your advantage. Become a one-woman lie detector."

"We just clarified that we can't read minds, only emotions."

"Right, which should be all you need to suss out a lie. My emotions should match my words. You should be able to sense deception if the two are conflicting."

Her shoulders slumped as she considered my statement. "So if I ask you a question, I should be able to tell if you're lying or truthful?"

"Yes, ma'am."

She narrowed her eyes. "No more OriginalSin southern drawl from you."

I smirked. "Sorry, darlin'." It was my first lie of the moment.

Her eyes widened. "You're not sorry at all."

"Looks like she's a natural," I said with a smile, pleased that she'd picked up on exactly what I'd been trying to explain.

"Is sex all you want from me?"

My chest tightened. "Yes."

Her eyes narrowed, and her head canted to the side as she waded through the conflicted feelings her question dredged up. "Lie."

Fuck. I hadn't lied on purpose that time. "Merri," I warned.

"Sinclair."

"Don't push your luck. I can put these walls right back up."

"Do you want to?"

"I don't know."

That little head tilt again. Fuck, she was cute.

"That was the truth. You aren't sure."

She leaned forward, her hair brushing my chest and the sweet scent of her overwhelming my senses as she brought her lips a breath from mine.

"What do you want from me if it's not just sex?"

She wasn't playing fair. Using her body to distract me.

Silly rabbit. I invented this game.

I grabbed her hips, digging my fingertips into the soft flesh there before taking charge and rolling us over. My walls came up as I kissed her, forcing her to stop asking me questions I couldn't answer honestly.

"Now who's cheating?"

"You started it."

"Sin," she whispered as I trailed my lips down the column of her throat.

"I just happen to be better at it," I added before giving her a soft nip.

She giggled and writhed under me, but Merri had made it clear sex was off the table, so instead of using my powers of seduction, I slid out from between her legs and got to my feet.

Merri blinked at me in confusion, so I held out a hand, waiting for her to take my offer.

"Come on, kitten. After a ravaging like that, we need a shower. Then you need a good night's sleep."

CHAPTER FOUR

GRIM

Flames danced in the hearth as I sat staring into oblivion. Malice was speaking, his sonorous voice registering, but the words could not find purchase in my brain. My thoughts kept returning to Merri and how upset she'd been.

Generally I didn't stick around after my work was done, but every now and then I'd come across a widow grieving for her lost love. That's what Merri had reminded me of. She'd been completely undone.

Over Sinclair.

It was unfathomable to me. She barely knew him. How had she come to care so much?

What had he done for her that made him worth her tears?

"Grimsby, did you hear a word I said?" Malice snapped.

My eyes flicked to his, my expression and posture radiating boredom. "You're prattling on about Merri."

Mal narrowed his eyes as he crossed his arms. "And?"

"Why should I bother to listen when you're constantly going on about the same bloody thing? I'll pay attention when you actually have something of consequence to say."

Chaos poured himself a fresh drink and knocked back the entirety in one long swallow. "She's a menace. A very pretty menace."

"Relying on camming isn't going to serve her well enough. We've seen evidence of that twice now." Malice flopped down in the leather club chair across from me. "But us working as a team seemed to suffice."

I sighed and dragged my fingers through my thick hair. "You seem to have forgotten one very important detail of why we were charged to keep her with us, Mal."

His unnerving purple irises locked on me. "I haven't forgotten. Neither has Sin, if the sounds from upstairs were any indication."

"Do you really think they were going at it again?" I asked, shocked at the suggestion. Merri had been devastated. How did one go from that to a romp in the sheets?

Chaos shrugged. "Don't underestimate the power of a beautiful woman."

"Beautiful succubus, you mean."

Chaos's sharp glare said he didn't like me reducing her to her species. I held his glare without issue. The distinction had to be made. Not only were the four of us not immune to her power, twice over, one of us had been rendered unconscious because of them. We could not afford to forget what she was.

Eventually Chaos sighed and scrubbed a hand down his face. "A woefully unprepared one. Malice, have you made any headway on those shielding sessions?"

Malice gave him an incredulous once-over. "And when exactly was I supposed to have done that? While we were fleeing London? While getting the château ready for five unexpected occupants with a need for internet access and security? During the orgy?"

Chaos held up a hand. "Okay, okay. I get it. We've been busy. But I do think we need to make her lessons a priority. I'll handle the hand-to-hand. You deal with the mental stuff."

"I don't care when you do it, but she needs sessions with each of you every single day until we are confident she can control and defend herself."

Merri was a liability in so many ways, chief among them how open she was to outside influence. That pride demon should have never been able to draw her away so easily. But a powerhouse like Merri with no protective skills was a prime target. She had been a sitting duck. The woman was basically a bowl of candy left unattended on Halloween.

Chaos nodded his agreement. After a beat, Malice huffed out a breath and did the same.

Under any other circumstance, he would absolutely refuse to assist, but we didn't really have a choice here. If we wanted to keep Merri out of Lucifer's clutches, she needed every advantage she could get.

"Fine," he sighed, reminding me of a put-out babysitter.

"You guys, you promised you wouldn't have book club without me again." Sin stood in the doorway, hair wet from the shower, shirt in one hand, jeans not even buttoned.

"Welcome back," Malice said, sounding not at all welcoming.

"Don't hate me 'cause you ain't me," Sin said smugly, tossing his shirt at Malice's face.

He had no idea how true that statement was at the moment.

"What happened to you?" I asked.

He gave an obnoxious wink as he sank back into the authentic rococo settee, his arms slung across the back. "If you have to ask, you're not old enough to know."

Chaos lost his temper first. "We don't care that you fucked her, asshat. Why did she knock you out cold?"

"She didn't. I just . . . overloaded on power. Had to sleep it off. Like after a Thanksgiving dinner."

"So you were in a sex coma?" Malice asked.

"Exactly. Best meal of my life."

"Is that what happened to Malice?" I asked.

Sin shook his head. "Nope." He made a point to pop the *P*. "Mal Pal wasn't strong enough to survive the experience."

Malice chucked a throw pillow at Sin's head.

"Children," I intoned, my warning clear.

"Sorry, Dad," Sin said without any hint of genuine apology. "Malice is still weakened from Hel's little game. He hasn't had the opportunity to recharge like Chaos and me, so when she fed from him without the rest of us there to share the burden, his body couldn't handle the energy drain. It powered down, just like one of his machines."

Chaos appeared lost in thought.

"What is it?" I asked, recognizing the look in his eyes due to years of familiarity. He was like a bloodhound scenting a new trail.

"Why should we trust Lilith?"

I wasn't sure what had led him to this line of questioning, but I knew that his strategist's brain picked up on things I didn't always notice right away. "Why shouldn't we?" I countered.

Chaos held up a finger, as if ticking off items on a list. "One, she's a demon. Two, she's a demon. Three—"

"Yes, fine. We understand. But we're not exactly the good guys either," Sin argued.

Chaos shrugged off his assessment. "I think we need to at least consider the possibility that Lilith is not to be trusted and that she sent Merri to us knowing exactly what would happen."

While it was true that Lilith was as manipulative as the rest of us and that a sneaky move like that was absolutely in her wheelhouse, something about Chaos's suggestion rang false to me.

"Lilith hates Lucifer. Why would she do anything to help him?"

"He has a point. A woman scorned and all that . . ." Sin spread his legs wider, and it seemed the satisfied smirk was a permanent resident on his face now.

"If she wanted to help him, she could have simply deposited Merri on Lucifer's doorstep. She has no quarrel with us."

"That we know of," Chaos muttered.

"I think you're missing the big picture, War. She didn't drain me. She boosted me. Your logic is flawed."

"And she didn't kill me," Malice offered.

"She fed on us all. Did any of you feel lingering weakness?" I asked, knowing the answer. No. Perhaps I'd been briefly incapacitated, but that could be said for anyone in the throes of pleasure.

Sin and Malice were quick to shake their heads. Chaos took a bit longer.

"I suppose you're right," he said eventually, but his expression was still uncertain.

"Enough of this. We're focusing on the wrong thing," I snarled. "Merri isn't a threat to us. She's ours to care for, and that means we need to all be at full strength before the next Prince is released."

As one, three sets of eyes landed on me.

"What?"

"Ours to care for?" Malice repeated, one brow raised. "Since when did impregnating the girl require catching feelings?"

My gut twisted. "Care for. Like one would care for a plant. Feed it, water it, keep it safe from harm."

"Uh-huh," Sin said.

I growled low in my throat, and a dark shadow flowed from beneath me, moving over the floor like an angry tide.

Sin spun sideways in his seat, lifting his legs off the ground to avoid coming into contact with the oily darkness. "Can no one take a joke anymore? Yeesh."

"You're pulling focus from the real issue at hand, Sinclair. The next Prince is due any day. Regardless of how any of us feel about her, Merri needs to be protected. We need to prepare."

"Prepare for what?" Malice asked. "They don't know where we are. And even if they did, we're already on an island. They can't exactly sneak up on us this time."

"You've said that before and have already been proven wrong," I pointed out. "At the very least, we should look into warding the premises. Making sure nothing can go undetected."

"My security system is the best available on the planet. It's already taken care of. Christian is in the process of checking all the sensors as we speak."

Chaos's frown and low grumble of dissatisfaction shook Malice's confidence. I could see it in his eyes.

Mal shot a glare at the warrior, who'd taken a sword off the mount over the fireplace. "Can you please stop touching things that don't belong to you?"

I snickered. "And you call me fussy."

"You are the fussiest fuck I've ever known," Sin drawled. "And I was an actor."

Chaos pointed the tip of the sword in Sin's direction. "You know the rules, Sinclair. Not a fucking word about the glory days."

"What are you gonna do, Chaos? Chop off my head?"

"Wouldn't be the first time."

Sin smirked. "Won't keep my mouth shut."

I sighed and shook my head. "Am I seriously the only one who cares that we are in imminent danger?"

"You mean Merri is in danger. We are immortal." Malice's tone betrayed his own worry. He didn't want any harm to come to her either. None of us did.

"I have never failed in any of my tasks. I will not fail in this one."

Sin snorted.

"What?" I snapped.

"Of course you've never failed. All of your tasks end with killing something or someone. Pretty easy when all you have to do is touch them."

"Are we just ignoring the one task that you've absolutely failed to complete, Mr. Horseman? Or does it not count unless it suits you?"

"Glass houses, Chaos."

"I'm not the one making claims of a perfect record, Grimsby."

"Enough," I snapped, my ire mounting at Sinclair's snickers.

They were getting entirely too comfortable and forgetting their places. I was the inevitable one. The oldest among us. The first of our kind. Yes, Pestilence came along moments later, but I had been first. And Death was pretty fucking final.

Malice blew out a breath. “What do you want us to say, Grim? She’s as safe as we can make her. I had this place warded centuries ago, but if it will make you feel better, I can have Christian strengthen them.”

“What would a groundskeeper know about wards?” Sin asked.

“He’s sworn to Hecate’s line. His family is blood-bound to the estate. It’s their wards that protect it. It’s also the reason they can never truly leave.”

“So he’s not loyal to you at all, then?” Chaos asked.

Malice’s eyes narrowed a fraction. “Why would you say that?”

“Because you are keeping him bound here. He’s forced to serve you.”

“Well . . . no. Not me, per se. I snagged this land from Hecate after a wild night of gambling. All I had to do was get rid of the occupant, spread a little plague to her enemies, and then it was mine forevermore.”

“What’s so special about this place?” Chaos asked.

“Ley lines.”

“What about them?”

“The five main lines all intersect here. It’s a place of immense power, which is why Hecate claimed it in the first place.”

“You’re not a magic user though, so why did you want it?” I asked.

Malice shrugged. “It’s picturesque and secluded.”

I raised a brow, not buying that for a second.

“What? You never know when you’re going to need an ace up your sleeve. I saw the potential.”

“You’re not wrong,” Chaos said. “And aside from things with wings, the ability to fortify and defend an island is much greater than a penthouse.”

I took umbrage with that. My penthouse was a fortress. Mostly. But now it was so much rubble, so perhaps he had a point.

"Are the wards strong enough to protect from above as well?" I asked.

"Technically speaking, yes. But the Knights are a different breed. It may not hurt to give them a boost. As I said, I'll have Christian look into it."

"Does he know what we are?" Sin asked.

Malice shook his head. "His family has been led to believe that I —or as they assume *my* family—descend directly from the goddess Hecate herself."

"And the fact that you have no magical ability?" I pressed.

Malice sneered. "Have you seen what I can do with a virus? I *am* magic."

Sin snickered and whispered, "I am the night."

"So his loyalty is misplaced, he's blood-bound to remain here, and he's potentially serving you against his will. Sounds bloody perfect. What could go wrong?" I said dryly.

"Oh ye of little faith," Malice countered.

"Where has faith ever gotten us?"

"Christian's loyalty is to his goddess and the land she's tasked his line with protecting. As far as anyone cares or is concerned, his values and mine are aligned. Anything that could threaten this land is something that must be dealt with. Therefore, a request to strengthen the wards against demonic entities seeking to claim this seat of power for their own nefarious deeds is not simply a request from me, it's an obligation to his goddess. There will be no issue."

Sin, who had finally donned his shirt, stood and walked over to the bar cart, poured himself a generous helping of whiskey—not Brimstone, unfortunately—then knocked it back.

"There better not be." His voice held such a serious note we all sat up and took notice. "You may not want to admit it, but Merri is important to us. She's important to me. Even if she wasn't the vessel, I'd care about what happened to her."

The declaration was so novel the three of us were rendered speechless. We were horsemen. We didn't care about mortals. They were sometimes tools, but always casualties. In other words, they were dispensable. Necessary evils. And while Merri was a succubus, she was still mortal in the sense that she could truly die. We would survive the apocalypse. She would not.

There was no happy ending here. Even if we did stop Lucifer, we were still who we were. All of this would start again. What place did she have in our lives?

I cleared my throat, not sure what to say to Sin. No matter how he felt about her, he couldn't keep her. It wasn't in our nature.

"She's not yours, Sin," Malice said softly.

"Not yet, but she could be."

Chaos and I exchanged a look, recognizing the mulish set of his shoulders. Sin was a child who'd just been told he couldn't have a toy. Now it was the only thing he wanted.

There was no winning this argument. Not now. Time to redirect.

"She can't be anything if she's dead." I trained my stern glare on Chaos. "Sin did his duty. It's time for you to do yours."

Sin smirked. "Not if I got one past the goalie already."

"That remains to be seen. But every day that passes is one day closer to Lucifer getting what he's after." I made a point to meet and hold each of their gazes. "It is imperative that we do not fail."

"Again with the we, like he's gonna step up to the plate," Sin said with a roll of his eyes.

I ground my teeth together, needing more effort than usual to keep myself in check. Sin was begging for a beating, and I wanted so badly to deliver it. But that would encourage his bad behavior. If he knew it got a rise out of me, he'd only redouble his efforts to do it again.

Chaos must have sensed the violence simmering within me. He moved across the room and snatched the highball glass out of Sin's hand, drinking the remains of the whiskey in one go. "Leave it to me."

CHAPTER FIVE
MALICE

"Oh, my little hellcat, what are you up to now?" I muttered as I watched the screen record of her computer from the comfort of my room. She had no idea I had this kind of access, but really, what kind of self-proclaimed protector would I be if I didn't make sure she wasn't getting herself into trouble?

She hadn't begun a session, so I couldn't see her, but watching her scroll through comments and messages was entertaining in and of itself. Especially when she got to a few of mine. Of course, she didn't know it was me, and she wouldn't if I had anything to say about it.

> TheSingularity: I like the pink, but I think purple would look better on you.

> Merri-Go-Round: And here I thought you were going to say you'd like it better on your bedroom floor. Way to keep me on my toes, cutie. 😉

I scrolled back up to her original post and the photo of her in nothing but a robe, holding up two options for the day. Her hair was in a thick braid, her face free of makeup, and she held a pink pair of leggings in one hand, a deep violet in the other.

Fuck me, she was striking. There was no question about that. A natural beauty by any definition.

MakeItClap22: Damn, baby girl. What if we just drop these options on the floor and you go naked?

URDreamLover: I'm with MakeItClap22. Let's have a naked day.

Magic_Fingie_Dingies: I could give you a massage. Then you could give me one . . . with your mouth 😊

EverySteve: Yoga? I love your yoga sessions.

OnMyKnees4U: Yoga is better with friends. I'll be your partner! We can practice some new positions.

These *supporters* of hers were nothing more than a bunch of lecherous bastards. It was a good job she was feeding from them. If all she was getting was money, I'd already have corrupted the entire website and burned it down.

Thankfully, not everyone was as disgusting. She had a few more respectable comments sprinkled in as well.

Brookec_reads: Okay, but where did you get those? They look so soft.

PrettyPenny: One for today, one for tomorrow. Why choose, baby?

bookwhore69: The bralette is cute, but will it actually keep the girls contained? 🙄 Mine always try to escape. 🤦‍♀️

Estar92: Can you link me to your favorite yoga channel online? I'm getting supes bored with my usuals.

Merri had made a point to respond to all of them with the requested links and information. Now that I was getting to know her, I could tell she enjoyed those interactions far more than the ones with her more . . . excited fans. Though I'd be willing to bet she was also a fan of mine. Her comments felt more genuine and less like her persona.

Unable to help myself from testing my theory, I typed out a quick response to her comment.

TheSingularity: You said it, not me . . . and it would be rude of me to disagree with a lady.

Her reply came almost instantly, a wicked sort of glee bubbling up inside me as I watched her type.

Merri-Go-Round: Is that an invitation? How forward of you. You haven't even bought me dinner yet and already you're trying to get me out of my clothes.

Before I could respond, a DM popped up on her screen, interrupting the flirty banter I shouldn't have been enjoying.

PRETTYPENNY:

Good job with the outfit tease today.

MERRI-GO-ROUND:

You were right. They love to dress me up like I'm their own personal doll.

PRETTYPENNY:

More like they love to feel included in your day. Girlfriend experience, remember?

Girlfriend experience? What the fuck did that mean? And why did the idea of it make me want to punch something?

MERRI-GO-ROUND:

I know, I know. Most of these people don't want that from me though. Just one in particular.

PRETTYPENNY:

ShyGuy. He really likes you.

MERRI-GO-ROUND:

If I'm being honest, I like him too. He's sweet. Different from the rest of them. He makes me feel seen, not just like an object.

And now I had a target for my fist. Who the fuck was ShyGuy? I already had a tab open and was about to launch a full-scale hack of his account when her next message came through.

MERRI-GO-ROUND:

It's probably a good thing the internet has been so unreliable. Otherwise I think I'd be in danger of catching feelings.

PRETTYPENNY:

What's so wrong with feelings? Haven't you seen Pretty Woman? Maybe he's your white knight and he'll come sweep you off your feet in a limo with roses and opera playing or some shit.

MERRI-GO-ROUND:

Who are you and what have you done with my friend? 🕵

PRETTYPENNY:

What do you mean?

MERRI-GO-ROUND:

Aren't you the one who made a point to warn me never to catch feelings for a client? 👀

PRETTYPENNY:

Well, yeah, but rules are made to be broken.

"The fuck they are."

I needed to put an end to this. Merri was typing, but I was done playing this ridiculous game of her fantasy man rescuing her from me. Fuck. From us. We were the ones doing the rescuing; she just didn't realize it yet.

With a few calculated keystrokes, I shut down her connection and changed the Wi-Fi password.

A sly grin twisted my lips as I heard the sound of her frustrated shout.

"Goddammit!"

My grin widened into a smirk as I heard a door slam shut and footsteps stomping down the long hallway.

Three.

Two.

One.

"Mal," she shouted as she opened my door.

"Hellcat," I said, failing to hide my smirk as I clocked her outfit. She'd gone with the purple.

Her eyes narrowed with suspicion. "I thought you said the internet is fixed."

I shrugged. "I must have been wrong."

She glanced at my computer screen and the very obvious web browser I'd purposely left open. "You did it on purpose."

"We had a date, hellcat. You were late. I was simply helping rid you of the distraction."

The way she had her hands on her hips, in some sort of display of defiance I supposed, only added to my amusement. Oh, I liked winding her up. If her eyes could flash with fire, they would have.

"We do not."

"We do so."

"I would have remembered you asking me on a date, Malice."

"Oh, but I didn't."

She flung her hands out in exasperation. "Then how the hell can I be late for something I didn't even know about?"

"You know about it now."

She huffed at me. "You are impossible."

"Among other things."

"I'm not just at your beck and call, you know."

I raised one eyebrow. "Aren't you? My mistake."

She made like she was about to leave.

"Sit down, Merri."

"No."

I made a show of standing. "Sit. Down."

"Why?"

"Because I said so."

She crossed her arms, which was more distracting than it had any right to be. "That is not, nor will it ever be, a good enough reason for me to do anything."

"We'll see."

There was no mistaking the threat laced through my words. Merri stiffened, finally seeming to remember who exactly she was mouthing off to.

"What are you going to do? Use your Pestilence power to knock me out again? That won't get you very far."

I strode toward her, my gaze desperate to drink in her luscious curves. Instead of giving in, my eyes remained steadfastly locked on hers. To her credit, she didn't back down. Not until I was a breath away from her and even then, it was only the slightest shift backward.

"Come in. Close the door. And don't argue with me again," I said against her ear, no small amount of command in my whispered words.

"Fine," she snapped, though there was a lack of strength in her agreement as she ignored my command about the door and stomped her way across my room to the armchair in the corner. On her way, she passed a bookcase and slowed her steps.

My chest tightened when I followed her gaze and discovered what had captured her interest.

Fuck.

It was obviously a child's toy. There was no disguising it, misshapen and faded as it was. The fabric had worn from age, but I'd kept it preserved as well as I could over the centuries. Looking at it now brought a rush of shame and betrayal. Foolishly, I'd hoped I could one day give it to Pan. Not that he had any need for such things now. But after all this time, I still couldn't find it in myself to part with the wretched thing.

"What's this?" Merri asked, fingers reaching for the doll. I was on her before she made contact, snatching her by the wrist and stopping her.

"Nothing," I lied.

She jerked out of my hold. "Mal, we're not going to get anywhere if you're not as open with me as I have to be with you."

"That's not true. I'm the teacher. You're the student."

"So lead by example."

"You want answers, you'll have to discover them yourself."

"What's that supposed to mean?"

"If you'd sit down like I'd asked you to, you'd already know."

"You're a shit teacher, Mal."

"And you might be the most trying student of all time. You're lucky I don't have a switch handy."

"Your age is showing. Beatings went out of vogue a long time ago, Malice."

"More's the pity. Now sit." I pointed to the chair and waited. "I have all day."

I saw one more spark of defiance light in her eyes before she huffed and finally did as she was told.

"Good girl."

My, my, she was a beautiful challenge.

But one I was more than up for. They'd named me Malice for a reason.

"All right, professor. I'm sitting. Now will you tell me what the hell we're doing?"

I indulged in a moment of fancy, picturing Merri in a short skirt and knee socks whilst I stood in front of a chalkboard. Tears were in her eyes over her poor grade, and she was begging me to show mercy.

I blinked and cleared my throat. No, I would not stand here with a throbbing erection at the whim of a succubus.

"Stop that," I grumbled.

"Stop what?" She blinked at me innocently.

"Using your power to distract me."

"I don't know what you're talking about. I'm not doing anything."

Closing my eyes, I pressed my consciousness into hers, instantly sensing she was being truthful. Fuck. That was all me. Annoyed with myself, I reopened my eyes and pushed harder into her mind, not giving her a chance to prepare for the invasion.

That was the entire point, if I'm being honest. She needed to realize what was at risk and how woefully unprepared she was. She needed to understand beyond all doubt why these sessions with me were vital to her survival.

Which meant I had to be absolutely ruthless.

I was the worst of them.

I'd show her how truly terrible I could be.

"Why are you looking at me like that?" she asked.

"Like what?"

I dug deeper into her head, latching on without her knowledge.

"Like I upset you."

"You did. You do. Now, hellcat, tell me . . . did you enjoy fucking my brother?"

Her eyes blew wide with shock, even as she answered. "Yes." The sound of her admission startled her, and she stiffened before adding, "I didn't mean to say that."

"Yes, you did. Now tell me how you really feel about your power."

"I love it. It's addicting, which is a little frightening, but when I'm in the moment all I care about is taking." Merri slapped a hand over her mouth. "What the fuck is going on?"

The question was only slightly muffled. I ignored it and asked, "Taking what?"

"Everything."

I grinned. "And how do you feel knowing you could take and take from us without killing us?"

"Ravenous." Her eyes widened.

"I suspected so."

"What are you doing to me, Mal?"

I didn't answer. Instead, I dove farther into her mind. "Tell me your most embarrassing moment. One you will never recover from."

Once again, she was speaking without a second's hesitation, the story pouring from her like water bursting through a dam. She couldn't get the words out fast enough, thanks to my influence.

"They called me Mary Magdalene in school. Even listed me under that name in the yearbook. All because when I finally fought the girl who bullied me relentlessly, the principal let me off with a slap on the wrist. They said it was because I was a whore who gave him a blow job to get out of punishment. But I didn't. He knew what was going on and that I was just defending myself. He was trying to be kind, but they didn't see it that way. It only proved what they all said about me. That I was a slut who fucked her way through the faculty."

A single tear dripped down her cheek, and a pang of guilt momentarily pierced me for making her relive such a memory.

"Lock that away and never think of it again, Merri," I said through a tight throat.

I didn't have the power to make her do that, but I'd still suggest it.

Confusion marred her brow for a moment before her eyes cleared and she really caught on to what I was doing to her.

"Mal . . ."

"Stand," I ordered, nearly done with my show of power.

She did, even if her face betrayed that it was involuntary. My essence was so strong, so able to infiltrate both the bloodstream and the unprotected mind, that I could have her writhing on the floor in untouched euphoria, hallucinating, or attempting to fly off a cliff if I chose. We weren't doing any of those today, although the first seemed like a viable option.

But, Malice, you say. Malice, you're Pestilence. You can't possibly control people's minds. To which I'd reply, it's called mental *health* for a reason, darling. I did warn you I was the most impressive horseman. Best not to ever underestimate me or my reach.

"Turn in a circle three times."

She did.

"Hop on one foot until I tell you to stop."

She did.

"Pat your head and rub your stomach while reciting the alphabet."

She continued hopping as she followed orders.

"Stop."

Merri went still and silent.

"Now, tell me the truth. Do you fear me?"

"No."

That both pleased and surprised me.

"How do you feel?"

"I want you."

Interesting. Very interesting.

"Just me?"

"No. I want all of you."

"Why? Because you're hungry and we're your only viable food sources?"

She blinked a few times, then licked her lower lip. "I . . . don't know."

Was that hesitation because she was finally catching on or because she truly didn't have an answer for me?

Only one way to find out.

"Strip."

Merri's cheeks flamed red as she reached for the bottom of her sports bra.

"Stop," I said before she could actually remove anything.

So she still didn't have a clue how to resist my influence. Which wasn't surprising. One rarely learned how to swim by being dropped in a body of water and left to their own devices.

I retracted from her so fast she swayed on her feet.

"You were in my head," she murmured. "I couldn't even tell until my body started moving without my permission."

"Yes. You have absolutely no protective barriers. You're ripe for plucking."

She looked a bit peaked.

"Sit," I ordered softly, making it clear that this was a suggestion.

The way her knees gave out, it looked more like a collapse than an intentional choice. She was reeling both from the mental assault and the revelation.

"Are you going to help me with those barriers then?"

"That is the goal, yes."

"And that little display you just did?"

"Proof of how badly you require my assistance. So that the next time I tell you to do something, you understand why it's in your best interest to do so."

She wrinkled her nose. "This is your 'because you said so' moment, isn't it?"

"You're a fast learner."

"Sure doesn't feel like it. How can I defend myself when I can't even tell that my mind is being fucked with?" She rubbed at her temples, discomfort evident in her posture.

"Headache?"

"Yes. I feel like I haven't slept in days."

"It'll go away in a bit."

She sighed. "I'm not even sure where to start. How does one build a mental barrier? Is it something I need to focus on at all times? What about when I'm sleeping? Or focused on something else? I'm a decent multitasker, but that seems impossible."

"No one creates a worldwide pandemic on their first go-round."

Merri stared at me. "Is that supposed to make me feel better?"

"I just mean to say that you must crawl before you run. Every plague begins with a sneeze, you know?"

"Pretty sure that can't be accurate."

"Oh, are you an expert now?"

"I'm just saying, some diseases aren't airborne, so how can they start with a sneeze?"

"You've missed the point."

"Have I? Or is your analogy flawed?"

"Now I have a headache."

She was returning to her plucky self, the infuriating brat I couldn't help but be drawn to. This back and forth with her was, dare I say, fun.

"So how do you build a wall?"

"Well, like most good defenses, first you must become familiar with what you are defending against. You need to *a*: recognize the threat level so you can respect it, and *b*: become familiar with the sensation—or symptoms, if you will. Once you can recognize that, you will instinctively understand how to block it."

"Now I know you're bullshitting me."

"I'm not. Think of your immune system. It has to come into contact with a contagion in order to create the defense required to resist it. Same idea."

"That . . . actually made sense."

I smirked.

"Did you know when I was little I used to imagine my blood cells like an army? The white ones were dressed like knights and rode white horses because they were there to save the day."

She might be the most adorable creature I'd ever laid eyes upon.

"Is that so?" I murmured.

She nodded.

"So work with that. When it comes time to start building your barrier, use your army metaphor. Eventually your white knights will know when it's time to patrol and when it's time to call in for reinforcements."

"Wow, you're really running with that metaphor, aren't you?"

I shrugged. "If it works for you, there's nothing wrong with it. They could also be a bunch of builders, laying the bricks one by one. Eventually shielding will become as natural as breathing. You don't have to think about it. You just do it."

"Can we try?"

Shaking my head, I took a long breath. She wasn't strong enough now for another test. Drained as I'd been from Hel's ritual, technically I shouldn't be either. But I felt great. Refreshed and strong in a way I hadn't since before she'd summoned me.

Of course.

I'd just flexed my Pestilence muscle, much like Chaos and Sin had done. This was the first time I'd actually utilized my gift since we'd gotten free.

I could have slapped myself for being so stupid. How had I not thought of this?

Then I smirked, my mind already running away with plans to use this to my advantage. Huh. Maybe ShyGuy needed a little computer virus?

*Mal*ware, if you will.

I chuckled.

"What's so funny?"

"Nothing. I think we've done enough for one day. We'll pick this up tomorrow. Run along now, hellcat. I've got work to do."

"Don't you mean plagues to spread?" she teased, having absolutely no idea how right she was.

"Just the one."

CHAPTER SIX

MERRI

Goosebumps pebbled my skin as cold winter air crept inside the drafty castle walls. Wait. Castle? A quick glance down at my body confirmed that I was, in fact, dressed as some sort of medieval lady-in-waiting. Or whatever I was supposed to be. I wasn't well-versed enough in the timeframe to identify the details that might tell me where I fell in the castle's pecking order.

The air smelled of woodsmoke and incense, a heavy sort of aroma obviously used to cover other, less appealing things. Glancing out the window, I took in the scene. A chilly, frost-coated morning greeted me, people milling about, dressed in garb I'd have been likely to see at a Renaissance Faire. Horse hooves clattered on stone, wagon wheels creaked, and the low murmur of conversations filtered around me.

Where the fuck was I?

A door creaked open to my left, and I spun in that direction. A startled laugh pulled from me at the sight of a very distracted Malice garbed in some sort of tunic and hose. I think maybe the jacket thing was called a doublet? And I had no word at all for the puffy short pants.

"What are you wearing?" I asked, unable to keep the giggles at bay.

His violet eyes locked on me, at first angry, then softening to something I'd never seen from him before.

"What are *you* wearing?"

Oh, dear. Why was he speaking in French, and why could I understand him?

His brows furrowed as he assessed me. "Why aren't you dressed for the lecture?"

Lecture? I felt like I was in some sort of play but hadn't received my script. What was going on right now?

The answer floated through my mind, there and gone before I had a chance to latch onto it.

Malice strode across the room, shocking me when he slid his palm around the back of my neck and pulled me to him.

"Do you think we were successful, *ma petite*?" he asked, his lips brushing my ear, the sensation making me shudder in pleasure.

"With what?"

He laughed, full and carefree, and I was struck by the sight. I'd already known Malice was hot; I could have been blind and known that much. But he was always so weighed down by the tragedy of his past. I'd never seen him truly happy before. It was stunning. Like beams of sunlight bursting through the clouds after a storm.

His other hand pressed to my middle as he brought his lips to mine. Then he pulled back and whispered, "I think we were."

Oh my gawd. My whole body lit up. Did I have an undiscovered breeding kink?

"Perhaps," I murmured, unsure what else to say.

"And if we weren't, we'll simply have to try again." He nibbled at my neck, his short beard tickling me in the most delightful way before his arms tightened around me and he sighed. "I'd suggest right now, but we're already behind schedule."

I leaned into him, giving myself over to the wildest dream my subconscious had ever crafted before reaching around and cupping his most excellent ass, even through the fabric of his ridiculous pantaloon things. "I think we can be fashionably late. It won't take too long to make sure your efforts aren't wasted."

A low growl of frustration left him. "I have wondered many times if you might be a witch, my sweet Merri. Now I know it's the truth."

Uh-oh. I may not be a historian, but I'd watched Outlander. I knew what happened to witches, and it was never anything good.

"Am not."

He chuckled. "Are so. But don't worry, that simply makes you my most perfect bride. Pestilence and his wicked little witch."

Okay, so he was French but still a horseman. Good to know. Did that mean I was still a succubus?

I reached for my power, sending out a few tendrils of lust to see if I could get us back to the fake baby making.

"Mmm, you are playing with fire, ma femme." His words were more tortured groan than anything, and he rocked his hips in response.

"Take those off so I can feel you . . . my lord." What? I was trying it on for size. When in Rome. Er . . . France?

He began tugging at the laces of my bodice, lips trailing over the swells of my breasts as he worked to help me out of this getup. Oh fuck. I really wanted him to touch me right now. I craved his caresses and tender affection.

"Merde, one day they will figure out how to make undressing simpler."

I snickered. "You could always just toss my skirt over my head."

"Tempting." He palmed my ass through my voluminous skirts and gave it a squeeze. "But I wish to gaze at your entire beautiful body, *ma chérie*. You are a gift. I want to tuck you into the space between my heartbeats so you never have to doubt that it beats only for you."

Jee-zus. When did Malice get so swoony?

"I'm sorry. Are you . . . in love with me or something?"

He laughed and fucking nuzzled my neck. “But of course, *mon petit chat d'enfer.*”

Did he just call me his little demon cat? Seriously. When did I learn French?

All of a sudden a lightbulb went off in my mind. I didn’t know French. Malice did. This wasn’t my dream. It was his.

What the actual fuck.

I sat up in my bed with a gasp. My breasts ached for his touch, and my body hummed from the memory of his lips on my skin and the sweetness in his words. Disappointment rushed in like the tide when I realized I’d broken free of the beautiful dream and was never going to get to see that side of Malice again. The only comfort I had was knowing he had that side at all.

If it was his dream, then those were his actual words and subconscious desires.

But how was any of what just happened even possible? I shouldn’t be able to just waltz into someone else’s dream. Was this some side effect of the mental acrobatics he put me through this afternoon?

I’d never been in another person’s subconscious while they were asleep. But I could feel the small bit of sexual energy from the brief interlude as it nourished me. Just a taste. A light snack, if you will. Everything about the dream burned brightly in my memory. How his touch had felt, the taste of him, the way the castle smelled, the cold air. This hadn’t been a shared fantasy, and the details weren’t fading from my mind the way dreams usually do. I’d been there. Really there.

Was this something I could do? A fucking succubus superpower?

In moments, my computer was powered on and I had a search engine running. I simply typed in succubus, and my God, there was a lot of shit to wade through.

Some of it was expected. Female demons who feed off their partner’s sexual energy.

Bo-ring.

But when I dug a little deeper, there was a wealth of information I'd never heard of before. Some of it was clearly bullshit. Like that our bodies were scaled and we had wings like a gargoyle or horns like a goat. Other details were steeped in truth, though they might miss the mark or be slightly exaggerated. Like that we hypnotized our prey and could enslave them. I mean, maybe I could do that. I wasn't actually sure. It's not like I'd ever tried.

And then there was my favorite. The articles that said we were a myth created to excuse infidelity. Ha! There was no excuse for that, succubus or not.

I scanned an article about succubus and incubus lore, skimming the details about impregnation and demonic behavior until I found what I needed. Dreamwalking. I added the new term to my search, and bingo! There it was. Over and over again, page after page, references to my kind visiting mortals in their dreams and awakening all sorts of sexual desires.

It was brought up too many times not to have a kernel of truth to it, and I'd clearly just experienced it. So why had Lilith never mentioned this to me before?

The best way to answer that question was to simply ask her. Pulling my phone off the charger, I dialed her number. It rang until her voicemail picked up, and I rolled my eyes. Who knew what my aunt was up to?

"You've reached the voicemail for your very own fairy sex mother. Unfortunately, I'm tied up . . . or rather, have someone tied up at the moment. Leave me a message, and I'll call you back—if you're a good little poppet."

"Auntie Lilith, it's me. Listen, I need your help with something. Uh, I think I just dreamwalked? Is that a thing? Have you ever heard of that before? It was weird and also felt so good. What does it mean? Is this something I can use to help me? Call me back."

After I ended the call, I sat at my desk for another minute, my fingertips drumming out a mindless beat on my thigh as all my unanswered questions danced in my mind.

The internet was only going to get me so far. It's not exactly like there was a trustworthy source of information available. Supernaturals were way too protective of their secrets to post something humans could find and use against them. So the only way I was going to get any answers was Lilith.

Unless . . .

Maybe I test the theory myself? See if I can make it happen on purpose this time.

As the idea took hold, excitement swelled within me.

"We'd need a good test subject," I murmured, standing and starting to pace. "Malice is out because there's no way to know if our connection is due to his lesson or my ability. And if it works with Sin, then that might just be because we're the same. I need someone else. Someone who I don't share any sort of link with."

Chaos's handsome, grumpy face appeared in my mind, a thrill rushing through me at the possibility. I wondered if I needed to be asleep for this to work or if I could simply choose to join him? It stood to reason that I'd be able to walk right in if this was how succubi typically fed. How else could we make our decisions and pick our targets?

Laying on the bed, I closed my eyes and pictured my angry warrior in all his broody glory. His scent, the warmth of his skin, the way his bearded jaw brushed my face when he kissed me. And then it was there, the path I needed to find him. I didn't know *how* I knew it was true. I just did. Chaos was deep in a dream, and all I had to do was go to him. I took one step down the path and appeared on a warm, sun-drenched balcony. He stood there, facing away from me as he stared out at pristine blue water.

He turned his head, his skin bronzed by the sun and glistening in the light, hair longer than I'd ever seen it, eyes blazing with desire as soon as they lit on me.

He stared at me, passion crackling between us as he said, "I've been waiting for you."

CHAPTER
SEVEN
CHAOS

My mystery woman was even more beautiful than I remembered. All I had to go on was the brief glance of her I'd snuck as she and the queen's ladies passed me by. This was likely to be my final day on this earth, the eve of war. My king knew he was asking all of us to pay the ultimate price to keep Sparta safe. In exchange, he was offering his men one final night of revelry.

I didn't intend to waste a second of it.

"Get over here," I ordered, turning so I faced her fully.

Her brows lifted in mild surprise at my demand, but she didn't seem put off by it. "What if I'd rather you come over here?"

Ah, she was fiery. Good. A challenge would make this even sweeter.

"If you wish to play, we can play. But I will win."

Her laugh was beautiful. "Ah, but you've never played with me. I thought you knew better than to underestimate your opponents."

"Must we be opponents?"

"I suppose that depends if our purposes are aligned or not."

Everything in me tightened as the woman took one step closer, her body swaying with the sensual grace reserved for a goddess.

"Our purpose is pleasure. And you were sent to me as a gift. One I mean to unwrap and enjoy."

Her eyes widened ever so slightly and she whispered something under her breath I didn't quite catch. Something about one night and bingo cards. Then she grinned, and I felt another answering swell of arousal.

"But I don't even know your name." There was a teasing note in her voice I didn't understand, but I pushed the confusion away.

"Nor I yours," I replied. "Nor do I want to."

She lifted one bare shoulder in a shrug. "As you wish."

Despite her easy acceptance, I felt compelled to explain. "Names are for lovers. You and I only have tonight."

"Then we better make it count."

I couldn't stand waiting for her. This game of cat and mouse had me aching. I needed inside her, to leave a piece of myself here in this bed so that when I died in glorious battle, I wouldn't be forgotten.

In three long strides, I closed the distance between us, snagging her by the nape and pulling until her soft curves were pressed against my hard body. A soft gasp left her, but her eyes were warm and inviting as she melted into me. Her lips were slightly parted, and I couldn't help but see that as an invitation.

I kissed her hard, laying a claim I had no right to. Selfishly, I wanted to ruin her for all future lovers.

She ran her hands up the hard wall of my chest, her palms coming to rest on either side of my jaw. Coming from me, the move would have been an act of dominance, but from her, it was unexpectedly tender.

"Are you going to have your way with me, warrior?" she asked, voice breathy as she threaded her fingers in the hair at the base of my skull and tugged lightly.

"Over and over again, until the last slivers of moonlight fade from the sky and the sun rises."

"I hope you're a man of your word. I'm going to be incredibly disappointed if you don't deliver."

A low growl was my only response as I unfastened the brooch holding her gown in place and let the fabric flutter to the floor. She was stunning, all soft skin and delicious curves. I was also fascinated by her long locks of flame-colored hair. I lifted a strand, letting it flow through my fingers like silk. "I think you must have been blessed by Aphrodite herself."

"Oh, really?"

"Tonight you are my goddess incarnate."

She smiled before taking my hand and placing it over one breast. "Then worship, warrior."

I gave the full orb a squeeze before adjusting my position and palming her ass. I didn't give her a chance to protest before picking her up and turning us toward the bed.

"Oookay, so you're not a boob guy. Noted."

I didn't understand what she meant, but I was too focused on the way she parted her thighs for me as I tossed her on the blankets. The triangle of russet curls drew my eye, tempting me beyond measure. I would have her writhing tonight, make her cry out and score her nails along my back and chest, leaving marks I'd wear proudly into battle.

I made short work of my tunic, kicking it aside before placing a knee beside her inner thigh.

She let out a low whistle of appreciation as she took in my manhood. "I knew you'd be a tripod."

"Excuse me?"

She beamed up at me, reaching out and sliding a warm hand along my bobbing length. "Nothing. Just enjoying the view."

Her touch had me sucking in a hissed breath, the sensation sending tingles to my balls. I wasn't an untried youth. I'd been with countless women in my life. But she affected me in a way I couldn't have prepared for. Everything felt more intense, not the least of which being my need to get inside her. I don't even think I'd been this desperate the night I lost my virginity.

I had to remove her hand before I embarrassed myself and came before we even started.

"Mmm, you're leaking for me," she whispered, swiping her thumb over the moisture on my crown. "Let's see what you taste like."

A groan escaped me as she took that thumb and sucked it clean, her eyes fluttering closed as she moaned.

"Pure chaos."

There was something wicked about the curve of her lip, and my heart thumped heavy in my chest. For the first time ever, I felt wildly out of my depth with a woman. If I let her, I'm pretty sure this one would eat me alive.

The knowledge sent a surge of adrenaline through me. Just that hint of danger was addictive. If I survived this war, I already knew I would hunt this woman down and make her mine.

Pushing her onto her back, I fit myself between her thighs and grabbed my cock, positioning myself at her hot, wet entrance.

"Wait," she whispered.

"Wait for what?"

"You . . . you'll have to pull out. I don't want you to leave me with your bastard as a reminder of you."

The thought of her pregnant with my child had me growling with primal pleasure. I knew it wouldn't be fair to her, but for a second, I flirted with the idea of leaving my seed deep inside where it could take root.

Fuck, I wanted it more than I should.

There was no guarantee I'd have the restraint to pull free of her welcoming cunt and spill anywhere but inside her. So, instead of sinking deep and taking her, I flipped her on her front and positioned my woman on all fours.

"What are you doing?"

"Taking you in a way that will ensure you are full of my spend but can't get with child." I pressed my thumb to the tight pucker of her ass, and by the goddess, she arched back into me.

"Get me wet first."

She was wet enough that I could easily use her own arousal for the job, but I had a better idea in mind. Spreading her cheeks apart, I let a long line of my saliva fall onto her hole. Then I sank two fingers inside her pussy and brought the glistening digits out again to coat my cock in her.

Sure she'd need to be opened up for me, I made to sink a finger inside her, but she stopped me. "I'm ready. Take me."

The way her voice filled the room, a needy and desperate sound, had my balls drawing up tight. I wouldn't last. I'd embarrass myself. But from the sound of things, she was in a similar state.

"Tell me if it's too much," I warned her, notching myself against her.

"You won't be."

"I'm not in yet."

"More's the pity."

I huffed out a disbelieving laugh and started to press in. My laugh turned into a hiss of pleasure as her body stretched to accommodate that first inch.

"Fuck, you're big."

A smirk twisted my lips even as I fought to keep from coming right then and there. "Perhaps you're tiny."

"Take the compliment, warrior. Oh God. Keep going."

I gripped her hips hard enough she'd see my fingerprints on her skin for days, then slowly sank inside her to the hilt. We both sighed in relief when I was fully seated, her ass pressed against my lower belly.

"So good," she moaned.

"So fucking tight," I bit out.

My cock twitched inside her, making her breath hitch in response. I slid out about halfway before slamming back in and making us both cry out.

She surprised me by glancing back over her shoulder. “Don’t feel like you have to draw this out. Come if you need to. We have all night.”

Her permission was almost enough to do the job. I’d never had a woman like her in my bed before. I wasn’t used to her brazen and playful ways. It was about to be my undoing.

“Fuuuck,” I groaned, hips pistoning as I thrust a few more times.

“Please, Chaos, give me your pleasure. I need it.”

She rolled her hips before reaching underneath her body and cupping my balls, fingers brushing the sensitive skin there and sending me hurtling over the cliff with no way to save myself.

I’d have been ashamed of myself if it wasn’t the best orgasm of my life.

“Mmm, delicious. Look at you, fucking my ass like you were born for it.”

Her words sent an aftershock of pleasure through me, my hold on her tightening as I gave a few more involuntary pumps of my hips.

“I knew you’d be a full meal.”

I blinked a few times, trying to make sense of her words, but as I came back to myself I realized she was gone and I was no longer in Sparta. I was in my bed at the château, alone and covered in my own cum.

“Fuck me,” I groaned, throwing my arm over my eyes. “Where the hell did that come from?”

CHAPTER EIGHT

MERRI

I wiped some of the steam off the mirror so I could see myself in it. I had to pop into the shower to rinse off after my unexpectedly hot dream session with Chaos. Who knew the God of War—as I now thought of him—had it in him? My ass was pleasantly sore, as though I'd really been thoroughly fucked and not dream-fucked. Then again, the set of fingerprint-sized bruises on my hips made me wonder just how real that tryst had been. Was it a two-way street? If I'd had the opportunity to scratch up his back, would the evidence be there when he woke up? Something to keep in mind for next time. Especially if these little visits were going to be secret.

And I was absolutely already planning on my next one.

For the first time I could remember, I was truly full. Comfortable and powered up in a way I hadn't ever felt. Smiling to myself, I pulled a brush through my damp hair and considered that this might have been the missing piece all this time.

A flicker of worry for Chaos sparked in my mind as I heard his phantom grunt of pleasure echo from my memories. I'd fed deeply. Was he okay? Would he even be able to train me today?

Fuck. I was over here feeling like a damn Disney princess with singing birds and sunshine and rainbows beaming out of my ass, and he could be in some sort of sex coma.

I was such an asshole. I should have gone and checked on him first thing. Malice too, for that matter. God, I was an idiot. How could I be so irresponsible?

Making quick work of braiding my hair down my back to keep it out of the way, I shimmied into a matching set of lime green workout clothes. Did I get stuck in my sports bra because I wasn't fully dry? Yes. Were we going to breathe a word of it to anyone else? No.

I adjusted the twins and gave myself a once-over in the mirror. I had a real Poison Ivy thing going on today, and I kind of loved it. My skin was glowing, eyes bright and vibrant, lips naturally plump and red. If Chaos wasn't down for the count, he might be once I walked into the training room.

One of his fingerprints was just peeking over the waistband of my yoga pants, and I grinned at the sight of it, a strange sense of possessiveness washing over me. He wanted me. I knew that already, but the proof of it was right there in the mirror. On instinct, I moved to adjust the waistband but then paused and tugged it down a little instead. Let him wonder how that mark got there.

Happy with my 'fit, I smirked and blew myself a kiss before dashing out of my room and jogging my way through the house and out the door toward the carriage house turned gym.

I heard him before I saw him, and there was no mistaking the tidal wave of relief that swept through me. Our little sexcapade hadn't done any damage. I could have cried I was so happy.

Grunts filtered out through the partially open doors and, fuck me, I liked that sound so much. Every one of them brought back reminders of how well he'd taken me. I knew without looking I had a full-body flush going on. It was going to be tougher than I thought to keep my focus today.

The second I stepped into the space, Chaos fumbled, almost dropping the heavy barbell he'd been using. I had to swallow back a laugh as he cursed and made a big show of righting it before finally turning to face me. He couldn't even look me in the eye. I'd never seen him so out of sorts.

"Everything okay?" I asked, batting my lashes and putting an innocent tone to my question.

"Fine. You're late."

He raked a hand through his hair, and his intense gaze trailed down my body, stopping on my hard nipples that were poking insistently through the Lycra of my bra.

"My eyes are up here, warrior," I muttered.

He coughed so hard he began to choke, and I mentally put a little tally mark under my name. Point for Merri.

"What was that?" he asked.

"Nothing," I chirped breezily. "What are we starting with today? We going to practice some takedowns again? Roll around on the mat a bit?"

"Jesus."

I snickered. Annnnd there was another.

"You know, my glutes are a little tender. Can we work those first? I think I need to loosen up."

He huffed, turned away from me, and pretended to be busy replacing weights on the rack, but I knew a discreet hard-on adjustment when I saw one. Or not-so-discreet as the case may be. I knew what he was packing down there; there was no way to be subtle about righting that monster.

I wish I wasn't enjoying teasing him so much. It was going to be hard to stop.

"How are you feeling this morning? You seem a little flushed."

I sauntered over to the mat he already had laid out for me and sat in a straddle, leaning over my right leg so I could stretch.

"I'm fine. Why do you ask?"

"No reason. You're just . . . on edge."

He grunted but wouldn't look at me. "Just finish your stretches so we can get on with it."

"Geez, you're testy. Have you orgasmed today? Maybe you should go rub one out and come back when you're in a better mood. It always helps me."

He started coughing again, and I had to dip my head to hide my laugh. It wasn't anything I hadn't said to him before, but after last night, everything was hitting differently.

"Get warmed up. I'll be right back."

"Have fun!" I trilled. "Feel free to think about me."

He flipped me off, and I laughed so hard tears came to my eyes as I worked through my usual stretches. I couldn't believe how successful my experiment had been. Not only was I bursting with energy, but Chaos was totally unharmed. And we'd had amazing, mind-blowing, filthy sex. It was all upside as far as I could see.

My chest was filled with warmth at the possibilities this new development presented. I could feed from all of them harmlessly, easily, and not ever have to worry about taking too much. I didn't even need to worry about uncomfortable relationship dynamics around the château because it wasn't technically real. Perhaps I'd need to be careful not to let them leave visible marks, but that was easily remedied with concealer and color corrector too. Idly, I wondered what this meant for my camming career. Would it even be necessary to keep it up if I could get everything and then some from my literal dream lovers? Something to ponder.

Unfortunately Luc couldn't feed me. He was a figment of my imagination. He was the dreamiest of dream lovers. The one who wasn't actually real. His energy would be no more than a wisp of my own. But the horsemen . . . Well, they were a horse of a different color.

Chaos was back before I'd completed my last set of stretches, his audible intake of breath making me grin before I leaned forward just a little farther and deepened my straddle. Yes, my ass was on perfect display for him, and I was going to take advantage as long as possible. Especially now that I knew he was such a big fan of the booty.

"All warmed up?" he asked, purposely not looking at me and ruining all my fun.

"Yup," I said, popping my *P* as I sat up.

"Then get over here. I want to work on your agility today."

"Oh, sounds fun," I said, making sure the sarcasm all but dripped from my words. "Can't wait."

"Brat," he muttered under his breath, but I still heard him.

"Did you not get enough sleep last night? Have bad dreams?" I batted my lashes at him as I positioned myself in front of the big guy. A flash of him with long hair and that short little Spartan dress thing he'd had on in the dream made my thighs clench.

"Total nightmare."

Even though he was looking me dead in the eye and delivered it with complete conviction, he couldn't fool me. I'd been there. I knew exactly how much he'd enjoyed himself.

I also knew exactly what it sounded like when he came, and I was more than a little addicted to it.

"Hmm, I see. Well, I hope you have more . . . satisfying dreams tonight."

His jaw ticked as those words sank in, but before I could tease him further, he lunged for me. I dodged his grasp, moving with a grace I'd never had before. I could only attribute it to the fact that I was fully fed.

"Good," he grunted.

The faint praise made me falter, and I was less prepared for his second attack. This time his fist connected, though he pulled the punch so it barely stung.

"Looks like I spoke too soon. Don't get cocky, Red. The goal is to evade the hits, not walk right into them."

"Ha ha," I said dryly.

He dropped his arms and glared at me. "Have you already forgotten why we're doing this? Because I don't need to train. I'm here to help you. But if you're not going to take this seriously, then I'm not going to waste my time. I've got better shit to do."

The sting his words left had me lashing out. "What's the point?

Seriously. A little Muay Thai is never going to help me defeat a demon."

"Maybe not. But it just might keep you alive long enough that one of us can get to you."

I hated that he had a point. And that he'd rightfully called me out for fucking around when I should be grateful he was trying to help me at all. With a sigh and a softly uttered, "Sorry," I got myself back into position and focused on what his body was telegraphing about his intentions.

Teasing Chaos wasn't going to help with anything at the moment. The two of us could play in his dreams. That was the safest option for both parties. It protected him from my appetite and me from forgetting what this was. Or worse, getting attached to men I couldn't have.

Squaring my shoulders, I stared him down. "All right, come at me, bro."

Chaos smirked. "Good girl."

It took everything in me to swallow the little gasp his words elicited.

Then he pounced.

LITTLE CLOUDS of my breath hung in the air as I strolled through the garden maze on this château's massive property. I snuggled deeper into the heavy coat I'd found in the wardrobe in my room, warm enough, save my cheeks and nose. I was certain both were pink from the cold, but I couldn't stay inside for one more moment. Could it be considered cabin fever even if I was in a castle?

"Castle fever?" I murmured, testing it out. "I mean, that's totally what Rapunzel had, right? So it must be a thing." With a laugh and a little nod, I decided I was the cleverest girl in all the land. "Ha. I can see it now. Grim standing under my balcony window"—I did my best impersonation of the surly Brit—"Merri, let down your hair to me."

"Why would I climb your hair when I could just come in through the door?"

My soul left my body. I'm sure of it. The sound that came out of me would put every living Hollywood scream queen to shame.

I spun around, hand on my heart and a scolding on my lips. "If you're trying to kill me, I'd much rather you just touch me."

His expression didn't change at all, but there was a flicker in the depths of those quicksilver eyes. I was sure of it.

He hummed softly in his throat, the wind sending that one forelock curl of his sweeping across his forehead. Fuck me, Daddy Death was sexy.

"Why aren't you wearing a coat?" I muttered, taking in his very un-wintery attire. The man was dressed in a black button-down shirt, dark trousers, and . . . were those gardening gloves?

"I don't need one."

"Are you gardening? Isn't it Christian's job to take care of all this?"

"It relaxes me."

I squinted at him. "If you get any more relaxed, you'll turn into a statue." I'd seen him angry before, but generally speaking, Grim was like a smooth lake. You couldn't ever really tell what was going on below the surface. There was probably a huge fucking alligator under there, ready to eat everyone.

"Isn't that a bit of a contradiction? Wouldn't I have to be tense to be a statue?"

Was he being playful? Was this his version of joking around?

"They're also emotionless, stoic, unmoving. Like you."

His brows furrowed ever so slightly. "I am not emotionless."

"Oh yeah? Have you looked in a mirror lately? You have the quietest face I've ever seen."

A small furrow appeared between his brows. "A quiet face?"

I nodded. "Yeah. Like some people have incredibly expressive faces. One look, and you know exactly what the person is thinking or feeling even if they never utter a word. Others, like you, have all the emotion of a porcelain doll." Then I leaned a bit closer and peered into his eyes.

"What are you doing?" he asked, immediately stiffening at my proximity.

"Not your eyes, though," I murmured, not answering his question but my own. "Your eyes can be incredibly loud if one cares to pay attention."

Those silver orbs were infinite molten pools most of the time, but right now they telegraphed every single thing he was struggling to hold back. I scared him. But I couldn't figure out why for the life of me.

What could Death possibly be afraid of?

"Step back, Merri." His voice was rough and tight, but he didn't break our eye contact.

"Why?"

"You are a breath away from ending your own life. Step. Back."

"You're wearing gloves."

"It's not my hands you should be worried about."

I snorted. "You can't kill me by breathing on me."

"No, but if you were to trip and stumble into me, your skin coming into contact with any part of mine would be the end of you."

I almost laughed at the ridiculous image that brought to mind. The only thing that checked the impulse was the sincerity in his gaze.

"Seems a little extreme."

He shook his head and trained his eyes on the ground. "Perhaps, but it's the truth."

"So even a slight touch from you kills?"

Without looking at me, he removed his gloves and reached out to the well-manicured shrub nearest us. One brush of his finger had the greenery turning brown and shriveling in seconds.

"Shit," I whispered.

He truly did want to keep me safe. From whoever was after me *and* from him.

"Comes with the territory."

"But you've touched the others. Why are they immune?"

"We're the same. Whatever it is that made us immortal protects them from the worst of me."

"But I didn't get sick when Malice touched me. Why is it different for him but not you?"

He shrugged and turned away from me, walking slowly down the path, clearly wanting me to follow.

"I'm not certain, but our talents are not the same. Pestilence is based on chance as much as anything. Mortals can come into contact with the same germs, but only one will fall ill. War is a choice, though men and women can be persuaded to fall prey to it, which is why Chaos fuels the urge for violence. And famine, well, it's an extreme, isn't it? Some will be drained by it, others may never feel its touch.

"Death comes for every mortal being, no exceptions. I was the first of us for a reason, as I am the culmination of them all. I am inevitable."

My heart gave a little pang of hurt for him.

"That sounds like a terribly lonely existence."

"You're not wrong."

He was so sad. Despondent.

Again, it wasn't so much what he said, or even how he said it. The truth lay deep in his eyes, at the heart of him.

These horsemen were all much more complex than they'd seemed. All of them broken. All of them missing something they craved—though they dared not speak the words aloud. The more I got to know them, the more I saw. I didn't think they realized just how clearly I could see through them now. Maybe it was part of my succubus nature to recognize and understand emotion, or maybe it was as simple as me finally being able to build real connections with people and not just through a screen.

The desire to fulfill those unspoken needs tugged at me. I didn't want to look too closely at why I felt so consumed by the urge. I knew I couldn't fix things. But perhaps I could give them all a version of what they wanted.

Even if it was only in their dreams.

Tonight I'd visit Daddy Death while he slept, and I'd show him how beneficial living with a succubus could be. No real-life touching required.

CHAPTER NINE

GRIM

It wasn't often Death had the opportunity to dream. I was a walking nightmare sent to haunt, rarely allowed the peace of my own subconscious haven. So when I found myself back in my penthouse with a computer screen filled with images of a mostly undressed Merri, I knew exactly what was happening.

By all accounts, the setting shouldn't have been idyllic. Lightning flashed outside, filling the dimly lit room with a blaze of radiance as a storm ravaged the city below. Sheets of rain pelted the floor-to-ceiling windows. But I found comfort in the storm and its darkness. It was home, as much a part of me as the spark that gave me sentience.

Here, I could be anything I desired.

Here, I could be hers.

If only for one night.

As if I summoned her—which I bloody well had—Merri walked through the door, her red hair flowing in waves nearly to her waist, face bare of makeup, eyes wide.

"You wanted to see me," she said, voice breathy and hitting me straight in the dick.

She was nervous, and I loved that little hint of fear. It meant that she knew exactly whose lair she'd just entered. To me, it was practically a sign of respect. Chaos and the others adored her defiance. It seemed I craved her submission.

"Yes. You're late. Come in and close the door."

Eyes downcast, she did as I instructed. "Did I do something wrong?"

"We need to discuss what you've been posting of late, wildflower."

Her gaze snapped to mine and then to the screen beside me. "You've been snooping."

I raised a brow. "Is it snooping when you post it for all to see?"

"It's no different from what I typically post. I don't understand why you have any issues."

Rising to my feet, I strode across the office, not stopping until I was inches from her, looming over the tempting succubus. "Oh, darling one, I have issues. The least of which are concerning you posting photos of what is mine for those lecherous pricks to enjoy."

"You know why I have to. I've never lied about how I feed."

I reached out and brushed a strand of hair off her face, tucking it carefully behind her ear. "But you don't need to feed that way anymore."

"I don't?"

I shook my head slowly, my eyes never leaving hers. "You don't."

Her perfectly arched brows pulled together, and a tiny furrow formed between them. "Wait. You said *what is mine*. What did you mean? I'm not yours."

"The hell you aren't."

"You won't come near me unless you have to. You can't."

A great crash of thunder shook the walls and Merri jumped, reflexively grabbing onto me and plastering herself to my chest. I stroked my fingers through her hair, then down to the bare skin of her lower back where her tiny shirt had ridden up. She was warm and soft and perfect.

She was mine.

"You're touching me," she murmured, pulling away just enough to look up at me. The wonder and appreciation shining in her eyes was breathtaking.

"I am."

"And I'm not dead."

"Of course you're not."

She took her lower lip between her teeth as my fingers traced the waistband of her sleep shorts. "But . . . how?"

"This is my dream, which means I can do whatever the fuck I want. Now"—I leaned close enough to run the tip of my nose along the length of hers so she could feel my next words like a caress against her lips—"get on your knees."

A shocked gasp escaped her a second before lust flared in her eyes. Her tongue darted out to wet her plump lower lip, and I couldn't resist diving down to trace the path with my own. She tasted divine. Like midnight and fantasies come to life. Or, more specifically, like her honey and strawberry lip balm.

"I knew you'd be sweet," I whispered against her mouth.

"I thought you wanted me on my knees for you." One of her hands pressed against my lower belly, trailing down until she cupped the bulge behind my fly. "Don't you want me to show you how sorry I am for posting my pussy online?"

Fingers threading in the hair at the base of her skull, I made a fist and pulled tight until she gasped. I released her hair as my wildflower gracefully sank to her knees and waited patiently with her eyes on mine.

"Would you like to taste me now?" I asked her, reaching for my belt with deliberate slowness.

"More than anything," she breathed. "This"—her cheeks bloomed a bright pink as she looked down, then brought her attention back to me—"this will be my first time."

My cock gave a happy twitch in my pants. A first we could share. My tryst with Hel had been fleeting and she was far too selfish to ever offer. But more than that, I'd grown too bored with her to ask and knew better than to trust her teeth around my dick.

Eager for the experience, I allowed my trousers to fall to the floor in a rustle of fabric, the only other sounds in the room the pelting rain and our mingling breaths.

"Well, what are you waiting for?"

"Permission."

My chest tightened, and I blamed it on anticipation, but I knew I was lying to myself even here in my dreams.

"Take my cock out, wildflower."

A wicked glint flashed in her eyes as she did just that. Her hot little hand stroked the length, pulling a groan from deep in my chest. It had been so long since a woman had touched me. An eternity.

"And what should I do with it, Daddy?"

Jaw clenched, I let a low growl escape before I fisted her hair and said, "Suck it."

She made a soft humming sound before leaning forward and wrapping her lips around the tip. The damp heat of her mouth had me seeing stars. If her hand felt good, then her mouth was fucking heaven. Or as close as a being such as I would ever get.

"All of it. I want you to choke."

A garbled moan was all she could give me by way of a response. Her hands went from the base of my thick cock to the backs of my thighs as she took me as deep as she could. I could feel her throat working, struggling as she fought the urge to gag around me.

"Such a good girl. Look at you, letting me feed you my cock."

Her body shuddered in pleasure at my praise. I ran my palm over the top of her head, reaffirming the words with my touch.

"Stay still," I commanded, holding her head in place as I slowly pulled out of her.

Understanding lit her gaze, and she gave me a little nod right before I thrust back in, taking full control of the situation.

She hummed around me, the vibrations racing through my dick and making me bite back a cry. Tears streamed down her cheeks, but her nails dug into my thighs, reminding me she was enjoying this as well.

"Fuck," I hissed, feeling the build of my climax on the horizon and not wanting this to end so soon.

The room exploded into light as another burst of lightning arced across the sky. For a heartbeat, Merri was cast in sharp relief, and the sight of her on her knees for me, mouth stretched wide, face flushed with desire, was nearly my undoing.

I didn't want this moment to end, but it was too good. Too perfect.

"I'm going to come," I warned her, giving her a choice in how she wanted that to happen.

She wriggled her hips, then gripped my arse and pulled me deeper into her throat before swallowing around me.

"Fuck, Merri. Fuck," I hissed as my knees nearly buckled. I stayed standing, but it was nothing short of a miracle. The orgasm this woman pulled from me seemed to never end as I pulsed down her throat and shuddered in euphoria.

It wasn't until my vision returned that I realized she'd sat back on her heels and I was stroking her cheek as though she were precious to me.

With a little smirk, she wiped at some of the saliva on her lip. "Am I forgiven, Daddy?"

"This time."

"You say that like there will be a next time."

"Because I know how much you love to get in trouble."

"Can you blame me? Look at how good my punishments are."

I helped her to her feet, not quite able to hide the smile in my words. "Perhaps I'll fuck you over my desk the next time you're naughty. I'll take you so hard you won't be able to walk the next day. Would you like that?"

"We could fuck around and find out."

I shook my head, pinching her arse just hard enough she yelped. "You misunderstand, wildflower. Punishments aren't to be enjoyed.

They're to teach a lesson. If you enjoy yourself too much, then you aren't learning anything. Which is why next time, I won't let you come."

She pouted. "That's not fair. Besides, one could argue that positive reinforcement is the only way to help a lesson sink in. Ergo, letting me enjoy myself is the only way to get the job done."

I laughed, pulling her close and nuzzling my face into her hair.

"Does that mean you agree?" she asked, wrapping her arms around me and holding tight.

"I guess you'll have to, as you say, fuck around and find out."

CHAPTER TEN

MERRI

A girlish giggle escaped as I spun around in my room, dancing to the music playing on my phone with abandon. I hadn't felt like this in so long. Whole. Healthy. Excited. My days had been little more than a series of carbon copies until a few weeks ago. There were brief sparks of enjoyment to be found in my routine, but nothing I looked forward to the way I did these new nightly visits.

As I sang along with the chorus of the song, I leaned close to the vanity mirror and used my fingers to swipe a honey-infused moisturizer across my forehead, cheeks, and chin. My skin was glowing, complexion clear and luminescent in a way one might use to describe the ethereal beauty of the fae. Hell, I was positive if I walked around like this, that's exactly what I'd be mistaken for.

I caught myself mid-cheek pinch and laughed. I was prepping as if I was about to go on an actual date. The butterflies in my stomach sure seemed to think that's what was happening, even if my partner for the evening had no idea about it. I had more of a physical connection with Sin than any of the other guys, that was undeniable, but something about being able to walk in their subconsciouses made this feel more intimate. Like I was peeking behind the curtain at things they kept from the world.

In only three days, I'd learned so much about the men I was cohabitating with. Things I'd bet they'd never willingly share. Maybe that made these visits a little unfair since I was essentially collecting their secrets without their knowledge, but it wasn't like I was using the information against them.

If anything, it was bringing us closer together.

And if Malice was allowed to spy on me via his cameras and computer spyware, then I say turnabout is fair play. Because there was no way he was keeping what he discovered to himself, so really, I was just creating an even playing field. Girl power and all that.

The itch of anticipation hummed under my skin as I glanced at the time, hopeful the late hour meant Sin would have finally nodded off for the night. He didn't need to sleep, per se, but all the horsemen did it by force of habit. Neither did demons, actually. Lilith had explained it to me once. She said it helped our brains handle the weight of our long lives and, in some cases, immortality. Those who didn't use these little opportunities to power down tended to go mad after a few centuries.

Settling myself in bed, I closed my eyes and homed in on Sin's energy. He wasn't hard to find, the feel of him distinctive, just as the others had been. Perhaps he was so easy because the two of us shared so many similarities. Or maybe it was simply because I'd gotten stronger. Either way, I could sense him before I opened the door labeled Stage Door and stepped into his dream.

The smell of the smoke machines hit me first, followed quickly by the heat of the spotlights, even though they weren't directed my way. From what I could tell, I was tucked off on the side of the stage, on which Sin stood front and center, cradling his mic stand as if it was a lover and belting out the final notes of one of the Apocalyptic Unicorns' biggest hits.

Good God, he was beautiful. Shirtless, in low-slung leather pants, sweat making his skin glisten under the lights, Sin was every inch the rock star of my fantasies. The song finished, and the crowd went wild. Sin smirked and silenced them with a single lift of his hand.

I'd heard the expression about holding someone in the palm of their hand, but until this moment, I don't think I'd ever seen it in action. Sin was in complete control of the crowd, and they trusted him fully. It was a powerful thing. No wonder he loved it so much.

"All right, we're just about to wrap up for the night—"

The crowd was immediate in their protest.

Sin laughed. "I know, I know. I'm having a blast too, but you see, I promised a very special lady that I wouldn't miss our date tonight." He looked over to where I was tucked behind a curtain and winked at me. I felt a flutter low in my stomach at the acknowledgment that I was said special lady.

There were a few cries of disappointment in response to Sin's explanation—fair enough, part of the fantasy was believing the rock star would fall head over heels as soon as he spotted his soulmate in the crowd—but most of his fans let out heartfelt swoons.

"You know," he started, holding his hand out and practically summoning a guitar tech from thin air. "I spend so much time as the frontman, running around on stage, singing for you all, and I love it. But what I really love is getting to show you the softer side of me."

He put the guitar strap over his head and strummed across the strings before beginning to pick out a tender melody. "Do you guys want to hear what I've been working on?"

A cheer loud enough to make my ears ring filled the arena.

He chuckled. "I'll take that as a yes." Then Sin looked my way, his eyes blazing as they locked with mine. "But only if I can get a guest out here."

My heart lurched as those words hit me.

"Well, what do you say, kitten? Come out here and let me serenade you so they can all see how much you mean to me."

Shock sent my heart tumbling in my chest. Of all the things I thought I might discover in Sin's dreams, a mid-concert serenade hadn't even made the top one hundred.

I pointed to myself and mouthed, *Me?*

He laughed and then turned to the crowd. "Looks like she's feeling a little shy. Let's make her feel at home, yeah? Will you show my girl how much you'd like to meet her?"

The audience erupted into applause, and a stool manifested out of nowhere next to Sin right as the stage lights dimmed so only two spotlights remained.

"Come on, baby. I want to show off my beautiful girl."

My knees shook as I stepped onto the stage, and Sin's expression morphed from a little unsure to absolutely beaming. I could feel the heat in my cheeks as a full-body blush swept over me. Thankfully the crowd was kind, and Sin didn't waste any time prolonging the moment. As soon as I was settled on the stool, he started to play.

Just like with his last song, his voice hypnotized the crowd. My whole body tightened as he bared his soul to all thirty-odd thousand of us through the poetry woven into the lyrics he wrote . . . about me. It wasn't all sex and rock 'n' roll like most of the Apocalyptic Unicorns' music. This was filled with yearning, hope, and happiness at finding the one meant for him.

Unexpected tears misted my eyes, and I was having a little trouble swallowing around the ball of emotion lodged in my throat. I knew this was a dream, which meant Sin's admission was subconscious at best. But I didn't have that same excuse to hide behind. My reaction to his confession was fully realized.

As the song ended, he lifted the guitar over his head and handed it back to the assistant, not even waiting for the crowd's applause to end before he pulled me into his arms and kissed me long and deep.

"God, I'd hoped you'd come. Did you like the song?"

I nodded, equal parts breathless and speechless because there was so much to unpack from what his song revealed.

"Come with me." He threaded our fingers and tugged me off

stage, and as is common in dreams, before I could process what happened, the two of us were in his dressing room.

"I know we're supposed to go out to dinner with the others, but if it's okay with you, tonight I just want you all to myself."

Since his request was made in between a series of drugging kisses, all I could do was let out a little hum of assent as I clung to him. I wanted him. Not only to feed from. I wanted Sin in the way I wanted Jimmy once upon a time. I wanted a future. I wanted to make plans and share the ups and downs that came with them. I wanted to be the girl in his song, not just the succubus he was protecting out of some weird sense of duty or obligation.

If you'd asked me even a week ago, I would have denied ever wanting to let myself get close to someone like this again, but Sin's song had revealed some long-buried truth inside me. I never stopped wanting that life; I'd just stopped letting myself believe it was possible.

"Sin," I whispered, looking into his eyes and finding nothing but hope there.

"Say you're mine, Merri."

"I—"

Before the words left my lips, I jolted awake to the shrill sound of my phone ringing in the pitch dark of my bedroom.

The disorientation was real. For several heartbeats, Sin's dressing room was superimposed over my bedroom, and I had to actively blink it away.

I made to sit up, but the room swayed, and I flopped back down on my pillow with a low moan. I'd say I felt drunk, but I hadn't had a drop to drink. The sensation was similar, though.

The phone continued ringing until I finally picked it up and managed a hoarse, "Hello?"

Lilith's voice was a blade of sultry steel. "What the devil have you been up to, pet?"

Irritation spiked through me at the interruption. "Well, I was in the middle of dreamwalking, but you interrupted me before I could get to the good part." And by good part, I meant the feeding.

Have you heard of being hangry? Try being horngry. Horny, angry, and hungry all at the same time. Do not recommend.

"Did you just . . . snap at me?" Lilith's tone sent a ripple of ice down my spine. I needed to rein it in.

"Sorry, Auntie. You know how it is when you are denied a very yummy meal."

"And who were we feeding from, my darling?"

I sighed and flopped back onto my pillow. "Sin. But sweet, sexy rock star Sin. With all the emotions and feelings. It was like a five-course Michelin star dinner just waiting for me to dive in."

Instead of approval, like I'd been expecting, Lilith sighed and murmured, "Oh dear. It's worse than I feared."

That dulled all my lingering sparkle. "What do you mean? I found a way to feed without hurting anyone. How is this a bad thing?"

"Merri, darling, you've been playing around with things you don't understand. Things best left in the past where they belong."

"Well, how the hell was I supposed to know that? It's not like you ever told me this was a possibility."

Lilith murmured something I couldn't understand before the sound of a door closing filtered over the phone. "It has been forbidden for centuries. That's why I never instructed you on the art of dreamwalking."

"What do you mean, forbidden?" That made no sense. If we could feed without doing harm, why would it be forbidden?

"I mean exactly what I say. The High Council forbade dreamwalking in the 1400s."

Something about the timeframe niggled at the back of my mind.

"It's no coincidence that the date corresponds with the start of the witch trials."

There it was. Give a woman a little bit of power or autonomy, and of course she must be a witch.

"B-but . . . why?"

"Well, darling, men being unfaithful, even in their dreams, has always been an issue. And women falling pregnant out of wedlock, or while their husbands were away, could only be the work of the demonic." Lilith snickered. "The Virgin Mary defense only works once, so witches were obviously the most convenient scapegoats."

"So you're saying dreamwalking caused the witch trials?"

"Precisely. And the Council wasn't wrong for the decision."

"How can you say that?" I sputtered, shocked to hear Lilith, of all people, agree with such a decision.

"Well, while we may not have done exactly what they accused us of, we were hardly free from fault. We were enslaving people, after all."

"Wait, what?"

That didn't sound good. So much for my "dreamwalking is harmless" theory.

"Every time we enter someone's dream, we attach a tether to them. A connection that grows stronger and more persistent with each visit. Before long, they become ours to control and feed from at our whims. We can use them for so many things. Nourishment, sexual pleasure, procreation. It's a most incredible power. But it doesn't come without a dark side."

Dread sat heavy in my stomach, turning my blood to ice.

"Dark side?"

"Yes, lovely. Obsession, madness, death. Once the bond is created, the mortal partner becomes addicted to their lover. The craving is unsatisfiable. A hunger that can never be sated."

What have I done?

"Is it reversible?"

Lilith made a musing sound. "Hard to say. Few survived after their bonded was executed. The mortals, I mean. It would hardly be much of a threat if our kind were at risk of dropping like flies whenever one of their mortal pets perished. But suffice it to say, even those who survived the passing were mere shells of their former selves, robbed of their happiness and will to live. Understandably so. Who wants to exist without that which gives their life meaning?"

"And that's why the High Council banned dreamwalking? Because the mortals were dying?"

Lilith's sultry laugh filled the line. "No, my sweet. They banned it because once the humans figured out our game, they hunted us to near extinction. Only a handful of us escaped with our lives. You're one of very few true succubi in the world."

"Is that like a pedigree thing?"

"Indeed."

A heavy sigh escaped my lips, the weight of the world feeling as though it was crashing down on top of me. I should have known something that felt so good and easy came with strings. Not even strings, but massive insurmountable chains.

"So I'm doing something bad?"

"Technically."

"And dangerous to them?"

"Have you been dreamwalking with all four of them?"

Worry twisted in my gut. "Yes?"

"My, my, you are a hungry little thing. Though that stands to reason, given how you've been surviving all this time. You've finally given yourself permission to thrive. Of course you're addicted."

"Do I need to stop?"

Please say no.

Please say no.

I felt guilty even as the words coursed through my mind. It was selfish of me, especially knowing what was at stake for my men if I continued.

"It is forbidden, darling. If you were to get caught, the penalty is death."

"And if I don't get caught?"

"The risk of building a bond you cannot break is still there." Lilith paused, her voice softening as she added, "Ask yourself this,

Merri. Are you willing to be tied to these men for eternity? Because that's the true danger."

I bit down on my bottom lip. To say I felt conflicted didn't begin to cover it. It had only been a handful of nights, so why did it feel like something precious was being ripped away from me? Memories flickered through my mind, each one bringing with it a fresh wave of loss. Malice calling me his wife as he held me tight. The way Chaos had worshipped me even when he thought it was a one-time thing. Grim's possessiveness over me and my body. Sin's confession and unexpected tenderness. I wasn't ready to give any of that up. I wanted more.

From all of them.

"After, with Chaos, I had bruises. Can I hurt them in these dreams?" I asked, already knowing the answer in my gut.

"Of course. Whatever happens in a dreamwalk affects the living body. How else do you think incubi spread their demonic seed?"

I screwed my eyes shut tight as a new stab of guilt hit hard. I couldn't continue this. Despite any upside, there was far too much risk. More than I ever could have expected. I never would have attempted it if I'd known how real it all was.

"I wish you'd told me about this sooner . . ." I whispered.

Silently adding, *if only so I didn't know all that I was giving up.*

That was the part that stung. Because of course I could continue to feed and build relationships with these guys in the traditional sense, if that's what I wanted. But I wouldn't get to uncover those secret pieces of them. The subconscious desires they'd never willingly share. I mean, for fuck's sake, Grim couldn't even touch me in the physical world.

"I am sorry, poppet. I never thought you'd figure it out. Dreamwalking isn't a skill easily tapped into."

Numb, I nodded before realizing she couldn't see me. "Thanks for calling me back."

There was a slight hesitation before Lilith responded. "About that . . ."

Oh God, what now?

"We can't speak like this again, Merri. It's too dangerous."

Goddammit. I needed more than just these four grumpy men who kept me on a need-to-know basis. I had no allies if Lilith wasn't even available.

"Who am I supposed to talk to?"

"Trust the horsemen, Merri. I chose them for a reason."

I opened my mouth to protest, but she hung up before I could respond.

"Ugh. Just great."

I'd lost my mentor and my meal ticket all in one fell swoop. Fucking perfect. Life hadn't felt so meaningless since losing Jimmy. Lilith might as well have left me locked up in Blackwood. At least there I could pretend to have some semblance of a real life and meaningful connections. No one had to hide who they were there. If anything, we were taught to embrace the truth of who and what we were. Lilith said to trust them, but how could I if I didn't know their secrets, their desires, their feelings? They sure as hell wouldn't offer that up willingly. And without access to their dreams to discover the answers myself, what could ever exist between us?

The answer made me want to curl up in a ball and cry.

Nothing.

Nothing real could exist between us.

CHAPTER ELEVEN

SIN

An odd heaviness sat in my chest as I ran through my morning routine. I'd woken up in the middle of the night filled with a sense of joy that quickly turned to loss as I realized it had just been a dream. One I could barely remember now but had felt so real at the time. The constant in my mind was *her*. Merri's presence permeated the fragments that remained, her presence and the feelings. *Feelings*? Fuck. Dream me wasn't simply lusting after her. Dream me had gone and caught feelings.

Feelings that weren't feeling at all dreamlike, come to think of it.

I rubbed at my chest, wondering what the fuck was happening to me. I had put aside mortal things like emotion when I'd taken up Famine's mantle, so what did it mean that they were returning now? Was it permanent? Was something wrong with me? Was this a side effect of Hel's ritual or the start of the apocalypse? Were we reverting to our mortal selves as the grains in the hourglass slipped away, counting down the end of us all?

Whoa. Okay. Calm down.

Get your shit together, Sinclair. Go get some coffee in you and stop with the stand-up philosophizing.

As I strode down the stairs, a weird ache took hold of my heart, kind of a twisting pain, an emptiness, and I realized what it was. Yearning. Oh dear God. I was *yearning* for Merri. I just wanted to see her. My gaze flicked to every corner, every doorway, in search of her. You'd think she was a fountain and I was dying of thirst with this desperate display I was trapped in. What had she done to me? Turned me into some lovelorn fool from a Jane Austen novel?

This had to be some sort of succubus love spell. There was no other explanation for it.

You know she can't do that. You're immune to those sorts of powers. This is your stupid human side.

The low sound of droning voices hit my ears as I came upon the kitchen. Christian was hunched over his phone, bags and boxes of provisions lying forgotten as he fixated on whatever the person on the other end was saying.

A man was speaking in an affected French accent.

"This is Jean-Marie Antoinette bringing you the latest in juicy news from around the world. I know I'm typically your source for catty gossip and scandals, but today we have to talk about how Parícutin needed to upstage Vesuvius and destroy not just a city but the entire state of Michoacán, Mexico.

"Pompeii who? Never met her. Rescue efforts are stalled since, so far, no one has been able to get through the cloud of ash without their aircraft's engines being damaged and the toxicity in the air making it unbreathable even with protective gear. Oh, and there's also that liquid-hot magma situation. I'm all for a hot stone massage, but this seems a little extreme."

Who the fuck was this asshole? Treating yet another lost wonder of the world like it was gossip fodder instead of a clear sign of the end times? And where was the compassion for all those lost lives—not that I particularly cared about that, but as one of their ranks, shouldn't he? I had half a mind to track him down and give him a front-row seat to what famine could do to a person.

"Like for part two, and remember, I might only be half French, but I'm aaaaall cake."

"Mon Dieu," Christian muttered under his breath. "He's an abomination. Someone should deport him."

"Amen, sister."

Christian shrieked and dropped his phone as he spun around, hand pressed against his chest. "You are like a terrifying cat, sneaking around and waiting for your chance to pounce."

I chuckled. "I said your name. Twice."

"I was busy."

"Yes, with the cake."

His expression went serious. "It's been all over social media. Another wonder of the world destroyed. Everyone is reporting on it. This is the third in as many weeks."

"Right on schedule," I muttered under my breath.

"Quoi?"

Ignoring him, I counted on my fingers. Victoria Falls, Everest, now Parícutin. Another motherfucking Prince was probably out there and coming after my Merri.

Our Merri.

No. Just Merri.

Fuck.

"I've got to tell the others. Thanks for the chat, Chris."

The Frenchman frowned and poured himself a cup of coffee. "Christian."

"That's what I said."

Turning on my heels, I made a beeline for the room we'd claimed as our gathering place, shouting for the others to join me. Chaos was already there, coffee in hand, scowl in place.

"What's wrong with you?" he grumbled.

"This," I said, grabbing the remote and turning on the TV. An episode of *The Golden Girls* appeared on the screen, dubbed badly in French. Blanche and Rose were doing their rendition of dirty dancing just in time for Dorothy and Sophia to walk in. Classic.

"Betty White offended you?" he asked with a smirk.

"Pfft. Not my Betty. Did I tell you we went on a date once? She was and remains an international treasure, thankyouverymuch." I rolled my eyes and clicked over to BBC News.

"What am I looking at?" Chaos asked, standing and walking closer to the screen. "Is that a volcano?"

"Yes. But more importantly, it's a signal. We need to be on the lookout for another attack. A Prince was released. Merri is in danger."

"What else is new?" Malice said from the doorway.

"Get Grim down here," Chaos said, his voice a dark rumble.

"No need," he said, stepping out of the shadows. "I'm already here."

"For your next trick, are you going to pull a personality out of your ass, or is that reserved solely for rabbits and hats?" I quipped.

A soft gasp dragged my attention to the redhead standing in the doorway behind Malice. Merri had a mug in her hands and pillow creases on her cheeks. "What happened? All those people . . ."

See? She wasn't even technically human, and she still had empathy. That Jean-Marie guy was a right prick. The sadder part of that revelation was how much money he probably made by being one. Because if his shtick wasn't getting him followers, then he would have dropped it a long time ago. When would the humans learn to stop rewarding bad behavior?

I couldn't help myself. I crossed the room and reached for her, needing to offer her comfort. The moment my fingers brushed her arm, she stiffened and flinched away.

"Sorry," she murmured, disguising her hasty retreat as an attempt to get closer to the television screen.

I narrowed my eyes as I clocked the move for exactly what it was. Why was she so jumpy this morning? Last I checked, we were good. Better than good.

"What does this mean?" she asked, looking from Grim to Chaos, then to Malice. Not me.

A pit began to form in my stomach. I didn't appreciate the distance—physical or emotional—that she was placing between us. There was no way I was letting this BS continue.

Because of the plan. Obviously. Not because of the *feelings*.

"It means the timeline is still progressing, and we need to keep up our sessions. Every time a Prince is released, we're that much closer to you being found and taken."

Malice wasn't wrong, but in my eyes, we were little more than sitting ducks. We needed more in place if we were going to protect her. No one was going to take her from me.

Us.

Because of the plan, like I said.

Yes. The plan.

We needed her barefoot and preggers, stat. There was an apocalypse to end and a Prince of Darkness to overthrow. Or something.

I scrubbed a hand down my face. In all the upheaval this morning, I'd forgotten to grab my cup of coffee. I was feeling the lack of caffeine. Or my brain cells were. Neurons were definitely misfiring.

"Sin?" Grim said, expression serious as always.

"Huh?"

"I asked you a question."

"Come again." I glanced around the room, realizing I'd missed the entire end of the conversation. Merri wasn't even in the room anymore.

"She's not pregnant. You need to try again."

I frowned. "How do you know that, weirdo? Does Death have X-ray vision now?"

The sigh Grim released was one I was intimately familiar with. "You know I can sense the spark of life. She isn't carrying. You and Chaos need to redouble your efforts."

"Is that your way of saying we need to have a threesome?"

"Fuck no," Chaos said, glaring at me.

"What are you complaining about? You haven't even had a twosome with her yet."

"I've seen enough of your dick to last me an eternity."

"Fine. I'll go redouble *my* efforts since the rest of you haters have made zero of them. And zero times any number still equals zero, you guys."

"Oh look, he's a mathlete now," Malice said.

I flipped him off. "Math is sexy. Chicks dig nerds."

I didn't give them a chance to retort because I had a woman to woo. Merri and I needed to fix whatever divide was between us. And what better way than with a little multiplication? See? Sexy math.

Did my heart squeeze at the thought of getting her alone? Yes.

Was it because of anything other than the plan? No.

Definitely not feelings.

I know my equations. Two plus two equals baby.

"Special delivery," I called out a beat before using the slightly open door as an invitation to waltz right inside Merri's bedroom.

"You're not holding anything," Merri said, eyes dropping to my hands.

That stole some of my thunder, and my winsome smile slipped before I redoubled my efforts. "It's me, I'm the delivery." I even added a saucy wink for good measure.

God, she was so fucking pretty as she stood in front of the wardrobe and pulled out a lacy floor-length robe and held it out for inspection. She hummed softly to herself before putting it back and selecting another option, this one a slinky black silk number.

"I like the lace," I offered, my voice a little hoarse.

"I wore that one recently," she said without looking away from her closet.

"That's the fun thing about laundry. You can wear it again once it's been washed."

Wrinkling her nose, she strode across the room and laid the

garment on the bed. "I don't do repeats. At least not so close together. They don't get as much of a reaction from my clients."

An unwelcome stab of jealousy hit me right in the gut at the thought of her being ogled online when I was right here, ready and willing to serve her.

"You're camming today?" I couldn't have kept the desperation out of my voice if I tried.

She stopped short and glanced at me. "I cam every day. Even when the world's ending."

"But why?"

Rolling her eyes, she huffed. "You know exactly why. I need to feed."

"Feed from me. We established this."

"No. Not unless I have to."

Ouch.

I rubbed at my chest and had to glance down to make sure there wasn't some sort of conjured dagger sticking out of it.

Was this what rejection felt like? Have to say, not a fan.

Usually my partners were banging down the door, begging me for repeats, not that I was known for an encore. Unless I was on stage, of course.

"Are you saying you don't want me?" I asked, adding a layer of bravado-shaped armor around my heart. "That's not what you said the other night when I was fucking you so well you could barely speak. Although, I guess technically you weren't saying much of anything."

"Sin, I can't do this."

A low ringing took up inside my head, and my palms started to sweat. "Can't do your camming session? Great. What are you in the mood for?"

"You know that's not what I meant."

I did, dammit. And I hated it.

"Merri, I don't understand what's happening here."

She glanced over her shoulder, her expression guarded and

distant. "Nothing is happening. I'm going to cam and feed so I don't have to take from any of you. We don't have to pretend this is more than it is."

"Pretend?"

"You guys protect me. I manage my needs on my own. We don't have to do this fake relationship thing. We both know you're not built for something real."

Fucking ow.

I mean, she wasn't wrong, but damn. Give a horseman a chance.

My chest tightened, my pulse thrumming rapidly in my ears. "Are you fucking serious?"

Her walls were up so high I'd need a Trojan horse to get past them. Maybe I should ask Chaos for help?

"Why wouldn't I be?" She huffed out a laugh. "You don't actually think I'm naive enough to mistake this for something else, do you? Lilith raised me, for crying out loud. Give me a little credit, Sin."

"Maybe that's all it was for you, but don't put your bullshit on me. I deserve better than some unhealthy situationship with you."

Her mouth fell open and she stared at me in shock, blinking a few times as my words landed.

"You . . . wait. You wanted more than sex?"

God, I felt like the world's biggest idiot. Shoving my hands into my pockets because I had no clue what to do with them, I shrugged and stared down at my feet. "Is there something wrong with that?"

"Well, no. Of course not. But you never indicated . . . How was I supposed to know?"

"I thought the whole not feeding on you and, you know, making sure you had everything you needed thing might have made that clear. Not to mention the way I let my walls down for you."

"But I asked you outright. I gave you an opening, and you never said so."

"Do you think that's maybe because you'd just said *you* didn't want more? I was trying to respect your boundaries. Also, this is fucking new to me, all right? I'm figuring this shit out as I go. And not doing a very good job, apparently."

Feelings, the anti-Viagra. My boner had officially left the building. Abandoned By My Boner was totally going to be my next single. A country song, I think.

Save a horse, ride a horseman.

I'd fallen so deep in my wallow it took me a beat to realize Merri was talking.

"Sin, I'm not sure I can be in a relationship. Not with anyone."

Fuck, this woman was really good at hurting my feelings. "Why not? Because if you're trying to say you killed the last guy you loved, I'd like to present exhibit Horseman. I can't die."

"Because I don't know how to let you in."

"And you think I do? I'm not exactly an expert at this, Merri. Fucking, sure. Grade A Stud, at your service. But the rest of it . . ." I shook my head. "I never had interest in any of it until you. No one makes me feel the way you do."

I was thisclose to begging her not to leave like Baby did in *Dirty Dancing*. All I needed was a rainstorm, maybe a lake in the distance.

She stared at me, her expression soft, her eyes conflicted. "Do you really mean that?"

Closing the distance between us, I reached out and took her hands in mine. "See for yourself." Then I dropped my walls and let her have access to everything.

No one could ever accuse me of doing things by half measure. I was an all-in kind of guy.

Her eyelids fluttered closed, and a shaky breath escaped her. "You're telling the truth."

"I'd say I told you so, but . . ."

Her lips twitched in the bare hint of a smile. I realized it was the first I'd seen from her all morning. It faded as quickly as it had appeared.

"You know I'm not built for monogamy, right? It's not in my nature."

I knew. Of course I knew. I was the one who'd suggested her feedings be treated as a team effort in the first place. Her appetite was too much for any one lover to handle. "That's what the other guys are here for. As long as I'm yours and I know it, the rest is negotiable."

That little smile was back. "Okay," she whispered.

There was no stopping my grin. "So does this mean we're official? Are you going to update your socials? Delete your apps? Do I need to give you an ID bracelet or something?"

"How old even are you? An ID bracelet?"

I shrugged. "Judy Blume wrote about them. I thought chicks were into that sort of thing."

"Just kiss me, Sinclair."

My heart fluttered like I was a kid at Christmas. "I thought you'd never ask."

OPERATION PFFN SUPER SECRET VIDEO CORRESPONDENCE: #5

Screen blinks to life, revealing a haggard-looking Asher sitting at a table with Caleb.

<<static>>

Asher: You ready, padre?

Caleb: I'm here, aren't I?

Asher rolls his eyes at the camera before glancing off screen and frowning.

Asher: I'll say one thing about priests, you know how to follow a schedule. Well, we might as well get started. ***clears throat*** So as I'm sure all of you are aware, the hits keep on coming. Or in this case, the wonders keep on falling.

<<door bursts open>>

Pan rushes into the frame, drops a book on the table, and does a double take at Asher and Caleb.

<<book falling onto table>>

Pan: You two have certainly looked better. I don't think I've ever seen you this disheveled, Caleb. I've definitely seen you this rundown, brother, but usually it's for fun reasons. Have you been remembering to hydrate? Do you need me to order you a multivitamin? Our Rosie is rather insatiable now that she's knocked up.

Caleb: You're late.

Pan: *scoffs* Impossible. A demon arrives precisely when he means to.

Asher: The last time I checked, you weren't a demon anymore.

Pan: More's the pity.

Pan opens the book and thumbs through the pages.

<<sound of pages turning>>

Asher: Are you demon enough to at least have something useful for us from that fucking book?

Pan: If you're going to be rude, I'm going to leave. I don't need to be here, you know. I have a pregnant mate I could be taking care of.

Caleb: So do I, demon. Can we move this along? The world is quite literally ending with every moment you waste yammering on.

Pan gets up and walks off screen.

<<footsteps walking away>>

Asher: Where are you going?

Pan: Satisfying my curiosity.

Caleb: I told you involving him was a mistake.

Asher: We don't have a choice. He's the only one who can decipher the Book of Ted.

Pan: *hums* Interesting. Vampires can be caught on film. I have always wondered about that. I knew the reflection myth was only in relation to antique silver-backed mirrors, but Gavin has never let us test the film theory.

<<footsteps coming closer>>

Pan comes back into frame.

Pan: And for the record, since this is supposed to be an educational program, it's not the Book of Ted.

Caleb: Have you figured out who the author is then?

Pan: No.

Asher: So Book of Ted it is. What have you learned?

Pan points to a passage in the book and stares directly at the camera.

Pan: That for each natural wonder we lose we welcome a Prince of Hell. Thus far we have seen Pride, Envy, and now Greed.

Caleb: How do you know that's who it was?

Pan: It says so here in this book. Our next Prince will be Lust, followed by Gluttony, Wrath, and finally Sloth.

Asher: *derisive snort* Figures that bitch would be last.

Pan: How apt. But none of them will be less dangerous than the others, no matter their names. They are the generals of Lucifer's army, each one bringing with it an unknown number of Knights to empower their ranks and fill their outfits with warriors infused with the power of each Prince.

Caleb: *scoffs* So we are not only up against Lucifer and his army of hellions.

Pan: I beg your pardon, *I* had hellions, not Luci. He refers to them as *legion*. ***snorts*** And you call yourself a priest. Seriously, did you study at all while you were at seminary? Or were you too busy flogging yourself and repenting for your hundreds of imaginary sins?

Caleb shakes his head, ignoring Pan's protest.

Caleb: Lucifer stands at the top, defended by his seven Princes, then their unknown number of power-boosted minions, with the *legion* of hell at the front lines.

Asher: Good ol' demon fodder.

Pan: An essential, albeit short-lived, position.

Asher scrubs a hand down his face before turning to the camera with a serious gaze.

Asher: Well, you heard it here, folks. We are in a bad way, up against a foe much more powerful than we thought. ***self-deprecating chuckle*** I feel a little like that one guy in that movie with the muscles and capes.

Remi: (shouts from off camera) 300!

Caleb holds one hand out, palm up toward Asher.

Asher: What are you doing?

Caleb: Pay up. I told you he wouldn't keep his mouth shut if you allowed him in the room.

Pan: Priests aren't supposed to gamble.

Caleb: I'm not a priest, just as you're not a demon.

Pan: What are you then?

Caleb: A father attempting to save up for my children's college funds.

Asher: Better hope there's still a world standing for them to grow up in.

Caleb: Why else would I be here subjecting myself to this farce?

Grunts and the sound of struggling precede the appearance of Alek Nordson with a tall, muscular man in his hold. Tor Nordson follows closely on their heels.

<<rustling of clothes>>

Jensen: *series of grunts*

Caleb: Jensen? Alek, what are you doing with a member of the Shadow Court?

Alek: I caught him as he was lurking about the property. Likely planning to curse one of us again. Fae scum.

Jensen: I was not lurking, you overgrown baboon. I was invited.

Alek: *scoffs* When?

Tor: That's what I was trying to tell you, brother. Kai invited him. Don't you remember our discussion earlier? We need every ally we can drum up.

Alek: Are you sure we want allies that can't even tell a couple of twins apart? We're liable to all end up casualties of friendly fire.

Jensen pulls out of Alek's hold and straightens to his full height, gathering his composure.

Jensen: Firstly, I had nothing to do with cursing your brother, Alek. Secondly, the Shadow Court is directly affected by the apocalypse, and Queen Maeve has sent me as her emissary prior to opening the portal between our realms so she can send every warrior we have to fight by your side. You don't want to make an enemy of me now, Novasgardian.

Tor places a hand on his brother's shoulder.

Tor: If I can let it go, brother, so can you. It's time to set our differences and past squabbles aside.

Alek's anger deflates before he nods.

Alek: Fine. But one wrong move and . . .

Jensen stares at the camera, confusion on his face.

Jensen: Are you filming this?

Asher visibly starts.

Asher: Shit. I forgot. You guys came in the middle of my sign-off. So, um, anyway. Things continue to unravel, are once again far worse than we thought, and frankly, if you were waiting for some kind of sign before getting up off your ass and joining the revolution, consider me one big flashing neon light. We need you here. Yesterday. If Pan's translation is correct—

Pan: Of course it is.

Asher: —then we have weeks left at best before the shit hits the fan for good. If we have any hope of righting this ship—

Pan: (as an aside) You really need to work on your metaphors, brother mine.

Asher: *heavy sigh* Just get here.

<<static>>

End of transmission.

CHAPTER TWELVE

MALICE

My phone buzzed in my pocket, incessant and demanding, but I didn't have time for distractions. I had an appointment with the one woman who would either end the world or save it. Snatching the device, I silenced the call and tossed the phone onto my neatly made bed. If it was important, they'd leave a bloody message.

A sharp rap on the door was my only notice before it swung open and Merri peeked around the corner.

"Am I interrupting?"

"Would it stop you if you were?"

"No," she said brightly, pushing the door the rest of the way open and waltzing inside. "Part of me was hoping I'd catch you being naughty."

I cocked one brow and looked her over. The woman just couldn't help being the most stunning creature in every environment. She wore her long hair loose today, spilling over her shoulders in a waterfall of red, but held back from her face with a thin sparkling headband. By all accounts, her cropped white t-shirt and jeans shouldn't have been sexy, yet they were.

Blinking rapidly, I cleared my throat and refocused on her face. "And what, pray tell, constitutes *naughty* for a horseman?"

"Oh, you know"—she waved a hand dismissively—"plotting the demise of the free world, rigging an election, planning the next major outbreak, or whatever it is you baddies do."

"We let the mortals make their own messes. It's beneath us to be involved in such petty games."

"Suuuure, Pestilence."

The fire in this one had me reacting before I could stop myself. "Are you sassing me, hellcat?"

A smirk made her lips twitch. "Do you want me to be?"

A resounding yes was on the tip of my tongue, but it wouldn't do either of us any good to give in to her game that easily.

"No," I drawled, infusing the single syllable with as much boredom as I could muster.

"That bulge in your sweats says otherwise," she said, offering me an arch look. "Really, Mal? Gray? Are you purposely trying to distract me this time?"

I glanced down at my black henley and gray joggers. "What's wrong with what I'm wearing?"

"Nothing," she said with more than a hint of appreciation. "That's the problem." And with that declaration, she flounced over and flopped onto my bed.

My eye twitched as one of the pillows tumbled off the side. "Do you mind?" I muttered, stalking around the side to retrieve it and put it back in its rightful spot, taking an extra second as I did to adjust the blanket she'd also knocked askew.

My phone lit up as it buzzed next to her hip. She glanced down and tilted her head to the side as she read the name of the caller out loud.

"Hades?"

Oh fuck. That couldn't be good. But I couldn't exactly accept the call with an audience. Hades didn't simply call to shoot the breeze. There was no telling what he would say.

Merri's eyes flicked to meet mine. "Hades, Hades?"

"Yes."

"As in the lord of the underworld? Greek god? Immortalized in one of my favorite movies of all time, Hercules?"

"Yes," I repeated, although I had no idea what she was on about. I rarely watched films, unless, of course, they were disease disaster movies or documentaries about my work. I smirked in memory as one of my favorite scenes popped into my mind. The candy striper and the teddy bear. Classic.

"Shut up! You are friends, like calling on the phone friends and not just acquaintances with the actual lord of the underworld?"

"I wouldn't exactly qualify it that way."

"But you two are friends?"

I blinked at her. "Why is that surprising? You know who we are and what we do. The jobs sort of coincide."

"Does he actually have blue hair?"

Oh, she was adorable. "No."

Disappointment flitted across her face as her shoulders slumped. "That is incredibly disappointing. Talk about hero to zero," she muttered.

"I don't see why you're so shocked by the news. You've seen him before."

It was her turn to stare in confusion. "Hades? When did I meet Hades?"

"At Blackwood."

She laughed. "Uh, pretty sure I would have remembered that. Nice try, though. You almost had me going for a second."

"I'm serious. He was admitted there while you were a patient. He's the one who found and freed us."

"Wait." She held up her palm. "You guys were at Blackwood too?"

If being magically kidnapped and caged in a subterranean bunker counted.

"In a manner of speaking."

She narrowed her eyes. "Why is this the first I'm hearing about it? How come we never ran into each other?"

"It's a long and, dare I say, irrelevant story."

She continued to stare at me. "Uh-huh."

"Believe me or not. It doesn't change the fact that Hades was a patient at Blackwood. Same as you."

"He was not. There was no one named Hades in residence. I would know. One of my super-secret spy tasks was snooping through the patient files for Auntie Lilith."

Had that sneaky bastard been at Blackwood incognito? Oh, Hades. Always hiding in some shadow or another. "I assure you he was. But that's neither here nor there—"

My phone rang again, Hades's name flashing on the screen once more, and another twist of dread gripped my gut.

"Are you sure you don't need to answer that?"

Shaking my head, I silenced the phone permanently and set it off to the side. "What I need to do is focus on you and your lack of ability to protect yourself. Last night's eruption is warning enough that they'll make their next attempt sooner rather than later."

Her expression soured. "I have been doing better."

"Better isn't going to keep you from being caught in a Knight's thrall, Merri."

She squirmed, letting out a heavy sigh. "Fine. Do your worst."

I cocked a brow. "Be careful what you wish for, hellcat. You can barely handle me at my lowest setting. You don't ever want to see me at my worst."

Merri paled, the reminder of who and what I was more effective than I'd intended. But that was for the best. She needed to remember what was at stake here. I wasn't doing this for shits and gigs, as they say.

"Do I need to close my eyes or something?" She stood, crossing her arms over her chest as she popped one hip. Bratty as ever.

"No. It's not going to be helpful practice if you are prepared for an attack. They'll come for you when you least expect it. Just like last time."

Merri gave a small nod. "Chaos said so too."

"Who better to listen to than the man who wrote the book on warfare?"

"Did he really?"

"May as well have," I murmured with a shrug. Then I attacked.

She gasped—just a soft, surprised intake of air—and attempted to raise her walls, but it was too late. I was inside her mind, infiltrating the parts of her she held most secret. She couldn't push me out if she tried at the moment, but I couldn't wait for her to gather her strength enough to make the effort.

Her mind was a veritable open book, each memory teasing me like a preview to an upcoming movie. A flicker here, a glimpse there. Merri as a chubby toddler, running into her foster mother's arms. Merri staring into the mirror backstage before a ballet recital, her gaze flicking to the other dancers, all willowy and lithe. Pretty waifs, certainly, but vastly different from Merri's undeniably sensual hourglass shape. Her instructor looking her over, shaking her head while tutting and murmuring, "I told you to lose ten pounds. If you think I'll allow you to audition for the company looking like this, think again."

My eye twitched as rage suffused me. Better to leave that one alone.

Another memory took its place, this one seeming well-worn. Like she returned to it often. Curiosity instantly piqued, I decided that was the one I was most interested in witnessing.

"No." Merri's soft protest barely registered as the memory took hold around me.

~

Merri

This was one of my most favorite moments to revisit. The beginning of me finding out who I really was and learning how to control my hunger in a way that helped me protect those around me. But more than that, it was also when I found the people I'd start building my own little family with. Auntie Lilith, for starters, and not too long after, Andi.

As the warm comfort of the recollection wrapped around me, I let myself sink into it and the respite it provided.

"Now, pet, I know this has been difficult for you to understand, but you mustn't be so hard on yourself. This is your nature. A succubus must feed." Auntie Lilith stood over me where I sat on the bed.

"H-how can I? I'll kill them."

"I know, darling. It's my fault for not anticipating your power being so strong."

"Are you going to send me away?"

Lilith tutted. "I don't want to, but if you won't try this as a means to feed, I won't have a choice. I cannot have you accidentally draining my patrons to the point of unconsciousness and without their consent. I have a reputation to protect, after all."

I mutely nodded, guilt eating away at me as I recalled yesterday's disaster. My succubus had taken things into her own hands, finding a way to feed without my knowledge. Sort of like a desert soaking up every ounce of moisture it came into contact with.

"If it's the only way."

Lilith rubbed my shoulders. "It is. And it's not going to be all bad. Or any bad. You'll see. I think if you give it a fair shake, you might even come to find that you enjoy it. There's power in coming into your own and accepting yourself for who you are." She booped the end of my nose. "Now, get your perky behind in that seat and get to work. Everything you need is available to you with a stroke of the keyboard."

She left me in a cloud of her enchanting perfume.

I took a few deep breaths, working to calm my racing heart as the weight of what I was about to do sat heavily on my shoulders. Cam work. I'd never even seen a camming site in action.

Clicking on a couple of things, I noticed that I already had a profile set up. Merri-Go-Round.

I snickered. Lilith had a wicked sense of humor.

She'd been busy. Not only had she created my profile, she'd also made my first post.

It was a simple picture of me in a tank top and shorts, my ample tits as pronounced as ever. The caption read:

Hi, I'm Merri and I'm new here.
Anyone want to help me get the hang of things?

My eyes went wide as I scrolled through the first few comments.

Tls4Tony: I'd sure like to go for a ride on your merri-go-round.

EverySteve: You need a real man to break you in, baby girl.

ShyGuy25: Nice to meet you, Merri. You're the most beautiful girl I've ever seen.

Already, little sips of lust worked their way through me.

"Maybe Auntie Lilith was onto something," I muttered.

Before I had a chance to scroll further, a chime announced an incoming message.

"Pretty Penny?" I asked aloud, accepting the message request.

PRETTYPENNY:

Hi! I'm Andi. Consider me your personal tour guide here on TwoLips.

MERRI-GO-ROUND:

Uh, hi. I didn't realize I'd get a tour guide.

PRETTYPENNY:

Oh yeah, anyone who signs up with the premium account gets assigned a liaison. I like to think of myself as a built-in bestie. I'll show you the ropes, get you all set up, and make sure you know how to keep yourself safe.

MERRI-GO-ROUND:

So you're being paid to be my friend?

PRETTYPENNY:

Well, when you put it that way, it sounds icky. Let's think of it more like a buddy system. Same as you might get at any 9 to 5. We chat around the metaphorical water cooler, lunch together, gossip about the assholes we work with/for.

MERRI-GO-ROUND:

I guess I could use someone in my corner.

PRETTYPENNY:

Can't we all? Now, tell me everything there is to know about you. I was serious about the built-in bestie thing.

It tracked. The way Auntie Lilith doted on me said the succubus would have absolutely set me up with the best, most supportive account level offered by TwoLips. She wanted to ensure I was successful. One, because if I wasn't, I might kill her clients on accident, and two, because I could tell she really wanted to take care of me. Andi was a welcome ally in a very small pool of positivity.

Just as I prepared myself to answer her question, a prickling at the back of my neck made me pause. I felt like I was being watched.

Turning my head, I glanced over my shoulder.

No one there. My room was exactly as Lilith had left it.

Frowning, I turned back to the screen, my unease only growing.

Something was off. This wasn't how the memory was supposed to go. This hadn't been what happened.

PRETTYPENNY:

So, have you ever done cam work before?

MERRI-GO-ROUND:

No, this is all new to me.

PRETTYPENNY:

From the look of you, you're going to be very popular. Take some time to peruse the other profiles on here. With your membership, you will have access to everything everyone posts. It's a perk. Learn from them and figure out what you like and don't like, then go from there.

PRETTYPENNY:

Though, if you want some unsolicited advice, I suggest you stick to the naughty/innocent thing. You have the face for it, and it drives them wild. You'll have to beat off clients with a stick. Don't pigeonhole yourself, though. Branch out every now and then, it's important to appeal to as wide an audience as possible. That way when your regulars aren't available, you still have income.

She had no idea money wasn't even on my mind. The only currency I dealt in was lust.

That uneasy creeping along my spine started up again, causing me to sit up straighter and glance around. Who the fuck was here?

That was when I caught him. Malice. He was there, like a ghost in the corner of my vision. I could feel his specific energy, oddly comforting even though it shouldn't be.

"No!" I shouted, shoving at him with my mind. He didn't get to have this memory or any other without my permission. No one did.

"Get out of my head!"

Malice

The sense of being flung back into myself was jarring, to say the least. Merri may be new at creating mental barriers, but she packed one hell of a psychic punch when she found her footing.

"Bloody hell, Merri. Where'd you get that kind of strength?" I wheezed as I tried to steady myself with a hand on one of the four posts of the bed.

She frowned, leveling her gaze on me. "That was rude."

I scoffed. "I'm sorry, do you expect the Knights to be polite?"

"No, but . . . last time you just did silly little parlor tricks and took control of my body. Why did you have to invade my privacy and go snooping around in my mind?"

"Typical," I muttered.

"Excuse me? What do you mean by that?"

"Your generation is so entitled. Do you really think an enemy is going to avoid doing something simply because you don't prefer it? No, Merri. No, they're not. They fight dirty. They will come at your weakest point and continue to batter it until you crumble because that's how battles are won. That's how they get what they want. There is no honor at the end of the world."

She was pouting and it was absolutely adorable, but I wasn't about to tell her so. Even if she'd have been receptive to it, now was hardly the time for such things. I had a point to make, and she an important lesson to learn.

"I know you're right, and you're only trying to help, but . . ." She rubbed at her chest as she trailed off. "I don't have to like it."

"You don't. You just have to learn how to protect yourself so that next time I can't get further than you want me to go."

"What if I don't want you inside my mind at all?"

"That would be the ideal. I want you strong enough to keep even me out of your head if I'm not welcome."

She blinked and then looked at me, a small furrow between her brows. "How did I know it was you? Was it just because my subconscious remembered we were in the middle of our session?"

"Perhaps. Though it's more likely it was because I've been in your mind before."

"What do you mean?"

"Each being has a unique psychic fingerprint. Once you've experienced it, you'll recognize it again. Sort of like spotting a familiar face in a crowd."

Understanding flashed across Merri's face. She knew exactly what I was referring to, and it wasn't just because my explanation was brilliant. I'd bet every Bitcoin I owned that it was from some other personal experience. Like I'd just given her the answer to a question she hadn't realized she'd had.

"My head hurts," she murmured, shutting down before my eyes. "Are we done here?"

Even if she was lying, I'd let her go. What she'd done, shoving me out of her memories, was more challenging than she knew.

"Yes. Go and rest. We will pick this up at our next session. Unless . . ."

She looked at me, her skin a little duller than before, eyes pained, hair less glossy. Merri needed to feed.

"Unless what?"

There was no ignoring the anticipation that flared to life as I offered, "Do you need me to feed you?"

She paled further, quickly shaking her head. "No. Thank you, though. I have a camming session soon. I'm all set."

Before I could protest, she was out the door and pulling it shut behind her. Camming wasn't enough. We'd already addressed that issue. I couldn't put my finger on it, but something had spooked our sweet Merri, and she was pulling away from all of us again.

I supposed I'd simply have to pay her a visit while she was working then. We'd all agreed to take care of her, and if that meant being one of her clients, so be it.

Snagging my phone, I began navigating to the app but stopped short when I saw the notification.

One new voicemail.

As soon as I clicked on it, my heart sank.

A familiar voice filled the room as the message played.

"Malice, it's Hades . . ."

CHAPTER THIRTEEN
CHAOS

"Malice, it's Hades. The one fuckin' time I need you, and you don't answer the godsdamned phone. Listen, I need to cancel the poker game we have scheduled. The shit has hit the fan, and I don't know when I'll be available again. You might have heard about the escapees, and well, that obviously needs to be dealt with. If you have any suggestions, I could really use a few good men on my side for this one. Anyway, if you could call me back to let me know that you got this, that would be great."

"What the fuck was that?" I asked, my eyes narrowed as I processed the weird-as-shit message from the god of the underworld. "Hades has never left any of us a *voicemail.*"

"Let alone asked us to call him back," Malice pointed out.

"We also don't have a poker game scheduled. Not for another twenty-five years." Grim paced in front of the bookcase, hands in his trouser pockets. "What is he playing at?"

My mind was a blur of possibilities. I considered and dismissed dozens before arriving at the only possible conclusion. "It's coded."

"Since when do we have a code with Hades?" Sin asked.

"We don't, but he's banking on the weirdness of the message to help us figure it out."

"Okay, so what is he trying to tell us?" Grim asked.

"It could be one of two things. A call for help or a Trojan horse."

Sin laughed. "I doubt he's got a bunch of Greeks hiding inside a horse just waiting to take us down."

"He does if he's actually Lucifer in disguise. The master of lies can do a lot of things. Trickery is his middle name."

Grim was studying me, his mercurial eyes dark and calculating. "And which do you think it is? A trick or a plea?"

I scrubbed a hand over my jaw. "With everything that's happening, it could be either. By mentioning the poker game, he was trying to convey something only the five of us would know about, which makes me inclined to think it's the latter."

"And the escapees would obviously be in reference to the Knights," Malice added.

I nodded my agreement. "A few good men would be us."

"He wants to go after the Knights?" Sin asked. "I know why we're on Team Keep the World Alive, but why is he? There's no upside. Think of how many souls he'd collect once everyone bites it. This isn't like him at all."

"Unless he's got something worth fighting for up here," Grim observed. "The lord of death may have found his Persephone."

"You mean the blonde he rescued?" Malice asked.

I shrugged. "Could be. We didn't exactly have time to sit down and chat."

"Then why don't we call him right now and get to the bottom of this?" Sin asked, pulling his phone from his pocket.

Grim snarled in response, his shadow expanding from under his feet and looming over Sin.

"Okay, okay, you don't have to get so grouchy. I'll put it away." Sin took one step back and returned the device to his pocket.

"You think it's Lucifer?" I asked, unsure myself.

Grim nodded, his shadow receding as he came toward the three of us. "The timing is off. Why is he contacting us now when we are hidden as deeply as possible? After each Knight has been released, there's been some sort of attack on us—"

"You mean Merri," Malice corrected.

If he was annoyed by the interruption, he didn't show it. Grim simply kept talking. "This is the first time one was released and hasn't had a lead on where to find her, or by proxy, us."

"He's trying to smoke us out," I murmured.

"I think he could be. Which means we can't take the bait. This might be the safest Merri has been since she's come under our protection."

"And if we're wrong?" Malice asked.

"Yeah, what if Hades really needs us?" Sin added.

I sighed. "Hades is a god. He doesn't need us. He will figure it out, or he'll find us."

"Chaos is right. We can't risk Merri." Grim settled himself in a chair, the antique wood creaking in warning as though protesting the use.

"Okay, so we ignore it," Malice summarized.

One by one, the rest of us nodded.

"Speaking of Merri," Grim asked, "how are the training sessions going?"

"She's getting better but still has a long way to go," I admitted. "She'll never be able to beat a Knight on her own."

"She doesn't need to beat one. Just survive long enough that one of us can get to her."

"She's getting there. We have something scheduled this afternoon. I have a couple of things planned that I think will help."

"Great. What about you?" Grim asked, turning to Malice.

"Well, she was able to push me out in half the time today. But not before I got fairly deep into her mind. Merri is strong, but . . ."

"But what?" Grim's brow lifted in question.

"But she hasn't been feeding like she should. She's not able to reach her full potential because she's refusing to feed deeply."

Sin cocked his head. "She's seemed fine the last few days. Bright-eyed and bushy-tailed."

"Not today. After she used so much energy to block me, she was winded and tired. She's doing a camming session right now to help her perk up."

Sin frowned. "She insisted on camming instead of feeding from me yesterday too."

"Did something happen?" Grim asked, looking around, accusation heavy in his voice.

"Don't look at me," I said, hands up in a placating gesture.

"Beats the hell out of me," Sin said.

Malice met Grim's gaze head-on, shrugging. "No clue. She definitely seems skittish, though."

Grim was quiet, long fingers stroking his chin as he stared hard off in the distance. "We might have to force the issue. We can't have her collapsing on us again. If Merri won't take care of herself, we'll do it for her."

"Sooo, you want us to just burst in and jerk off for her? Like a dick flash mob?"

Everyone glared at Sin.

"What? It sounded like that's what you were suggesting."

"We need to convince her to take from us. And someone needs to get to the bottom of why she's pulled away."

Sin rolled his eyes at Grim's logical response. "Dick flash mob was way more fun."

"That won't get you any closer to breeding her."

"It's called foreplay, Grimsby."

"If you think surprising a woman by bursting into her room and whipping your dick out like some sort of psycho stalker is foreplay, then there's no hope for you," Malice said.

"Oh, I dunno. Could be fun. And I'm willing to bet she'd even be into it under the right circumstances. I might float the idea as a role-play scenario."

The hell he would. A wave of possessiveness hit me from out of nowhere, making me grind my teeth together. I'd already laid my claim as her next potential partner. Sin needed to sit the fuck down and shut the fuck up.

"She's mine," I growled, causing them all to look at me. I cleared my throat. "I mean, it's my turn. I already said I'd be the next to take her."

Sin snorted. "Take her? Buddy, she's not going to be tooken. She's got to choose you. Merri holds all the cards in this scenario and she doesn't even like you that much."

Oh, she liked me. She liked me a whole hell of a lot. Sin just hadn't been paying attention. But he had a point. Merri needed to want this with me. Just like she had in my dream. The one I couldn't get out of my head.

I'd have her. But before that, I had to make sure she wanted me.

Then, and only then, I'd make that dream a reality.

"MMM, you like that, huh? You are so naughty today. What else do you want me to do for you?" Merri purred into the camera.

Watching Merri like this was its own special kind of torture. I was equal parts turned on and furious. Each time one of those fucking clowns wrote to her, I wanted to reach through the screen and strangle them.

> EverySteve: Show me your pretty pussy, baby.
>
> PimpinAintCheesy: How wet are you after using that toy?

Yes, the toy, the one she'd trailed across her panty-clad cunt over and over as she let her audience dictate the vibration levels . . . for a price, of course. My girl wasn't going to give anything away for free. Not to them, anyway.

BigMan69: Make yourself cum 4 us, pretty girl.

Bob1212: Yeah. Give us the payoff we've been waiting for.

ShyGuy25: Watching you make yourself feel good is all I need.

TIs4Tony: What a fucking beta.

I couldn't remain quiet. Usually when I spied on Merri's camming sessions, I kept to myself, but watching these assholes treat her like she was their personal toy now that I'd claimed her as my own had me seeing red.

ThisIsSparta: Just proves how bad you are in bed. Anyone who's actually experienced a female's orgasm knows that her pleasure always matters more than your own.

I didn't miss the flare in Merri's eyes, the flush that raced up her cheeks. She was excited to see me in her chat.

"Well, friends, it looks like our time is up for this session. I hope I'll see you all soon. This has been the most fun I've had in a long time." Merri leaned close to the camera, giving her clients a perfect view of her ample cleavage as it threatened to spill out of the top of her sheer pink babydoll negligee.

"Finally," I muttered, closing down the computer and striding purposefully out the door.

I hadn't wanted to interrupt her feeding, but I was itching to get her alone. I'd told the others that I would see to our mission, and I was nothing if not a good soldier.

I stood outside her room, forcing myself to remain patient. I knew she'd come out eventually, but after a few minutes, I lost the battle with myself and let myself inside. She was there on her bed, lying on her belly with her feet kicking in the air as she scrolled through the comments and left little heart emoji on each one.

Her eyes widened when she snapped her gaze to me, mouth open in a little O of surprise. She almost looked like a pinup illustration I'd seen once.

"What the hell, Chaos? Don't you know how to knock?"

Ignoring her question, I glanced at the watch on my wrist. "You're late."

"Late for what?"

"Training."

"How can I be late for something that didn't have a set time?" She repositioned herself on the bed so she was sitting on her knees, facing me with fire sparking in her pretty eyes.

My already hard cock ached at the sight of her like that. It took everything in me not to close the distance between us and fist my hand in her hair.

"It starts when I say it starts."

"That makes zero sense."

"Are you defying me, Red?"

One russet brow lifted in challenge. "What if I am?"

Fuck. I loved her spirit. No one ever dared challenge me, knowing they wouldn't survive the experience. No one until her.

"Get off the bed and come with me. We're wasting time."

"No."

"I'm sorry, I think I misheard you. What did you say?"

"I said nooo." She drew out the word and slipped off the bed, strolling past me without even a glance over her shoulder.

"We have training."

"It's not on my calendar, big guy. I don't know what to tell you."

"It's a standing date. Every day unless I say otherwise."

"Tough titties."

As she stood in front of her wardrobe, she made an exaggerated show of bending over to pick up a scrap of lace that had fallen to the floor. Her little nightie rode up and offered me a perfect view of her ass and the plump lips of her pussy covered by obviously damp silk. She couldn't see me—thank the gods—so I reached down and adjusted my throbbing dick.

"Mmm," she moaned, looking back over her shoulder with a grin. "Like what you see, Chaos?"

Fuck. She'd tasted my arousal. Of course she fucking had.

"Stop fucking around," I growled, storming over to her and lifting her up and over my shoulder.

"Hey!" she protested, feebly pounding on my back. "Put me down, you big bully!"

"You've been enough of a brat for the day. Don't make me put you over my knee and show you exactly who is in charge here."

Her pussy was so close to my face. I could probably bury my face in it if I let go of my hard-won control. Instead, I turned my head and sank my teeth into the globe of her ass.

"Ouch! Did you just bite me?"

"Do you have a problem with that? And before you try lying, you should know that it doesn't smell like it to me. Your arousal is intoxicating."

She squirmed and let out a little whimper. "I edged myself all session. You know that. Fucking creeper."

"You can say whatever you want, but your body has already betrayed you. I saw your reaction when you realized I was there. And I can feel what my touch is doing to you now. Deny it all you like, Merri, but you want me. And not just to watch. You want to know what it would be like if I split you apart."

The image of me balls deep inside her had my body tensing as that fucking dream I had replayed in my mind. I'd been out of my head with need for her, desperate to be inside her any way I could. I couldn't remember all of the details, but I specifically recalled her asking me not to spill inside her. In my dream, I'd conceded. But in reality, that was exactly what I had to do.

She was more than a little breathless as she replied, "If the lust coming off you is any indication, it's you who's wondering what it would be like."

"What if I am? What if I told you that I came in my sleep dreaming about that very thing?"

CHAPTER FOURTEEN

MERRI

Little did Chaos know, he couldn't have said anything worse than those words in that very moment. Any ounce of desire was doused by a metaphorical bucket of ice water, and I stilled, going cold in his arms.

"Put me down, Chaos."

The mention of his dream, the one I'd invaded and fed from, had all of Lilith's warnings shooting through my mind. This wasn't true desire. It was a side effect. I'd caused this. I'd begun binding him to me through my misguided attempt to feed without consequences.

His arm tightened around my thighs. "Not gonna happen, Red. I told you, we have a session."

Heaving a sigh, I went limp in his hold, knowing he could and absolutely would overpower me if needed. Hell, that was essentially what he was doing right now.

"Can I at least change first?"

"I have half a mind to make you stay in this," he muttered, finally setting me back on my feet.

"So you can ogle my boobs?" I scoffed, brushing my hair off my face so I could glare at him properly. "Come on, Chaos, be serious. I'll be flopping all over the place. You can't expect me to train like that."

He smirked in response, and I wanted nothing more than to slap that smile off his lips. "Can't I? It would certainly make our session entertaining."

"You pig."

"Are those fools lusting after you on your site any better?" he growled, taking one step forward before stopping himself.

"At least they're paying me."

His jaw clenched, making a muscle tick on the side of his face. "Get changed. But remember, there may come a time when you have to fight your way out of a situation with your perfect tits on display. It's very possible, given your preferred method of feeding, that you might not be wearing anything at all." He let out a soft hum, lust floating off him in waves. "Might be in your best interest to do a couple of nude training sessions just to get used to it."

"Your dick would be so hard you wouldn't be able to focus, and you know it."

Said dick twitched behind his sweatpants, betraying him. "If you think I couldn't fight in nothing but my skin, then you're a bigger fool than I originally thought."

I clocked his use of the word "originally" and wondered if that had changed over time or if my actions with the Knight in the penthouse had only confirmed it.

"No naked fights. That would spell disaster for both of us." I smirked. "That whole joke about just slipping and falling on your cock might be a little too real."

Hunger flashed across his face. Oh shit. He liked that a lot.

"It just might."

"The last thing we want is you accidentally knocking me up. Or smacking me in the face with your balls." I laughed.

He didn't.

"Would that really be the worst thing?"

"You teabagging me?"

"You pregnant with my child."

Oh, sweet mother of God. I really didn't want Chaos to see the way that made my nipples tighten.

"Wh-what?" I spluttered.

He reached out, one large hand sliding around the nape of my neck before he tugged me against the hard line of his body. Very hard.

"Think about it, Red. I could fuck you for hours and fill you over and over. Leave a piece of me behind so everyone would know you were mine. Mmm. It's a very tempting idea."

I stared up at him, rendered mute by his words for several heartbeats. My hands were resting over his chest, my breath coming in uneven pants. "B-but you d-don't even like me."

"I like you just fine, Red."

"Chaos . . ."

"Yeah, Red?" His lips were hovering over mine, his eyes blazing and hooded.

"The world is fucking ending. Getting pregnant would be the most irresponsible thing I could do."

He dipped his head and trailed warm lips over my ear. "Would it? Or would it be the hope we all need?"

"What do you mean?" I whispered, because I couldn't manage more than that.

"Let me feed you, Merri. You're hungry. I can feel it in the air."

The temptation to say yes and give in was so strong I was weak with it. Besides, what would be the harm in letting him try? Succubi weren't known for being Fertile Myrtles anyway. That was reserved for the shifter community. Those creatures reproduced like . . . well, bunnies.

"Well, Red. What do you say?" His finger trailed across my shoulder, slipping the strap of my nightie down.

Images filled my mind. Chaos driving deep inside me, filling me with his cum as I fed from him. It sounded really damn fantastic. If not for the ghost of Lilith's voice haunting me, I think I would have surrendered then and there, damn the consequences.

Instead I steeled myself and shoved him away. "You're mistaken. I just ate. Couldn't possibly have another bite. Besides, it's a terrible idea to train on a full stomach."

A low chuckle rumbled from deep in his chest. "Liar. Pretty little liar. I'll either feed you now or feed you after we train. You can choose, but it is happening. You and I both know the meal you have from one of your camming sessions is not enough to sate you."

He wasn't wrong. And if I was being one hundred percent honest with myself, ever since I'd had that night with all four of them, nothing had come close to sating me.

As if he could sense that he'd won some ground with that comment, he pressed on. "I've been doing some research about your kind, Merri. Learning all about the best way to ensure that you are well cared for."

I opened my mouth to comment, but he just kept on talking, his eyes locked onto mine and promising all sorts of wicked, dangerous things.

"Did you know that a feeding between a succubus and male partner is only ever truly satisfying when he fills her with his cum?"

"Wh-what? That's not true."

"Yes, it is. Think about it. When you let Sin fuck you, how did you feel afterward?"

My thighs clenched at the memory of the moment Sin came inside me. The way I'd fed was unlike anything else. I'd chalked it up to the two of us being the same and some kind of magic between us. But I'd felt so good after, energized and whole.

There was, at the very least, a kernel of truth in Chaos's declaration.

"You know I'm right. So let me take care of you, Red. Let me fill you with my cum. Let me finish what you started and put all that sweet slick between your legs to good use."

A groan escaped me entirely without my permission. I'd never been pursued like this. Usually I was the one with the dirty words and sexy innuendos. Apparently, real-life Merri was much less of a sexpot when she wasn't behind a screen. I could dish it out, but I sure as shit couldn't take it.

I reached out and pressed my palm to his chest, needing to touch him even though I knew it was leading me down a path I wasn't ready to walk. "Chaos . . ."

He stared at me, yearning in his eyes. "I dreamed of us. Of us coming together and me claiming you. It was so real. Almost like a vision of what I could have if I let myself."

Just like the last time, mention of his dream was all it took to send me plunging back to a sobering reality. His interest in me was wrong. Fake. Completely and utterly unnatural.

There was no way I could take advantage of it.

Not even two weeks ago, Chaos could barely stand to be around me, and now he was making declarations about knocking me up? Did I need a fucking neon sign to spell out the truth for me? This was all a direct result of my playing around in his mind.

It was one thing when I didn't know better, but now I did. If I allowed myself to take him up on his offer, I would be the worst sort of monster. I could not use him like that.

"No, Chaos. I'm not yours. This"—I motioned between us—"is a bad idea. It can't happen."

Frustration settled across his face. "You're wrong. It's not an if. It's a when. Resisting the pull between us is futile, Red. We both know it."

I tugged myself free of his orbit once more. "I'm going to change."

Chaos didn't follow me as I gathered some clothes and went into the bathroom for privacy. Once the door was shut, I leaned against the wood and heaved a sigh as the weight of reality set in.

He might be right. We may be fighting a losing battle. But not for the reason he thought. I couldn't tell him he was under the influence of my out-of-control power. That his body thought we were supposed to be together for one reason and one reason alone. I'd turned him into some sort of unwitting addict.

He'd never forgive me if he found out I'd caught him in my snare.

Just like I'd never forgive myself.

CHAPTER FIFTEEN

LUCIFER

"When I find her, I want you to do everything in your power to bring her to me. Everyone else has been a failure so far." I shot a pointed look at Famine, who was still bound to the wall though I'd since gagged her for good measure, then returned my attention to Greed.

She was the most beautiful of the Princes, interestingly enough. One might have expected Lust or Pride, perhaps even Envy, to claim that prize, but it was Greed. My theory was that when she was being created, her nature stole just a little bit more than everyone was given. Although I suppose the reason why didn't really matter. It was simply fact.

"My Knights and I are ready and waiting, my king."

So deferential. Just the way I liked my Princes.

"Of course they are. You want all the glory for yourself, don't you?"

She smirked. "Is there any other way to claim it? Sharing is for suckers and the bleeding hearts. The winner takes it all is a saying for a reason."

"Oh, how I wish you'd been first to be released. We'd likely already be registering for baby gifts," I mused.

"There's still time, my king. I only need to be pointed in the right direction."

"Yes," I drawled. "And I think I know how we can do that."

Her smile stretched. "Of course you do. Shall I leave you to it, then?"

I waved a hand. "You might as well stay and watch. This shouldn't take long."

Oh, wait a bloody minute. A beyond brilliant idea sparked to life as I prepared to step into my Merri's dream. Holding out my hand, I glanced from Greed's palm to my own. "What are you waiting for? Come on, then."

"You want me to dreamwalk? My king, I can't. I don't have that—"

"I don't want you to join me. I simply want to show you what I'm seeing. Two sets of eyes are better than one. Now take my hand before I chain you up the same as Famine."

Her skin skated over mine, hesitant at first.

"Oh, don't be so precious. I'm not going to bite." I grinned at her and snapped my teeth together. "Not yet, anyway."

To her credit, she didn't shy away. "If that's what you require of me, my king."

Such a good pet.

Closing my eyes, I took a deep breath and reached out to find Merri's subconscious. We were linked now, so it wasn't much of a struggle. Before long, she'd be all mine. I was tired of being a figment of her imagination.

The first thing that registered was the sensation of sunlight playing over my face. Next was the flower-kissed breeze. Instead of the beach this time, she'd chosen a blooming garden with a giant house in the near distance. It would seem sweet Merri was tired of the winter weather, her mind craving the warmth of early summer.

In fact, I'd never experienced a dream with her in anything but an idyllic temperate location. Perhaps the heat of hell wouldn't be received as poorly as it typically was for surface dwellers.

Aside from the locale, there was one notable difference to this dream versus the others I'd joined. Merri wasn't alone.

My lip curled back as an unexpected wave of jealousy rolled over me. My vessel was not supposed to be dreaming of other men. *I* was her perfect lover. She should fantasize about none other. None.

"The château has been my family's responsibility for generations. I am happy to share any of its history with you, mademoiselle. All you need do is ask," the handsome Frenchman said as he walked alongside her through the gardens.

"I wouldn't even know where to start. I had no idea there were islands in France. Certainly not ones that housed places like . . . this."

The man grinned at her, nothing but abject lust in his eyes for my —MY—woman. If I could kill him in a dream, I would, but unfortunately for me, he was not real. At least not presently.

"Oh, oui, mademoiselle. There are many."

"So how did your family come to find themselves attached to this one?"

The swoony bugger, who did not yet realize his days were numbered, wove his arm through Merri's and led her down a gravel path away from me. "Well, that is a rather long and complicated story. One that I think is best told with a cold glass of rosé."

"You'd better not let the others hear you planning to wine and dine me. I don't think they'd take well to adding anyone else to the mix."

He chuckled. "You do have quite a lot on your . . . how do you say it? Plate?"

Her laughter twined with his as they wandered farther away.

I made to follow, but the world around me became as insubstantial as mist. The dream had disappeared, which meant Merri was awake and there was nothing to connect my subconscious to hers any longer.

The man's flirtatious demeanor was burned in my mind even as my throne room came back into focus. "You'd better hope you're just a character she came up with, Frenchy. If I find you, I will kill you so thoroughly you won't remember your name as I drag your soul to hell with me."

"Did you recognize where they were, my king?" Greed asked, drawing me out of my murder plot.

"No," I said with a noticeable pout. "My knowledge of French islands housing châteaux is sadly lacking."

Famine made a noise of protest behind her gag, thrashing her head in a pitiful attempt to gain my attention. She was truly the most annoying of her sisters. If I could kill her, I would.

"Do you think it's simply a place she dreamt up?" Greed asked.

I let out a musing hum. "With that level of detail? No, I doubt it."

Famine groaned behind her gag, struggling even harder against her bonds. I sighed loudly, peering up at the ceiling as I spoke. "What can you possibly want now, Sabine? I know it's not my attention. That never ends well for you." She made another pitiful moan that had me looking at Greed conspiratorially. "Never lower yourself to working with a horsewoman. You'll regret every second of it."

"Shall I begin researching the inhabitable islands in France?" Greed asked, keeping a fair distance from me as though she worried her question might have been stupid.

It was.

Of course she should start researching inhabitable islands in France.

Famine stomped one foot, her chains rattling as she screamed behind the gag.

Shaking my head, I turned away from the disappointment of a horsewoman and looked into Greed's eyes with a measured calm I didn't think I had in me.

"Yes. Go find out everything you can about those islands. Some may be small enough to be privately owned."

The clink of chains drew my focus once more to where Sabine

was restrained. But instead of the bloodied, pathetic woman I expected to see, all I found was empty shackles and a dirty gag on the floor. Famine was gone. She'd abandoned her post. I hadn't taken her for a coward.

"Well, can't say I saw that coming."

CHAPTER

SIXTEEN

MERRI

I wrinkled my nose as I noticed the fresh dump of snow that had accumulated overnight. I was so ready for winter to be over. Letting the curtain fall back over the window, I sighed and glanced around my room. The truth was, I didn't have to stay in here, locked away from social interactions. I could be downstairs right now, talking with Sin, making Grim teach me about plants, ogling Chaos, or asking Malice to help me test my mental barriers again. But that would mean I'd need to make myself vulnerable to all sorts of other things. Namely, the risk of getting attached to these handsome horsemen.

And that could not happen. Not under any circumstance. Chaos had proven yesterday just how fragile my self-control was.

Thus my self-inflicted exile.

Was it an exile when you didn't leave a specific place? What was the word for exiling in the same spot? Quarantine? Internment? House arrest?

Just as my thoughts truly began to spiral, there was a brief knock at my door. I didn't even have a chance to respond to it before the door cracked open.

"Mademoiselle? Are you decent?" Christian asked, his voice hesitant but not unwelcome.

I was more than decent. I'd bundled up in the warmest sweater available in my wardrobe, as well as a pair of fleece-lined leggings, wool socks, and soft slippers. "Yes. Come in."

He pushed the door open a bit further but remained firmly on the other side of the threshold, his arms filled with a large stack of something.

"Ah, this will not do. Your fire is dying. No wonder you are so cold." He set the bundle on my bed and rushed to the fireplace, which looked fine to me, but what did I know?

In minutes, he'd stoked the wood, added more, and the flames had gone from meager to robust.

He stood, dusting off his hands and beaming at me. "There. Much better. You should be warm in no time."

"Thanks. I guess I should've realized something wasn't right when the windowpanes frosted over."

"It's these old houses," he said with a shrug. "Even with the improvements, they aren't the most insulated." As if remembering something, he straightened and picked up the stack of what I could now tell was clothes. "Which reminds me, these finally came for you."

"What are they?"

"Outerwear. Gloves, a hat, and a heavy winter coat to ensure you are properly bundled for when you take your afternoon stroll through the grounds."

"You noticed," I said, touched he'd been paying attention enough to realize I'd been enjoying the outdoors even with an ill-fitting coat, hat, and gloves.

"Oui. It is my job to notice these things."

"Well, thank you. That was really kind of you."

Christian shrugged again, as if it was no big deal. "And if there's anything else that you need during your stay, please do not hesitate to ask. I am here to help."

There was a moment where I thought about exactly how Christian could help me, but I immediately snuffed the idea out. *No. Bad Merri. He wasn't offering to be your own personal buffet. He's human. He can't handle you. It's horsemen or camming, and you already decided that all things horse are off the menu.*

A pang of hunger protested, but I pushed it away. I could cam later. I would have to. Maybe Cole would be around for some one-on-one time. And I needed to check in on 1N3V1T@BL3 and see how he liked his personalized content. There was a good chance he'd have something to say about it that would tide me over.

Christian excused himself, shutting the door behind him and leaving me alone with my thoughts and the crackling fire as my only company.

I had to admit, the coat was pretty. Puffy and stuffed with down, I could tell from first glance it would keep me as warm as possible the next time I went outside. What a thoughtful gesture on his part. I was glad I'd controlled myself and resisted the urge to go all succubus on him.

I was just trying on the gloves—leather but lined with the softest fur—when a chime on my laptop announced an incoming message. I hadn't planned on working quite yet, but you had to make hay while the sun was shining, right?

Tossing the gloves and coat aside, I moved over to the desk and clicked on my messages.

There was no faking my smile when I saw it was from Andi and not one of my clients.

PRETTYPENNY:

Hey girl heeeeyyy.

MERRI-GO-ROUND:

Well, hey there. What are you doing up at this hour? Isn't it like the middle of the night?

PRETTYPENNY:

I'm an all-hours opportunist. Sleep is for the weak.

MERRI-GO-ROUND:

Fair enough.

PRETTYPENNY:

What about you? What have you been up to with those handsome bodyguards of yours? Please tell me there's a sexy forbidden love square happening by now.

MERRI-GO-ROUND:

Love square? Lol I wouldn't say that. There have been some . . . developments, though.

PRETTYPENNY:

OMG tell me everything. I'll get a glass of wine.

Part of me shouted to keep it private and not kiss and tell, but honestly, I really needed some girl talk. I was drowning in a sea of testosterone, and I needed an estrogen life preserver right now.

MERRI-GO-ROUND:

Well . . .

PRETTYPENNY:

Babes, if you don't spit it out, I'm going to reach through this screen and throttle you. Now spill!

MERRI-GO-ROUND:

I slept with one of them. A couple of times.

PRETTYPENNY:

Oh. Is that all? 🥱 I was hoping for an orgy.

MERRI-GO-ROUND:

Are you serious???

PRETTYPENNY:

Uh, yeah. Sex is what we do. Did you guys at least get kinky? Ooh, did he leave marks?

I thought about my first dreamwalk and the bruises on my hips.

MERRI-GO-ROUND:

there were some marks

PRETTYPENNY:

Yessss! Thatta girl.

PRETTYPENNY:

And did he wrap it up, or did you have him finish on you?

My cheeks flamed as the memory of Sin's cum dripping down my thighs replayed in my mind.

MERRI-GO-ROUND:

Um . . .

PRETTYPENNY:

Anal?

Now I was thinking about Chaos.

MERRI-GO-ROUND:

Um . . .

PRETTYPENNY:

MA'AM. I know I taught you better than that. Cum shots are great, but a baby bump is the worst thing you can do for your career right now. Tell me you were smart.

MERRI-GO-ROUND:

I'm fine. He's shooting blanks.

God, I was a liar. I had no idea if Sin could get me pregnant, but it wasn't likely.

PRETTYPENNY:

Did he show you proof? Because that sounds like a line to me. 'No, baby, we don't need a condom, I'm sterile.' *insert jack-off gif here* You should get tested. Stat. Just to be sure.

MERRI-GO-ROUND:

Okay. Okay. As soon as I can. Are you happy?

PRETTYPENNY:

Not really. No orgy and you might have gotten yourself knocked up.

MERRI-GO-ROUND:

It was really great, if that's any consolation.

PRETTYPENNY:

Consider my ears perked.

MERRI-GO-ROUND:

And he's not the one who has a breeding kink anyway.

PRETTYPENNY:

J'scuse?!

MERRI-GO-ROUND:

One of them tried to turn me into a puddle with his dirty talk. He really laid it on thick once he realized the risky behavior turned me on.

PRETTYPENNY:

My my, how the plot thickens. No wonder you let that dude blow his load in you. SMH baby has a breeding kink.

MERRI-GO-ROUND:

I didn't have an opportunity to think about it before. There's no way any of my clients could ever do it.

PRETTYPENNY:

Well, I guess it's not the worst thing. Minus, you know, your line of work and the state of the world. But, in general.

PRETTYPENNY:

Does this mean if you *are* pregnant, you'll keep it? Am I going to be an auntie?

MERRI-GO-ROUND:

Jesus, Andi. I'm not.

PRETTYPENNY:

You could be.

MERRI-GO-ROUND:

I'm not. I'd know by now.

Truthfully, I would have no fucking clue. But I needed to say something that would appease Andi and get her off this topic.

PRETTYPENNY:

Have you gotten your period?

Succubi didn't have the same reproductive cycles as human females. It was part of the reason my kind was so notoriously infertile. Basically, the stars had to align under a very strict set of circumstances for the window to even be open. It wasn't impossible, but it was far from easy. Understandably so. With as much sex as we were supposed to have, we couldn't very well be at risk of being impregnated every time. It was pretty counterintuitive to our base function in the world.

But I couldn't tell Andi any of that, so instead, I did what I seemed to be best at. I lied.

MERRI-GO-ROUND:

Any day now.

PRETTYPENNY:

Hmmm. You'd better tell me the moment Aunt Flo arrives. I'll start knitting some booties just in case.

MERRI-GO-ROUND:

Please don't.

PRETTYPENNY:

Oh, what about a cute little hat with devil horns? Something tells me any baby you make will be just as devilish as he is adorable.

With Famine as his potential father, that wasn't entirely far off. Not that I was thinking about Sin as the father of my nonexistent children. Or any of the horsemen for that matter.

Nope.

Definitely not.

Remember when I said I was good at lying? Yup. That even applied to myself.

Or maybe especially to myself.

A notification popped up on my screen, and the name that appeared made my heart flip just a little. Cole. If I didn't know better, I'd say I had missed him.

MERRI-GO-ROUND:

GTG. Client wants a private.

PRETTYPENNY:

Kk. Let me know if I'm gonna be an auntie! 💋

MERRI-GO-ROUND:

🙄 don't hold your breath. I wouldn't want you to die

PRETTYPENNY:

And miss out on my hot paramedic moment? Rude!

I laughed and closed out of our chat so I could maximize Cole's.

SHYGUY25:

There you are. I was hoping you'd answer.

MERRI-GO-ROUND:

😉 I haven't been gone that long. Did you really miss me that much?

SHYGUY25:

I always miss you when I'm not talking to you. You're my favorite part of the day.

MERRI-GO-ROUND:

Aw thanks, handsome. You're definitely the highlight of mine.

SHYGUY25:

Really? Do you mean that? 😍

Currently? Yes. But only because of my situation. Outside of that? Not really. I'd had a lot of highlights recently. Most involving Sin and Chaos.

SHYGUY25:

Merri??

MERRI-GO-ROUND:

What are you up to right now? Did you meet your deadline?

The guilt of lying to him made my skin itchy, so I went with a little redirection, hoping it might work in my favor.

SHYGUY25:

Not yet. I have some more time before I have to get everything done, but I'm on track.

MERRI-GO-ROUND:

That's great. I'm really proud of you.

Dots bounced on the screen and then stopped. It went on long enough I could tell he'd typed something and deleted it.

MERRI-GO-ROUND:

Since when are you shy with me? What were you going to say?

SHYGUY25:

It's nothing. Honestly. I just couldn't remember the last time someone told me they were proud of me.

MERRI-GO-ROUND:

Well, that's a shame. You work hard. You're kind and gentle. You're a good man, I can tell. You deserve someone in your life who tells you how proud they are.

SHYGUY25:

Maybe it's you.

MERRI-GO-ROUND:

Me?

SHYGUY25:

Maybe you bring it out in me. The goodness and kindness.

MERRI-GO-ROUND:

I don't believe that. You've been the same sweet guy since I met you. So the math doesn't math.

SHYGUY25:

Math is gross.

MERRI-GO-ROUND:

Facts. It's clearly an instrument of the devil.

SHYGUY25:

Hey, don't put that on him. He gets blamed for all the bad things.

MERRI-GO-ROUND:

. . . he's the devil . . . King of Bad Things.

SHYGUY25:

🤔 hear me out

MERRI-GO-ROUND:

Fine, I'm listening.

SHYGUY25:

God is literally "the creator." He created everything. Therefore, God created math.

MERRI-GO-ROUND:

That's a surprisingly good point. But didn't man technically invent math?

SHYGUY25:

Man discovered math. But fine, need another example? God also created the Pacific Hatchetfish. And I don't know if you've ever seen one of those things, but it's terrifying. Probably best not to google it if you haven't. It's not called a dead-eyed ghoulfish for nothing.

SHYGUY25:

Also spiders.

MERRI-GO-ROUND:

Wow, you've really put a lot of thought into this.

SHYGUY25:

I do a lot of research.

MERRI-GO-ROUND:

I was actually smiling even as I sent the emoji. Cole and I hadn't had a conversation like this in a long time, but it reminded me exactly why I liked him so much. He was insightful and sweet, but also incredibly intelligent. It gave me such a competency boner.

SHYGUY25:

Sorry, I went on a bit of a tangent.

MERRI-GO-ROUND:

No, don't apologize. I loved it. I'm sitting here with my chin in my hands, waiting to see what other knowledge bomb you're going to drop on me.

SHYGUY25:

Did you know camels can't have sex by themselves?

MERRI-GO-ROUND:

You mean they can't masturbate?

SHYGUY25:

lol, no. They need human assistance to do the deed.

MERRI-GO-ROUND:

How did they reproduce without humans before humans found them? That can't be true.

SHYGUY25:

Divine intervention?

MERRI-GO-ROUND:

So there was some poor angel assigned camel sex duties?

SHYGUY25:

His name was Frank.

MERRI-GO-ROUND:

😂 Frank? There's an angel named Frank?

SHYGUY25:

The name had to start somewhere.

MERRI-GO-ROUND:

All right, smartguy. Any other fun camel facts for me?

SHYGUY25:

Well . . . they're polygamous.

MERRI-GO-ROUND:

Of course they are.

SHYGUY25:

And the males bite the females' genitals as part of the courting ritual.

MERRI-GO-ROUND:

😱 now you're just messing with me. Also ouch.

SHYGUY25:

Annnnnd they come 4 times in one go. So you know. Dick humps are a thing I guess.

MERRI-GO-ROUND:

Dick humps?!?!?!

SHYGUY25:

Well, they store water in their humps, so they must have extra dick humps to store all that jizz. Or they just want to really make it count when their good buddy Frank shows up.

I let out a cackle loud enough I had to stop and wait to see if any of the horsemen were going to come check on me. When I was certain the coast was clear, I refocused on the screen, another little snicker escaping me as I reread his last message and typed my reply.

MERRI-GO-ROUND:

So . . . testicles.

SHYGUY25:

Well, yeah, if you want to be pedantic about it.

MERRI-GO-ROUND:

Big testicles?

SHYGUY25:

Come on, admit it, dick humps sounds so much more on brand. And it has flair.

MERRI-GO-ROUND:

You've got me there.

SHYGUY25:

Shit. I have to go take care of something unavoidable. Can we pick this up again later?

MERRI-GO-ROUND:

Sure. But . . .

SHYGUY25:

But what?

I bit my lower lip as the idea percolated. I'd never taken my conversations with any of my clients off the site, but Cole was more to me than just a John who paid for my time. He was my friend, as this conversation just proved. It wasn't sexual at all. Well, not unless you counted camel sex facts as foreplay. Which I didn't.

MERRI-GO-ROUND:

Can we stop messaging like this here? I'd rather you text me instead.

SHYGUY25:

😱 Really?

MERRI-GO-ROUND:

Is that okay with you?

SHYGUY25:

Yeah. Of course it is. I'd love that.

MERRI-GO-ROUND:

Great. 😘

I sent him my number with my heart in my throat. In seconds, my phone dinged with a text from an unknown number.

UNKNOWN ID:

It's me 🩶

I programmed him into my contacts, but instead of using his name, I simply set him as C.

ME:

Hi there.

C:

I'll talk to you later, Merri. Thanks for letting me in.

ME:

I'm glad I did.

C:

You won't regret it. 😉 🩶

Realizing what I'd just done and the possible implications, my tummy gave a nervous flip. I sure hoped he was right.

CHAPTER SEVENTEEN

GRIM

I was keenly aware that there was something ominous about the image I cut—a dark figure standing out in the pure white snow amongst the bare trees and frozen pond. I was the danger lurking not in shadow but plain sight.

Unbidden, my eyes shot to the ground where my shadow rippled, moving like a marionette although I remained still. He was restless. My power had returned in leaps and bounds over the last few weeks. Admittedly, it had been slow going in the immediate aftermath of Hel's ritual, but now that I was out here surrounded by nature my power reservoir was nearly overflowing. Unlike my brothers, who had to go out in order to rebuild their strength, I merely had to exist. The circle of life continued no matter where I was. At any given moment, *something* in my proximity was in a state of decay. That was all I required.

Sin liked to remind me how categorically unfair it was that I could be replenished so easily. I'd given up trying to make him understand that with this power, I also suffered the crippling knowledge that I'd never know the touch of a friend or lover without killing them. And while, yes, I could refill my reservoir by walking into a room and killing everyone in sight, I alone knew how fragile mortal lives were. How precious. So I preferred not to. Instead, I reaped souls when I had to in order to serve a greater purpose.

My footsteps crunched across the frozen ground as I made my way back from my stroll. Disappointment threaded through me at the knowledge that Merri hadn't come out as she usually did. I'd accompanied her daily, though she was none the wiser. I enjoyed watching the way her breath made little clouds as she walked, the sight of her hair blowing in the wind, the scent of her that was left in her wake. She'd become my obsession ever since the dream I'd had.

Oh, who was I kidding? I'd been obsessing over her from the moment we took her. But now? Keeping her in my sight was damn near a compulsion. The longer I went without seeing her, the stronger the itch beneath my skin. Even now it scratched at me, urging me to go seek her out and discover what had kept her indoors today.

A gentle tugging in my belly drew my attention from the ice-covered pond. It was a sensation I was intimately familiar with, and at first, panic gripped my chest. Someone was dying, and the pull was coming from the direction of the house.

"Fuck."

I didn't even bother with walking the relatively short distance, calling on our preferred—though less used—method of teleporting. Between one heartbeat and the next, I was at the door. Just as I went to enter, that tugging came again, this time pulling me away from the door.

Brow furrowed, I turned, my shadow lengthening and stretching like a sentient compass, leading me in the direction I was meant to go. The soul I would be reaping wasn't inside. But who was it?

I followed, rounding the corner until I came upon the broken body of a raven, its wings twitching, neck bent at an unnatural angle. The poor thing must've flown into a pane of glass but hadn't hit quite hard enough to avoid a slow and painful death.

"Hush now, I've got you," I murmured, sending the shadow form of my hand out to the bird.

It struggled for only a moment before I carefully scooped its soul from its body, leaving the remains silent and still on the snow. Before returning to me, my shadowed fist opened, releasing the flickering soul. I watched the spark fly away, its spirit form taking shape the further it flew. Relief filled me as the soul was given back to the universe. Contrary to popular belief, Death wasn't a sinister enemy. Not always. I preferred to think of myself as the close of a chapter. A necessary break before starting again. There was peace in that. And mercy.

Although, of course, there didn't have to be. That gift was mine alone to offer or withhold.

Energized from the power boost, I made my way back to the front of the house, my mind still weighing the role I played in this world. It wasn't until I was halfway up the stairs that I caught the sound of Merri's laughter and that infernal itching beneath my skin came roaring back.

"What's so funny, wildflower?"

I hated knowing someone was making her laugh when I couldn't even touch her. It sent jealousy blazing through every cell in my body to think Sin or Chaos was in her room with her right now.

"No fair, man. You sunk my battleship. You always fucking win this game." Sin's voice filtered from the den, followed by Chaos's satisfied laugh.

"Strategy is not your strong suit."

Peeking around the corner, I saw that they were alone. No Merri.

If not them causing her mirth, who?

A more rational man would not have taken that as an invitation to go and discover the answer.

Another giggle came from upstairs. There was no way it could be Malice making her laugh. He didn't entertain anyone.

"Who do you have in there with you?" I murmured as I ascended the rest of the staircase and made my way to her closed door.

With barely a whisper of sound, I cracked it open and peered inside. Merri was sitting at her desk, computer on, fingers flying over her keyboard. From the way she'd been giggling, I couldn't surmise whether she was working or playing. Fuck me, but I wanted her to be playing with *me*.

You could always log in and watch.

As far as ideas went, it wasn't terrible.

"Mmm, but do you have big ones?" she murmured before she typed something and let out another giggle.

Oh, I'd show her big ones. The walls and door around me darkened as my shadow expanded along with my jealousy. All I wanted was for my dream encounter with Merri to be real, and hearing her flirting with some knob online only drove home the point that I would never have her.

I'd have to settle for the pieces of her that were available to me.

With that thought in mind, I stalked down the hall, my shadow swelling behind me like a billowing cloak.

Just ahead, Sin turned the corner, heading to his room. He took one look at me from his doorway and snickered. "Looks like the 'I am the night' portion of the day has begun. Go on. Say it. I'm Batman."

Without a word, I sent my shadow at him, shoving him inside and slamming the door closed in his face.

"Ow," he whimpered from behind the wood. "My nose."

I smirked, then pulled my darkness in closer. He'd be fine. Unfortunately.

With Merri's sweet giggles still echoing in my head, I stormed into my room and made a beeline for my computer. The curtains were already drawn, blanketing the large space in comforting shadows, and as the screen came to life, I gave myself a moment to gather my composure.

"If you're going to be distracted, wildflower, it's going to be because of me."

I logged in to my account on TwoLips and navigated straight to the only page that interested me. Merri's.

She wasn't live.

A sneer curled my upper lip. Was she in a private session?

No. She wasn't logged in at all. The little green circle at the bottom right of her picture was gray.

So who the fuck was she talking to?

Before I had a chance to follow the line of thought, I noticed the little 1 icon next to the envelope symbol at the top of my screen. I had a new unread message.

That could only be from one person.

I clicked on the icon, and my mouth ran dry at the video that began auto-playing.

"Oh hi, Daddy," Merri purred into the camera.

Her voice went directly to my cock. I'd already been half hard since spying on her in her room, but now? Fuck, I was done for. It was like a pulse of lust was trained straight between my legs.

My gaze wandered over her form, the sweet-as-pie pair of braids trailing over her shoulders, the pouty pink lips, her spray of freckles. But what really got me was the crisp white men's button-down she wore. It was many sizes too large for her, only held closed by two buttons in the middle of the shirt, the fabric gaping open and showing tantalizing glimpses of her silken skin.

"I hope you don't mind," she continued, fingers lazily playing with the placket of the shirt, drawing my attention to her cleavage. "I snuck into your closet and grabbed one of your shirts."

I glanced at my closet before my brain reminded me that she didn't actually know who I was, so she couldn't have done that. But the thought that she had . . . fuuuck.

She brought the collar to her nose and inhaled. "Mmm, it smells like you. God, I miss you, Daddy." Her bottom lip pushed out into a little frown.

Annnd my palm had somehow found its way to my rock-hard erection. I gave myself a squeeze and groaned as my dick throbbed in response. If she was anywhere as good with her mouth as my subconscious had made her out to be, I wouldn't make it out of a night with her alive. What a twist that would be.

"Such a good fucking girl for me," I rasped out, knowing she couldn't hear me but desperate to say it nonetheless.

She leaned closer to the camera, and I swore I could see a tiny sliver of dusky nipple. "I hope you can find some time for us soon. I'd really love to talk to you and make sure you're getting all your . . . needs met. Just let me know when you want to see me, okay, Daddy?"

"How about right now, wildflower?" I murmured.

"Hope you're having a great day, or if not, that my little message made it better," she continued, blowing a kiss into the camera. "Bye for now . . . Daddy."

The message ended and I already missed the sound of her voice. I didn't care that she didn't know she was speaking to *me*, Grimsby. That message was still created for me, which only sent every feral, obsessive part of me into overdrive.

It took all of a heartbeat for me to pull my aching cock free of my trousers and press play on the video again. I might not be able to touch her, but I could still remember the way her hot little mouth felt as she sucked on me like I was her favorite thing in the world.

Closing my fist around my length, I began a slow rhythm as I focused on her. The way her eyes sparkled when she spoke, the shape of her mouth, the play of fingers over her delicate throat. I was already keyed up from earlier, but now? Fuck, now I was wound so tight I knew it wouldn't take much more before I found my release.

Merri had just blown me her second kiss when a hand touched my shoulder.

"Inevitable, huh?" Sin asked from behind me. "I knew you wouldn't be able to stay off her site."

"Motherfucker!" I snarled, jumping up from my chair. "What the hell are you doing in my room uninvited?"

"Uninvited?" Sin asked, a smirk on his mouth. "I wouldn't say that." He closed his eyes and inhaled deeply. "My nose doesn't lie."

“You could smell my dick?” I glanced down at my now flagging erection.

“Gross. No. But I sure as hell could smell your lust. I’m sure Merri could too. Maybe I should call her in here?” He glanced over his shoulder. “Oh, Me—” his words cut off on a grunt as I elbowed him hard in the stomach.

“If you say another word, I’ll string you up by your balls and leave you outside for the ravens to pick at.”

Sin frowned for a beat and then shrugged. “Wouldn’t be the worst way I’ve spent a day.”

“Get the fuck out of my room.”

His eyes fluttered closed and he took another deep inhale. “Thanks for the snack.” Then the bastard winked and added, “Daddy.”

CHAPTER EIGHTEEN

SIN

The scent of warm tobacco and smoke curled in my nose as I walked into the billiards room to meet the boys for "book club." Yeah, that's right, I'd gotten an invite this time. As I should have from the start.

Okay, to be fair, it was less invite and more summons, but whatever, I'd take it.

"You're late," Grim grumbled from around the cigar in his mouth.

"I'm exactly on time. Also, has anyone ever told you it's rude to talk with your mouth full, Grimsby?"

Malice snickered as he straightened, the ball he'd just aimed at sinking effortlessly into one of the corner pockets. "Is that your way of saying we should gag you, Sinclair?" Moving around the table, he made another shot, this one missing.

"He'd probably like it. Don't tempt him," Chaos offered, lining up his own shot before sending two of the striped balls into the center pocket on the left side of the table.

"It's true," I agreed, earning scowls from all three of them. Laughing, I shrugged, "What? Can't blame a guy for being open-minded."

Grim sighed, shaking his head. "Now that you're here, we can get to business."

"She's still not pregnant. We know." I stared pointedly at Grim, not understanding why he needed to reiterate the fact that I failed in my first attempt.

"And why is that?"

"I don't know, why don't you ask Chaos? He's just over there playing with his stick and balls instead of trying to up the odds of success."

Chaos swore as he scratched, his eyes flashing with fury as he glared at me. "I tried. She wasn't interested."

I crowed. "What was that about seduction and foreplay? You're not the master you thought you were, after all? Do you need some tips? I can draw you a diagram if that's more helpful. The clit can be found—"

I barely ducked in time as he used his pool cue like a javelin. Instead of impaling me, it went nearly halfway through the wall behind me.

"Hey! That could have left a scar."

"I know."

Chaos might've acted like he hated me, but I knew the truth. He only strongly disliked me.

Malice handed him a fresh stick before moving to sink his next shot. "She's been distant ever since you two slept together."

"Not true," I said, though on second thought, he was sort of right. Kinda. A little. "She was really affectionate and sweet with me. I thought we'd made some headway, actually."

"We'd broken down some barriers as well during our training sessions. There's undeniable chemistry between us, but still she refuses me." Chaos's lips twisted in a frustrated frown.

"Are you sure the chemistry is on both sides?" I asked.

"I'm fucking sure."

I held my hands up in surrender. "Just asking."

"What did you do?" Grimsby accused. I hadn't been paying

attention to him, so I'd missed him standing and sneaking up behind me.

"Nothing! Nothing! It's not my fault if she fell in love with me. Obviously she's decided to be a one-horseman succubus."

The eight ball soared across the room as Malice overshot the cue. Grim caught the ball with one of his shadows, holding it up with a question in his eyes. "If that logic stands, then why isn't she feeding from you? Why is she avoiding you, as well as the rest of us?"

"She's not."

All three of them gave me varying expressions of disbelief.

I sighed and raked a hand through my hair. "I mean, yeah, she hasn't invited me back to her bed, but she's not, like, avoiding me or anything."

The air of incredulity in the room shot up several notches.

"Seriously. You know how big a deal it was for her to be intimate with someone without a screen between them. I think she's just adjusting to it. She needs a little time to make peace with the shift or whatever."

They didn't need to know she'd told me she couldn't be monogamous. In my heart, I knew it was more than that. The truth was that she'd gotten scared. Her feelings for me were just too powerful, and Merri didn't want to be vulnerable with anyone. Not truly vulnerable.

"I think there's more to it," Malice drawled, echoing my own conclusion. "She's afraid of something."

"What did you say to her, Sin?" Chaos bit out.

"Why is this all on me? Everything was fine until she was alone with you, Chaos. She was feeling great, looking all glowy and healthy. Then you tried to smolder her to death, and she stopped giving any of us real attention."

A soft snarl escaped Chaos before he muttered, "Everything was fine until I admitted that I'd been dreaming about her."

One by one, the rest of us went still.

"You dreamed about her?" Grim asked, his voice carefully neutral.

Chaos's brows furrowed. "Yeah. Why?"

"So did I," Malice admitted.

"Me too," Grim finally said.

They all turned to me expectantly. "Yeah. So? I had a dream about her. What else is new?"

"Is it a coincidence we're all dreaming about her?" Chaos asked, putting his pool cue away before leaning his hip on the side of the table.

"It's not that strange. Especially since we're all under the same roof with a succubus. Her power calls to us." Malice wandered over to the chess board and knocked over the white queen with a smirk. "It stands to reason she'd infiltrate our dreams. That is the nature of fantasy, after all."

"Perhaps," Chaos said, clearly not convinced.

"You think it was something else?" Grim asked.

Chaos shrugged. "Seems significant that it happened to all of us in a short span of time. Do you know of any reason that might happen?" he asked, pinning me with his gaze.

I shook my head. "No, but then I didn't exactly have a mentor in the sexual demon arts, so my education is spotty. I can look into it, though, if that would make you feel better."

"I think that might be for the best. If only to confirm Malice's theory," Chaos said.

"Do you think she was feeding on us while we slept?" Grim asked.

"Doubtful. My dream wasn't sexual. It was . . . kinda sweet, actually." I smiled as flashes of the fantasy filled my head. Without meaning to, I started humming the melody of the song. My fingers itched to put it to paper.

"Same here. For the most part. No sex, though. Not much for her to feed off of." Malice cut a glance at Grim. "What about you?"

Death looked uncharacteristically sheepish.

"Aw, he's blushing," I teased.

"I am not."

"Are so."

"Am not."

"Are s—"

"Shut up!" he snapped. "Yes, okay. Mine was sexual."

"Did she call you Daddy?"

He shoved me so hard I went over the back of a sofa.

"So that's a yes, then," I said as I got to my feet. I snickered, recalling how potent his lust had been every time she'd called him that in his little video. God, his arousal had been a much-needed snack. My mouth watered as I realized how hungry I was. I needed to feed. ASAP.

"Chaos, you're awfully quiet," Malice observed.

"Mine was sexual. Very sexual."

"We're gonna circle back to that in a little bit," I said.

"No. We're not."

Malice made a soft, considering sound. His arms were crossed and his gaze averted as he surmised, "So only two of us had sexual dreams. That means we can't say with any certainty that Merri was behind it."

"But we also can't rule it out," Chaos said.

"Well, something has made her take a big step back from us, and whatever it is, we need it fixed." I dragged a hand through my hair and sighed, fighting the slightly woozy feeling threatening to make me sway. "I have to feed, and soon. So does she. She's not getting what she needs from her camming sessions but won't come to us for help. If this goes on much longer, she's going to accidentally kill Christian in the kitchen."

"He's off-limits," Malice warned. "We need him."

"I'm just stating the obvious. If she and I aren't feeding off each other or you three, he's the only viable candidate left. Sex demons gotta fuck, or however the saying goes."

"That's not a saying," Malice said.

"Should be."

Grim let out a frustrated breath. "The bigger issue here is that we have to breed her. Sex is an obvious and vital part of achieving our goal. There is no time to waste. It's a matter of when, not if, he finds her. Her womb cannot be empty when he does. And with every Prince that's released, Lucifer grows stronger, and his army swells. The sooner she's bred, the weaker he will be, thus the easier to defeat."

A beyond brilliant idea came to blazing life. "I have a plan."

The annoyance rolled off the three of them in waves. "Enlighten us," Malice said.

"I'll join her cam session."

"Watching her perform won't get her pregnant," Chaos protested.

"No, no. I mean *I'll join in.* IRL." I waited a beat, staring at their blank expressions. "In real life."

"So you'll fuck her for an audience," Grim stated, his tone betraying how much he didn't like this idea.

"Well, if she won't let us feed her as a team, I'll need to bring in some bigger numbers to her camming session to make up for the difference. Which will be easy as soon as I post on my socials what's about to go down. That way both of us have more than enough to keep us full. Two birds, one bone." I waggled my eyebrows.

"I really do hate you," Malice murmured.

"You say that, but I'm the only one contributing here." I stretched and let out a pleased sigh before cracking my neck. "If you'll excuse me, boys. I have to see a succubus about scheduling a rendezvous with a rock star. That's right, I'm coming out of retirement and giving the world the Sin sex tape they didn't know they needed."

CHAPTER NINETEEN

MERRI

"Okay, so tell me more about this hottie who may or may not have knocked you up," Andi said, her voice coming from my phone's speaker as I continued putting away the outfit options I'd discarded.

My cheeks burned as I thought of Sin and the way he'd touched me.

"He's a musician," I finally said.

"Yu-um," she said. "Tell me he's covered in tattoos."

"He is," I admitted, though I hadn't really gotten a chance to study any of them in detail. I'd been sort of preoccupied the last time he was naked. "They're just hidden most of the time."

"And what kind of music does he play?"

"Well, he plays guitar, but he's mostly the frontman."

"OMG, is he in a band? One I might know?" Her excitement sent her voice up to a register I was pretty sure only dogs could hear.

"No," I said with a nervous chuckle. "He's retired, and now he's part of that security firm. Which is why he's one of my bodyguards."

"Oh." There was no missing her disappointment. "Wait, does

that mean he's a silver fox? Does he call you his good girl? Ohmygawd."

I thought of Grim and had to fan my face.

"You're ridiculous."

"You know, I think this is good for you. You've been so hesitant to let anyone in. He might not be *the one,* but he's sure showing you there are worse things than giving your heart to someone. Maybe now you'll find the guy you're really made for."

I scoffed. "How do you know he's not *the one*?"

"You said he's a musician. Definitely not known for their staying power."

I made a soft sound that wasn't really an agreement or dismissal.

"You know what they are good for, though? Sex. And making babies. Speaking of, did you take that pregnancy test yet?"

"No, because I'm not pregnant."

"Silly goose, you take the test to find out whether you're pregnant. Not once you already know."

"Exactly. Which is why I'm not wasting the money on buying one."

"You're being stupid. For the record."

"Your grievance is noted."

"I'm just saying, putting your head in the sand is not going to suddenly make you un-knocked up."

"I'm not knocked up!" I shouted with exasperation just as Sin popped his head into my room.

"Phew, that's a relief. Not that I wouldn't love to see you with a mini-me, but I'd like it if I knew about it before whoever that is on the phone."

God, the man's voice sent a shiver down my spine that had nothing to do with fear.

"Oh, is that him? Please tell me it's him." Andi's hushed whisper was still audible across the room.

"Andi, you're on speaker."

Sin smirked and sauntered farther inside. "Yes. It's him. As long as being him is a good thing. Otherwise, my name is Mal."

I bit back my smile and shook my head. "What are you doing in here, Sinclair?"

He leaned against the bed frame, hands tucked into his pockets. He looked entirely too edible. "I came by with a business proposition for you and your site."

"Oh?" I said, curiosity piqued.

"I was going to offer my services."

"What services?"

He pointed at himself. "I'm a household name. I figured if we teamed up, we'd get a metric fuck ton of followers. You know"—he eyed the phone on my bed—"rake in those big bucks."

"Is he saying what I think he's saying?" Andi interjected.

"He is," Sin answered. "You and me, Merri. Live, on camera, for a price."

The thought of how well the two of us could feed made my stomach growl audibly, and I reflexively licked my lips.

"Do it. Do it. Do it," Andi chanted. "It will be absolutely huge for your following. Any time you can cross promote is always a good thing. Also . . . how household is household? Are we talking a Rock and Roll Hall of Famer or something?"

"Pretty much," I rasped, unable to come up with anything else that might be helpful. I was still too stuck on the idea of letting Sin fuck me for an audience. I swallowed to try and get some moisture back in my mouth. "You don't think it will piss some of my regulars off? Seeing me with someone else?"

"I think they will be too busy fantasizing that they are the ones doing it to you to care. And if you lose a couple, think of how many more you will gain. So it's a net positive, really. I would just make sure that the cum shot is perfect, though. They want it big and messy. On your tits or face. These people don't want a creampie."

Sin frowned a little, but I was already nodding my agreement.

Before I could wonder what that was about, his signature smirk was back in place. "So what do you say?"

I shrugged. It was a good idea, and I wouldn't be taking advantage of Sin. He had something to gain from this too. Also, that amount of people watching, plus the boost he'd give me, potentially meant I'd be full far longer than usual. Maybe even longer than I had after dreamwalking.

"I guess I say I'm in, partner."

TWENTY-FOUR HOURS LATER, I still couldn't believe I'd agreed to this. Or how seriously Sin was taking it. True to his word, he'd posted on all his socials, sending his fans behind a paywall of a certain site to get a tease about what was coming. Namely him. Currently, he was chatting with Malice about the cameras set up in my room and something about ensuring everyone watching would be redirected to my site for full potency.

Apparently, Sin and I were way more alike than I initially thought.

"So the feed will be direct from Merri's site, but there's a link on yours that will send your followers straight to it as well."

"Right. We don't need their money. We need their sexual energy. They've already paid me plenty." Sin flopped onto the bed and spread his arms and legs wide. "Come on, Merri. Hop on so we can make sure the angles are good."

I sighed, feeling a bit like one of those characters in *Love Actually*. This was the fourth time we'd done this.

"Fine, but if you ask me to be tits out for the *lighting* again, I'm going to throat punch you."

He snickered. "I can't believe you fell for that the first time. You're adorable."

"You're an ass."

"Can confirm," Malice muttered, playing with the settings on one of the cameras.

"I'm waiting, Merri-go-round."

The way Sin was so unfazed by all of this could have come off as uncaring. Instead, it felt a lot like he was doing everything he could to make sure the two of us had what we needed in a way that served us both. He cared about whether I fed and how I did it. He knew intimacy freaked me out, so he was approaching it in a way that made it seem like it was just another day at the office. And it was working.

Mostly.

I'd only had two minor freakouts so far.

I think part of the difference between when Chaos approached me versus Sin was that Sin had been trying to get in my pants since day one. This was nothing new for him. It didn't feel out of character or like he had been unknowingly manipulated into it. With Chaos—or the others—I didn't have that distinction.

Climbing onto the bed, I positioned myself so I was straddling Sin. He grinned at me and slid his palms over my hips.

"You look good up here. Very good."

A thrill raced up my spine at the praise, but also the tone he used. Genuine desire.

"Yes, that's great. We'll get an excellent shot of the two of you as long as whatever position you use keeps you in the center of the bed." Malice sounded bored out of his mind, but that wasn't new for him. Knowing about his mental and emotional barriers, I wondered how much was a front for what was really going on inside there.

Curiously, I sent a little mental tendril his way, seeing if I might be able to deliver a sneak attack of my own as a bit of retaliation for our session the other day. Instantly, he went still, his eyes snapping to mine and a knowing smirk on his lips. He wagged a finger at me, and his voice filled my mind. *"You're going to have to do better than that, hellcat."*

"You gonna watch?" Sin teased.

Malice's gaze slid to him. "I have to keep the feed going. You two are likely going to crash Merri's site without my help."

"Soooo, yes?"

He crossed his arms and gave Sin a deadpan look. "Who else is going to make sure the camera angles are changed at the appropriate time? Would you like me to have Chaos do it and likely ruin the whole thing before it begins?"

"I didn't realize you were an erotic filmmaker in addition to being a hacker. You're holding out on us, Mal."

"Do you want this to be a success or not?" he snapped.

"Obviously."

"Then shut the fuck up."

I had to bite back a smile. Their bickering was one of my new favorite things. They were like an old married couple. The thought of them dressed up like Lucy and Desi Arnaz had me snickering.

Sin's fingers flexed into my waist, making me squirm. "What's so funny?"

"Nothing."

"Little liar."

"I'll tell you later." I would *not* tell him later. He'd probably start busting into the room shouting Desi's signature line. Although Malice was clearly the Desi in this fake relationship. Sin was classic Lucy—always up to something.

I giggled again, picturing Sin stuffing his mouth full of chocolates or squishing grapes with his bare feet to make wine.

Malice walked past to check on one of the lights. As he did, his eyes caught mine and he muttered, "You've got some 'splaining to do."

I. About. Died.

Also, dammit. I really thought I had my walls up that time.

"So we open with a bit of heavy petting," Sin began.

"And you need to take off my outfit. You still want me in that red nightie?"

"Absolutely. And don't forget the fishnets. The ones with the seams up the back."

I nodded, and he continued talking through our plan.

"From there, we'll get in some real good making out."

"And then move to oral for you."

"I thought we were gonna do you first?"

"You first, then me. Then . . ."

"No, no, no," Malice interjected, pinching the bridge of his nose.

"Yes, director Mal?" Sin teased.

"Merri first, then Sin, so she can be on top. After that, you switch to missionary, doggy, or anything that will give you the best opportunity to finish where you're supposed to."

Mal gave Sin a pointed look, at which the incubus nodded. It really irked me that I couldn't get into his head to see what he was signaling.

Sin slapped me on the rear. "Okay, baby. We've got an hour to showtime. You'd better get your pretty little ass ready for a good ravishing."

I got off him with a smirk. "If I'm riding you, you're the one getting ravished, Sin." I leaned over and gave his thigh a gentle pat. "Don't worry, I'll make it good for you."

He clutched his heart and looked over at Malice as I moved away from the bed. "I think I just fell in love."

Mal snorted. "Just?"

Laughter bubbled up as I flitted off to the bathroom, but deep down, a weird twist of excitement took hold. Whether it was because of what we were about to do or what he'd said, I wasn't sure. But either way, I couldn't wait to be with Sin again.

CHAPTER
TWENTY
CHAOS

It took every ounce of strength I had not to storm out of my room and into Merri's when I opened the link to her video feed and saw the graphic displaying her adorable cartoon avatar blowing a kiss. I was not a *watcher*. I was a fucking *doer*. Especially after I decided I was going to do something.

I quite literally could not recall the last time I'd been stuck on the bench. I was used to being the number one draft pick. So, to say that I was not handling my loss to Sin well . . . I glanced at the remains of what used to be an antique bookcase. Whoops. Malice wouldn't be pleased to find I'd destroyed one of his many pieces of furniture, but it was that or go steal her away and keep her for myself.

It didn't make me feel any better knowing that I was stuck here among all the other riffraff as well. Merri had opened the chat early, and there was a little countdown at the top of the screen signaling the start of tonight's livestream.

Already, comments were pouring in from some of her most loyal fans.

CallMeMommy: The antici . . . . .pation is killing me 💀

TIs4Tony: God, baby. I can't believe you're doing this for us.

EverySteve: Do you need to warm up first? I can get you wet with my words if you want.

BigMan69: My lotion and tissue are on standby. Things are about to get messy. 💦

TheRealMan: I never thought she'd fuck someone and let us watch.

OnMyKnees4U: Does anybody know who the guest star is?

TheSingularity: If only something existed where you could search for that information. 🙄

PrettyPenny: This is going to be so fucking good!

1N3V1T@BL3: Of course it will be good. She's too perfect for it not to.

Bob1212: It would be better if she was there with @PrettyPenny instead.

ShyGuy25: I'm just hopeful she stays safe. Why does she need to do this?

Bob1212: Stop complaining, you tosser. She's doing it for all of us who need more than what we've been getting.

ThisIsSparta: Or maybe she's doing it for herself.

BigMan69: Looks like she's graduated from camgirl to being a whore. That's good for us, boys. Maybe there will be a signup sheet for her next partner. We could run a train on her.

CallMeMommy: Don't hold your breath. Actually, scratch that. Definitely hold your breath.

Rage boiled in my veins at the word *whore*. Who was he to call her a whore?

"Your mother should have swallowed," I growled, gripping the arms of my chair hard enough the wood creaked. Before I could type exactly what I thought of him, the screen changed and Merri walked into the frame.

"Oh, hi there. I'm so glad you all could join me tonight," she said as she sat on the end of her bed, her eyes sparkling with mischief. "I guess you're as excited by yesterday's announcement as I am. There are"—her eyes darted to the side of her screen and then widened—"Wow! So many of you."

My eyes flicked to the same place she must've been looking, the little icon on the left of the video feed. Upwards of ten thousand people were watching, with more joining every second. Malice had been right to be concerned about them crashing the site.

"You get them all warmed up for me, baby girl?" Sin said from somewhere off camera. "I know they're really here to see you, but I've got a few sparklers in the audience."

The screen filled with floating reactions from the *sparklers* in question. A fuck ton of them. They were the superfans of Sin's band, The Apocalyptic Unicorns. Rabid, feral, and thirsty AF, as he so often said. And they were proving him correct.

#1Sinner: OMG. Sin you sound so gooood.

TIs4Tony: I thought that guy was dead.

Baberino22: Stop teasing us and come on camera.

CherryPie: I bet he looks as good as ever.

ACourtOfLadyDeath: Forget how his face looks. I was promised some dick. 🥒 I mean, that's really why we're all here, right? To see if it's as big as they say?

OnMyKnees4U: Is he really even here?

SinStan: Of course he is. Sin never lets us down. Swooooon.

ShyGuy25: Really, Merri? A washed-up rock star? If you wanted to have sex for an audience, you could have asked me.

SparkleGirl4Life: Oh look, it's a pick-me boy.

Gumdrop: Haters gonna hate. No one is sexier than Sinclair St. James!

ApocalypticUnicorns#1Fan: Sing us something, Sin. Do it while you're naked!

PrettyPenny: God, you guys are good. I can't wait to see what happens when you actually get the show started. 🥵

SinEater: Say my name when you cum, Sin.

SinEater: It's Amy.

LadyPancakes: Dead. I'm officially dead. Someone notify my next of kin. It was good knowing you. 👻

Anxietea: OMG I'm pretty sure that was his shadow in the bathroom doorway.

TheSingularity: And people wonder at the state of the world.

ThisIsSparta: You're just jealous he's getting all the attention.

1N3V1T@BL3: Aren't we all?

ShyGuy25: He doesn't deserve her.

TheSingularity: And you think you do?

ShyGuy25: At least I care about her.

TIs4Tony: Boy, this ain't about feelings. It's about pussy.

Sin took that moment to saunter into view. He was dressed in a mesh shirt and ripped black jeans, his hair tousled and a smirk on his face. It was no wonder he'd so easily become a rock star. The man probably defined the look. The chat exploded with his fans, who were foaming at the mouth for any sort of acknowledgment from him, but he only had eyes for Merri.

I couldn't blame him. She was an absolute smoke show. Her skin was glowing, her long hair up in a perfect ponytail. I wondered if Sin would wrap it around his hand so he could tug her head back. It's what I would have used it for. A pretty handle to put her where I needed her.

"Miss me?" he asked, reaching for her and sliding his hand along her waist before he tugged her against him.

"Of course I did."

"Should we give these good people a show?"

Merri bit down on her bottom lip and nodded. "I think that's what they're here for."

ShyGuy25: Merri, please. We love you without all this. Just come back to doing what you've always done.

Bob1212: Shut the fuck up. Don't ruin this for the rest of us.

TIs4Tony: No one is forcing you to be here. Sack up or fuck off.

SinStan: Shhhh! He's taking his shirt off! 🥵

EverySteve: His shirt was transparent. What's the big deal? Take off your nightie, Merri.

TheSingularity: Seriously. Does no one realize that the world is literally ending? How are you this obsessed with some has-been's state of undress?

Anxietea: It's called disassociation. Look it up.

I laughed out loud at Malice getting roasted by one of Sin's fans. It almost made up for having to watch Merri perform with him.

ThisIsSparta: 🔥😂

LadyPancakes: Do you SEE the way he's looking at her? Are they really in love? I think they might be.

ACourtOfLadyDeath: Forget the way he's looking at her. Do you see that bulge in his pants?

SinEater: Amy. A-M-Y. Just once. Please, Sin.

"Then give me some sugar, kitten," Sin breathed before claiming her lips.

Once again, the chat exploded, but I ignored it in favor of watching her. The way she melted against him. The way she curled her fingers in his hair. The soft sigh she released when he nipped her bottom lip. I memorized all of it.

And I coveted it.

"Mmm, you smell so good," she whispered against his mouth. "It might be my favorite scent."

The chat continued flying across the screen. People complaining they couldn't hear. Others begging them to get the show going. And then, one lone sad man telling Merri she didn't need to be with Sin for money.

What a judgmental prick.

With a smirk, Sin started walking Merri backward toward the bed, his finger hooked beneath the strap of her red nightie. The fabric floated to the floor, but he stood in front of her, offering us nothing but a tease of her bare hips. Fuck, she wasn't wearing any panties.

The chat was visible in my periphery, moving at a rapid pace as people interacted. I didn't pay it much mind. I was too busy watching as Sin shoved her back until she had no choice but to fall onto the bed. Then, with a quick look at the camera, he winked and dropped to his knees, showing us everything Merri had on display.

A soft groan escaped me at the sight of her glistening folds. My cock ached, begging me for relief. I knew it was a futile wish, but part of me hoped Merri could feel what she was doing to me. That she would be able to differentiate my lust from the thousands of others falling in love with her right now.

The memory of what her perfect cunt smelled like was a phantom that teased and taunted me as Sin's head blocked my view. I wanted nothing more than for him to get the fuck out of my way and let me see her open and wet, all swollen with desire. Until she arched her back and cried out for all of us to hear. Sin had closed the gap between them, and though I couldn't see what exactly he was doing, it was evident he was doing it well.

Slender fingers threaded in his hair, tangling in the strands just before she pulled him in closer. Her painted toes curled as Sin groaned against her, and she cried out his name. Curse the gods, I wanted to hear my name from her, not his.

From the flurry of activity on the chat feed, others felt the same. One comment in particular jumped out at me.

> 1N3V1T@BL3: Hard to be a brat when you're being such a good girl and moaning so sweetly for us.

Glad to see I wasn't the only one of my brothers so affected by her. Not that it was news at this point. Just a nice reminder that I wasn't suffering alone. My cock gave a throb, as though reminding me it was still there, still waiting for some friction.

Usually this was the point where I stubbornly refused to give in to my desire. But I was done with that. Not only was it futile, but the whole point of this exercise was to give Merri what she needed. And I was done denying her anything.

Reaching down, I palmed my cock and rocked my hips upward in a few shallow thrusts. On instinct, I hissed in pleasure, a damp patch already growing on my basketball shorts. Fuck, Sin was a lucky bastard.

"Make her come, Sinclair," I grumbled. "She needs it."

Her fingers tightened in his hair, and she whimpered, thighs shaking as a climax began to roll through her. How did I know that? Because I fucking felt it. It was just like the first time she'd come and I burst into Sin's room, wondering what the hell had happened to me. We were rooms apart, but her energy still swept over me like a wave, starting at my feet and building as it moved up my body.

"Fuuuuck," I groaned, long and loud. I didn't care who heard me.

She continued her desperate whines as Sin ate her like a starving man, and I barely had time to pull my cock free of the confines of my shorts before my own orgasm stole my ability to breathe or think. My body was awash with conflicting sensations, warm and blissful while somehow being almost painful at the same time.

My eyes rolled back in my head, and everything went dark as euphoria pulsed through me. Hot jets of cum landed on my stomach, but my hand continued to shuttle along my length as the orgasm swelled and continued far longer than I was used to. That was the power of Merri. She took us all with her when she fell, and we went like sailors called by a siren.

Little aftershocks of pleasure continued to ripple through me as my brain switched back on, and the world around me came into focus once more.

The first thing I noticed was that the camera angle had changed. It was zoomed in now, and Sin was no longer on his knees.

He stood over her, rigid cock in his hand. "Spread your legs wide, sweetness. Show them what I did to you."

Merri did as she was told, and the comments in the chat became nothing more than a blur. Her pussy wasn't just glistening. It was so wet she dripped for us. A damp trail down the bedspread betrayed exactly how much she'd enjoyed the orgasm Sin had given her. Fuck me. Our girl squirted.

"Sin?" she asked, one finger running a slow circle around her clit.

"Yeah, baby?"

"I need more."

Even though the words were for him, it was like she'd whispered them directly to me. My cock was immediately hard again, ready to go like I hadn't just spilled all over myself less than a minute ago.

"Fuck," I muttered, feeling more than a little out of control of my own body as my balls gave an insistent throb.

"More?"

"Please."

"Oh, kitten, you don't have to beg." The camera angle changed again, and Sin smirked at his audience. "I'm always up for an encore."

CHAPTER TWENTY-ONE

MERRI

The amount of sexual energy coming through the feed was insane. The closest I'd ever come to this many different sources was *Iniquity,* and that was still a fraction of what I was feeding off right now. My body was buzzing, tingles racing through me like the pulse of an electrical current. If I didn't know better, I'd have said I was high.

It took Sin all of two seconds to remove every stitch of clothing before he held out a hand for me.

"It's my turn. Use me to get exactly what you want." His eyes burned with pure desire.

Behind the intensity in his stare, I could see his urge to feed me, to give me everything he could so I'd be sated. So we both would.

I knew there was more than enough energy pumping through the room that we could both feed and be full, but all that lust didn't hold a candle to what Sin and I would get from each other. I didn't have much to compare feeding from him to, but I couldn't help but wonder if what was happening between us was normal for our kind or if it was something else.

Something . . . *more.*

"Then I need you on your back, Sinclair."

He winked, a cocky smirk on his handsome face. "I like it when you try to be dominant."

Sin pulled me up as he moved to take my place on the bedding, and I used the exchange as an opportunity to glance at the monitor Malice had set up for us. Comments were pouring in. Some excited, and some surprisingly upset. I guess not everyone liked watching me perform with a sex god. My eyes landed on a couple of familiar names.

TheSingularity: There's a good girl. Making sure we can all see you.

ThisIsSparta: Fix the camera angle so I don't have to see him.

ShyGuy25: Merri, it's not too late to stop this. You don't have to start making sex tapes to get attention.

1N3V1T@BL3: Stop teasing and show us how you like it.

I bit the inside of my cheek to try and hide my reaction to the last comment. My newest Daddy must have liked his video. I gave the camera a little wave and blew it a kiss. "I hope you're enjoying yourselves as much as I am."

There was a flurry of activity in the comments, but I turned my attention back to Sin. God, he was beautiful, all lean muscle and ink. And I hadn't even gotten to the long, thick erection waiting for me between his legs. Fitting myself right where I was supposed to go according to our pre-arranged choreography, I made sure my ass was in prime view of the camera before licking a line up Sin's rock-hard shaft. The groan he let out was somewhere between tortured and euphoric.

"God, yes, baby. Do it again," he grunted.

His hand found my head, fingers fisting in my hair, ruining my ponytail. I licked him again, but this time when I tried to take his swollen crown into my mouth, he used my hair as a handle and dragged me away from his cock.

"Sin," I gasped, confused. "The plan . . ."

"I can't. I won't last, and if I'm not inside your pussy in the next few seconds, I might explode."

He wasn't lying for the benefit of the show. His legs were tense, jaw tight, eyes pleading. Sin really needed this. I couldn't give him slow and sweet lovemaking, filled with tender touches and intense eye contact. And frankly, this wasn't about that anyway. No one wanted to watch me make love to my boyfriend. They wanted to watch me fuck or get fucked by a rock star—all while pretending it was them or they were me.

Nodding my understanding, I shifted my body, turning away from his pleading stare as I straddled his hips. His hands immediately grasped my ass.

"Such a pretty view," he murmured.

From this vantage point, I could see us reflected in the video feed. My entire body on display, his fingers wrapped around my hips, face just visible behind me since he'd propped himself up on the pillows. It was perfect.

The chat thought so too.

> Bob1212: Fuck yes. I can see everything.
>
> EverySteve: Sink down on him. Take him raw.
>
> TIs4Tony: I bet your cunt is so hot and tight.
>
> PrettyPenny: You've got them eating out of the palm of your hand. Don't forget to give them the big finish! 💦 🐚
>
> 1N3V1T@BL3: Touch yourself. I'm taking notes.

Sin released my hip with one hand, and as I lifted up, he positioned his dick at my—as TIs4Tony said—hot, tight entrance. For a second, the positioning reminded me of one of my favorite toys. It was a grinding pad that had a spot where you could place your favorite dildo or vibrator. Then I sank down on him, and all I could think of was the man under me. Sin felt so good. Sex wasn't always like this, was it? Because every time Sin filled me, it was like I'd found a missing piece.

And I didn't just mean because his dick seemed to hit every single erogenous zone inside of me. This was something else, that something more.

"Oh my God," I breathed, my eyes fluttering closed as I adjusted to the feeling of him stretching me.

"Fuck, yes, Merri. Ride me." Sin's voice was as tight as his grip on my waist. I was sure I'd sport bruises tomorrow, and the idea sent a wash of pride through me.

The chat was flying by, fast enough I knew they liked what they saw. As I moved my hips and gave myself over to the pleasure of taking Sin's dick in this position, I watched the two of us on screen. My tits swayed with the motion of my body, Sin's fingers flexed, and his expression contorted as he worked to control himself.

"Let me in, Sinclair," I hummed, needing him to drop his barriers so I could feel more. I wanted to be closer. As close as I could possibly get.

He was so lost to the sensation of my body gliding over his that it took him a second to register my demand.

"Wha—" He stopped himself mid-question and then the walls came falling down.

It was as though floodgates had opened and sent Sin's emotions rushing over me with the force of a rogue wave. So many complicated feelings—quite a few that mirrored my own—hit fast and hard. Confusion, affection, fear, and most notably, that sense of rightness when we were joined. My incubus was just as connected to me as I was to him.

Any sense of unity was swiftly replaced by fear. What had I done to him?

My pace faltered as my mind worked to sabotage everything we were doing, but Sin took over, moving me with his hands and thrusting his hips upward as he chased the release barreling down on him.

"Fuck, Merri. Don't stop. God, it's so good."

His fingers snaked around my front until he found my clit, and he began rubbing tight circles over that tender flesh. I whimpered, throwing my head back and letting my own pleasure build. It was as if our orgasms were spurring each other's on. With his mental barriers down, I could feel his climbing as if it were my own. That, combined with my own spiking pleasure, was too much to process. I tensed down on him, my orgasm hitting like a fucking freight train at the same time his did.

I fed. I fed so deeply from him and the audience we'd all but forgotten. For a few beautiful moments, I was nothing but a being of light.

There was a soft buzzing in my ears and a damp sheen of sweat coating my skin when I finally came back to myself.

"Wow," I whispered.

Sin traced a line down my spine with one of his fingers. "You can say that again."

I shot him a grin over my shoulder, my voice low so it wouldn't be picked up by the microphone. "At least you didn't pass out this time."

He pinched the top of my ass. "We need to close out the live."

Glancing at the monitor, I watched as the number of participants began to rapidly decrease.

"Thanks for joining us," I said coquettishly. "We'll have to do it again sometime."

The feed ended before I could even attempt to shut it off myself. Malice must've taken care of it. My heart lurched as I leaned forward and Sin's still hard dick slipped out of me. The chat was still open, but the comments were slowing. One in particular stood out in sharp relief.

ShyGuy25: You're breaking my heart, Merri.

My reaction to his words was complicated. I wasn't sure if it was guilt or something else that gnawed at my insides. Before I could worry too much, Sin nipped at the back of my neck.

"I told you it was a good idea. I haven't feasted like that in, well . . ."

I glanced back at him as he trailed off, noting that he looked sheepish.

Rubbing a hand over the back of his head, he shrugged. "I guess it doesn't really matter." He slid a palm up my spine before kissing my shoulder. "Come shower with me?"

I wanted to, but at the same time, I needed to address what had happened with Cole. My phone was buzzing over and over on my nightstand, and I knew without a doubt it was him. I couldn't ruin things with him. He was my friend and one of my most steady sources of sustenance. I didn't want to hurt him.

It also wouldn't hurt to put a little bit of distance between Sin and myself. I know I told him I would explore something more with him, but now I needed to unpack what the hell that was I felt between us. More specifically, if it was real, or just another side effect of the dreamwalking. Fuck, this was such a mess. I never should have agreed to perform with him. What if I just ruined everything?

"I'm going to stay here and bask in the afterglow a little longer. You go ahead."

"Have it your way. I'll be in there, naked, soapy, and wet. You're welcome to join me if you change your mind."

A half-hearted laugh escaped me. "Tempting."

Then the handsome horseman sauntered into the bathroom and shut the door behind him.

I grabbed my phone as soon as I could, guilt clawing at me from all sides. I was hurting them both, and perhaps worst of all, Sin didn't even realize what I'd done.

C:

Did he force you to do this?

C:

Merri. I hate that you think sex for money is the only way you can get what you need.

C:

Please call me. Text me back. Something.

I needed to fix this. Dammit. Cole didn't deserve for me to leave him on read, not after he had been there for me time and time again. And while I didn't love the jealous and more than a little judgmental slant to his messages, I did understand it. That was reason enough for me to reach out to him.

ME:

I'm sorry you're disappointed with me. This was a business decision. A very lucrative one. But I am sorry that it hurt you. That was never my intention.

I hit send, my stomach twisting uncomfortably. The live was an absolute success. I should be celebrating. Or at least enjoying the feeling of being fully sated. Instead, I was miserable.

C:

So giving your body to him is just a business transaction? You didn't even use protection.

Resentment fueled by anger sparked to life at his words. My fingers flew across the screen before I fully registered my response.

ME:

You sure are assuming a lot of things right now. Both about me, and about your place in my life.

ME:

It was a mistake to give you my number. It blurred the lines.

I tossed the phone away from me, my pulse racing from an onslaught of conflicting emotions. It immediately buzzed with a new message, and I couldn't resist seeing his reply.

C:

Merri, don't say that. We don't have lines between us, not anymore, and you know it. I'm just worried about you. You've never done this before and you deserve so much more than some rock star who is going to throw you away after he gets what he wants.

C:

Please don't ignore me. You know I'm right. You deserve love. He doesn't love you, not if he'd share you with the world like that.

ME:

Just because that's not a choice that you would make doesn't mean it was wrong. Some people love to be watched. Some people also love to share.

ME:

And you're hardly one to judge. You know exactly what I do for a living, and you pay me for the privilege of watching. So do us both a favor and get off your high horse.

I bit my lip as I read my message back. I was supposed to be smoothing things over, not picking a fight. But I wasn't wrong, dammit. He didn't get to be a judgmental hypocrite.

C:

I'm sorry.

C:

It's just . . . this doesn't seem like the Merri I know. But maybe that's because you don't let me know the real you. I've fallen in love with you and now I realize that might all be a lie.

ME:

It's not a lie.

My head was reeling over the confession he'd just laid at my feet, so I really didn't have anything else to say to him. He was in love with me? Andi had warned me about the dangers of getting too close to clients for this very reason. But Cole was different.

I squeezed my eyes shut when his next message came in. I wasn't ready to look at it yet. I'd told Cole the person I was with him wasn't a lie, but I'd been lying to him since the day we met. No matter what he thought he felt for me, he'd never know the real me. He couldn't.

I was a succubus. He was a human. That was the start and end of our story.

For a lot of reasons, not the least of which was that I would never not need to feed off the sexual energy of my partners, and he alone would never be enough to sustain me—assuming, of course, I didn't kill him outright. I would never be able to give up camming and have the white picket fence happily ever after he was clearly envisioning.

I should put us both out of our misery and end this right here, right now. Block him from my contacts and my site. Cut him off for his own good.

Before I read his response, I typed one of my own.

ME:

I'm never going to be the girl you really want, Cole.

God, why was my lower lip trembling? Had he really worked his way past my walls without me noticing?

I guess it shouldn't be that much of a surprise. He was the only person, other than Andi, who I'd had any long-term contact with. Besides Lilith, but she didn't count. She was family. They were the closest thing I had to friends. You know, for people I'd never actually met face-to-face.

My phone buzzed in my hand, and this time I read his message and the one before it.

C:

I love you.

ME:

I'm never going to be the girl you really want, Cole.

C:

You don't get to decide that for me.

C:

I mean it, Merri. You are the only person I've ever felt safe enough with to fully be myself. You know how limited I am because of my situation. You also know what it means for me to offer to share my space with another person. And if the words alone aren't enough to convince you, maybe this will help you understand just how serious I am about us.

The next message he sent was an address. *His* address, I assumed.

Los Angeles, huh? Somehow that felt fitting for him, even if he never left his house to enjoy the sunshine.

ME:

Cole, I can't.

C:

This isn't a now or never offer. If you need me, if you need a place to crash when that dick decides he's gotten everything he can from you, just come. I'll be here, ready and waiting to help you pick up the pieces and show you what love should be.

I set my phone down and shook my head, at a total loss. I couldn't make any sort of commitment to Cole. Hell, I didn't even know what he looked like. He was confused, mistaking lust for love, as so many people do. Especially when a succubus was involved.

So why, then, if I was so sure about that, could I not just cut him loose?

Why did his offer make my heart feel squishy?

Goddammit.

I swiped across his message thread and let my finger hover over the little trash icon that would clear all traces of this conversation, but I hesitated. If I deleted everything, I wouldn't be able to find him if I ever needed to. Was that wise? It was the end of the world, after all. Having a safe place to land might not be a bad idea.

With a few decisive actions, I copied his address and saved it to his contact information. Then, with Malice on my mind, I deleted the message thread. The last thing I needed was Mal snooping and questioning my texting habits. Or why I was texting with a client, specifically one who felt he was allowed to comment on my site activity. He'd probably start rooting around in my brain to get the answers I'd refuse to provide.

Fuck that.

For some stupid reason, tears misted my eyes.

Don't you dare start crying, I ordered sternly. Because that always works.

One rogue tear dripped down my cheek, and I angrily brushed it away.

There was zero reason for me to be crying. I had a naked man in the other room, and I was better fed than I had been in days.

Oh shit, Sin would be done soon, and then he'd come in here and wonder what the fuck was wrong with me. I was not a pretty crier. My eyes got all red and my lips puffed up. It wasn't something I could easily hide. And even if I could, he'd probably be able to smell the shift in my mood with his stupid incubus mojo.

I scrambled off the bed, grabbed a pair of sweats, and pulled them on without paying attention to what I was doing. It wasn't until I tried to tuck my phone into my pocket that I realized my bottoms were on inside out.

I heard Sin whistling in the bathroom, a clear indication his shower was over. No time to fix the pants now. If I ran into one of the others, the worst they'd do was judge me.

As I scurried out of the room, my phone buzzed once more, making my heart lurch.

C:

I'm not abandoning us, Merri. Take time if you need it. I'll be here when you're ready.

CHAPTER
TWENTY-TWO
MALICE

Merri breezed into the room with a smile on her face and an energy I hadn't felt from her since the last time we all fed her together.

"Morning, Mal," she chirped, claiming the seat by my desk.

"Someone's in a good mood," I stated dryly.

She gave me a heavy dose of side eye. "Wake up on the wrong side of the bed, Mal?" She tapped her lip thoughtfully. "No . . . you're this delightful on a regular basis."

"I wouldn't want to shock you with a deviation from my typical constitution." I had to force myself to look away from her luminous skin and bright eyes. "I take it the live stream was fruitful? I can only assume, since I wasn't directly participating."

"Uh-huh."

I spun back around. "I wasn't. I was too busy handling the cameras."

"Whatever you say, Mal."

My eyes narrowed. "It's true."

She gave me a saucy salute. "I totally believe you, Mr. Singularity."

Spine stiffening at her use of my handle, I set my jaw and forced myself not to react. She was baiting me. Merri knew exactly which of my buttons to push.

"Is that something you'd like to do more often? It seemed to suit you and see to your needs quite well." In truth, if we could get her to live stream with Sin or Chaos on a semi-regular basis, that just might get us where we wanted to be. Namely, her pregnant and the apocalypse thwarted.

Her eyes grew distant and she shrugged. "I dunno. Maybe. It was good for feeding, but I'm not sure how my core audience would feel about it."

That reaction wasn't what I expected. She seemed . . . hesitant. While Merri had always been guarded when it came to sex with a partner—until Sin proved she wouldn't kill him—she'd maintained a very sex-positive attitude and wasn't ashamed of her profession. For the succubus, sex was a necessary part of life. It wasn't something dirty or shameful. So why would she have even a hint of shame or caution now? Perhaps during our training today I could uncover exactly what caused that response.

She seemed to return to herself, noticing that I was studying her. She straightened and blinked at me. "What? Do I have something on my face?"

Latching onto the excuse, I nodded and moved closer to her. "A little toothpaste . . . right here." I used my thumb to brush at an invisible spot beside her lower lip. If she caught the spark of sexual interest that blazed to life within me at the small touch, she thankfully didn't call me on it.

I needed to get a hold of myself before I forgot who and what I was. I couldn't go around touching her face and closing the distance between us like she was my lover if I expected to keep myself safe. I already cared about her far more than I should. Certainly more than I ever wanted to. My feelings for Merri were a complication neither of us needed. Especially since I had to watch her be impregnated by another man. Jealousy burned in my gut, but I doused the flames. *Feelings,* blech. They ruined everything.

The last time I allowed myself to care like this, I sired a son. And look where that got me. I'd been made a fool, a piece of me stolen, and above all, weakened.

"Well, are you just going to stand there and stare at me, or are we going to practice?" Merri's sweet and sass-filled voice yanked me back into the moment.

It was my turn to straighten. I took a few much-needed steps away from her. "Ready when you are."

"You're giving me advance notice this time? How gentlemanly of you."

I sneered at her, my lack of amusement dripping from each and every word. "I thought it was time to see how far you've come in building your mental barriers since, until now, your mind has been as easily accessed as a Whitechapel whore."

Merri pressed a palm to her chest and made an exaggerated O with her mouth. "Not the Jack the Ripper references! How scandalous."

"Oh, excuse me. I meant sex worker. Though I doubt Jackie boy called them that."

She rolled her eyes. "You probably were the Ripper, for all I know. You seem like the type."

"Do I?"

"Yes. Sneaky, quiet, arrogant . . . horny."

There was no missing the challenge in her blue irises or the smirk curling her lips. Fuck. I knew she'd clock my lust the second it bubbled up.

"The Ripper was hardly horny. He hated women."

"Or he wanted one he couldn't have. Hate is but the other side of love, is it not?"

"And she's a philosopher."

Her eyes lit with mirth. "I'm telling you, the guy had blue balls."

"Or perhaps he was aroused more by killing than he was fucking."

"So . . . exactly like you then, Mr. Horseman, sir."

A little growl built in my throat, and Merri snorted.

"I didn't mean to touch a nerve. Sorry, we can start whenever you're ready."

"I've been ready."

She beamed at me. "Great. Come at me, bro." Then she squared her shoulders and shut her eyes.

Just as I sent the first tendril of my consciousness toward her, something yellowed with age sat on the shelf just behind her pulled my focus.

It was the little poppet I'd made for Pan. The one I'd never been able to get rid of.

Maybe it was because I'd already been thinking about my estranged child, or maybe it was all this talk of breeding that I'd been forced to participate in recently, but I couldn't seem to look away from the toy. Nor could I let go of everything it represented.

"Well, if you aren't going to play by the rules, why should I?"

It took more energy than it should have to tear my gaze away and look at Merri. "Wha—"

The little poppet in my hands seemed to weigh so much more than it possibly could as I agonized over the meaning behind it. I'd nearly finished making it for him. Him. My child. I still couldn't believe Odette tried to keep him from me. I knew she'd been up to something, but she always had been a sneaky bitch, so I hadn't thought too much of it. Not until I'd been told about the baby.

She'd successfully hidden her pregnancy and the birth until a week ago when Chaos spotted her wandering through the streets of London with a bouncing aubergine baby on her hip as she spread yet another plague. Subtlety never had been her strong suit. Which was part of the reason I was still so fucking shocked she'd managed to keep a secret of this magnitude.

Chaos was certain of the child's parentage. He'd said he could sense my aura tangled with hers. Not to mention, the baby had my eyes, and the last time I'd been with Odette lined up with the child's arrival.

My fingers clutched at the silky fabric in my hands, and I sat back in my seat.

A child. I'd sired a child.

How?

I was supposed to be a means of destruction, and yet somehow I'd helped create life. It was unbelievable. I'd never considered myself father material. My existence was for one sole purpose: to bring about the end of the world through pestilence. But knowing I'd created a being who would live on and continue my line until such time came that the apocalypse ended it all was . . . thrilling. I could show him how to do so many things. We could create and spread disease together. He'd be a chip off the old block. The greatest and most fearsome gift I could give to humanity. Maybe one day he could even take up my mantle.

But first, I had to meet him. Which meant, unfortunately, I'd need to see Odette.

I stood, pocketing the toy as I turned to check my appearance in the mirror. Some unpleasantness could be tolerated in exchange for getting to hold my son for the first time. Realizing that a three-month-old would neither remember nor care what I looked like, I turned away from the mirror and took the step that would lead me out of my house and bring me to Odette's doorstep. I could arrive directly in her room, but it seemed rude, and I needed her in good spirits. She so rarely was.

My hand shook as I rapped my knuckles on the door, the other shoved in my pocket and clutching my gift for the baby.

Then she was there, her demonic form hidden under the guise of a beautiful woman.

"Malice. So you've heard, then?" She looked me over and sneered. "I don't know what you expect from me."

"My son, Odette. I expect to see my son."

"Your son?" She cocked a brow. "I don't recall you carrying him in your womb and then shoving him out nine months later. All you did was donate a little sperm. Hardly worth giving you any credit."

"It would be a much different story if you'd informed me we were expecting him."

Surprise widened her eyes. "Oh, would it? You would have, what? Made me your bride and created a happy little family?" A disbelieving laugh escaped her. "Doubtful."

"You didn't give me the chance."

"I would never give you the chance to chain me to you. I have plans for this little one. They do not involve you."

I stared at her, dumbfounded. "But he's my son."

"No, Malice. He's *my* son. As far as he will ever be concerned, you do not exist."

I snorted in disbelief. "A son needs his father. He'll come looking for me."

"Why would he? He's never going to know who you are. And when he asks, I'll tell him you're dead. War, perhaps," she added in a musing fashion. Then she tossed me a grin that was all teeth. "Or maybe the plague. How poetic."

"You cannot keep him from me. I won't allow it."

"You won't allow it?" She threw her head back and laughed. "Hilarious. As if there's anything you could do to stop me."

"I'll take him from you. You and I are matched in every way. All it will require is for you to turn your back for one moment."

Her eyes narrowed, power flaring within them. "Attempt it and I will kill him faster than you can blink, Malice. I would rather he be dead than tainted by contact with you."

The world felt as if it had dropped from beneath my feet. "You cannot be serious. He's a child."

"He's a means to an end, Malice. But if you leave me with no choice, I will kill him."

She was serious. This was no bluff.

"I thought you needed him. You had big plans, you said." Panic curled in my chest.

Shrugging, she inspected her fingernails, which were more like talons. "I'd hate to have to start over, but I will. I've proven I can carry a child successfully. I certainly can do it again."

"Odette, please . . ."

Her laugh grated like claws over glass. "If I'd known this was how to make you beg, I'd have tried it centuries ago."

My voice was strangled as I tried one last time to make her see reason. "He's my son."

"And if you care for him, as you seem to, then you will stay far away. One hint of you nearby, and I will slit his throat without blinking. Do you understand?"

Misery and dread threatened to mow me down beneath their weight. Along with something unfamiliar. Something that didn't belong to me.

Shock.

I was only half aware as Odette slammed the door in my face, my consciousness fracturing into two pieces. Then and now. One remained slumped against her door as I'd been so long ago. The other registered the foreign presence in my mind.

"No," I whispered, the cold air of the London streets biting at my skin.

"No!" This time, a shout, but not aloud. I screamed in my mind and shoved at the intruder, who was seeing something I hadn't invited them to witness.

I closed my eyes and when I opened them again, gone was the past. The air was warm and sweetly scented with Merri's perfume. She stood in front of me, eyes swimming with unshed tears, sympathy etched into her features.

"Mal—"

"That's quite enough."

She reached for me, gentleness radiating from her. I couldn't bear it. Not her pity and definitely not her touch.

"I said that's enough! Leave me be."

"I'm sorry, I didn't mean—"

"Get the fuck out!" I roared, feeling far too raw to be around anyone right now.

That memory was one I'd locked away in the deepest recesses of my mind. She shouldn't have been able to access it. But that fucking toy had drawn it to the surface, and with the influx of power she had in the wake of her session, it had to be as easy as plucking a ripe piece of fruit off a tree.

But there was a reason I'd locked that particular moment away.

A reason I couldn't bear to relive it.

It was the one thing in my entire immortal existence that had the power to undo me completely.

Storming across the room as soon as she was gone, I grabbed the poppet and stared down at it, rage burning within my heart. I could not afford any more weakness, and that's what love was. A tumult of emotions sent me to the window, chief among them desperation to free myself from this agony clutching at me. I opened the glass and threw the ancient child's toy into the winter storm. It wouldn't be long before the elements claimed the bit of fabric and straw. And perhaps then, I could be unburdened. Or perhaps I was simply fooling myself. I'd lived with the pain of that day for millennia, and it still had the power to flay me wide open. Odette had chosen her trap perfectly.

And it seemed I would never be free from its snare.

CHAPTER
TWENTY-THREE
GRIM

These little mid-morning walks of mine were becoming increasingly tedious. I was typically a being who kept busy. Instead I spent my days wondering what Merri was doing, who she was with, and what I could do to protect her. Like I said, tedious.

With an annoyed huff, I lengthened my stride, intent on putting an end to this nonsense and going back inside where I could at least use one of my brothers to distract me from these incessant thoughts. Before I could make the turn that would lead me back to the house, I caught a flash of red in my periphery.

Everything in me tensed, my body going tighter than a piano wire. Merri.

Without conscious thought, my body moved toward her, its new destination set.

Fuck me. I couldn't recall a time in my long existence I'd ever been so out of control of myself. I couldn't even touch the woman, but being near her was enough. It was all I had.

For now.

I grimaced at the voice in my head, reminding me that while I was the equivalent of a god, I was also a man. One who hadn't tested the waters of complicated human urges in a very long time. Until recently.

Fingers balling into fists so tight the leather of my gloves creaked in protest, I fought the wave of desire that rolled through me. I'd been captivated watching Merri be fucked by Sinclair. So aroused I'd been in pain until I finally allowed myself to come when they did. As much as I might wish to be the one doing the fucking, I'd long ago made peace with my reality. I think it was that acceptance that allowed me to set aside things like petty jealousy and just appreciate the beauty of her in the throes of pleasure, regardless of who might be giving it to her.

Or I could be lying to myself. Not that I'd ever have a chance to put it to the test.

Soft sniffles from Merri doused the flames of lust caused by my memories, the sound setting me on alert. What had made her cry? Who did I need to kill?

Part of me hoped it was that insufferable Frenchman, if only so she could watch me rob the bastard of his soul. If it was one of my brothers, it would be a bit harder to enact justice.

"Wildflower?"

Merri startled, spinning around and dropping the object she'd been holding in the snow. I'd never thought much of a woman's tears, but the sight of her with the crystalline beads hanging from her lashes robbed me of breath. I wanted to capture this moment, find a way to mount it on my wall. Not because she was sad, but because she was the single most exquisite creature I'd ever known.

And I'd known them all.

She knelt down and scooped the scrap of dirty fabric out of the snow, dusting it off with deliberate care.

"I can't believe he threw it out," she murmured. "It's my fault."

More tears slid down her cheeks, and it was all I could do to pull out a handkerchief rather than use my finger to wipe away the moisture.

"Here, love. Dry your eyes, and then tell me what all this is about."

She accepted the scrap of silk with a soft snort of amusement. "I didn't take you for a Boy Scout."

"Pardon?"

"Always prepared."

I lifted one shoulder in a shrug. "You never know when you might—"

"Stumble across a damsel in distress?" she offered, dabbing at her cheeks and then delicately blowing her nose.

"Something like that."

Merri tucked the now dirty cloth into the pocket of her unbuttoned coat. It was my turn to snort, though mine was annoyance rather than amusement. As if on cue, she shivered.

"What am I going to do with you?" I grumbled, stepping closer and grabbing the lapels of the thick coat before fastening each button until she was as bundled as she could be.

"Take care of me, apparently."

She looked up at me with those big blue eyes and smiled faintly before sorrow overtook her expression.

The still-wet tracks of tears on her cheeks beckoned to me. She hadn't done a very good job of drying her face. Merri wasn't very good at taking care of herself at all. Which I supposed made her earlier comment correct. If she wouldn't do it, I would.

"What has you so upset?" I ask, brushing a gloved finger down the side of her cheek.

"I . . ." She flicked her gaze down to her hand, which held what I now recognized as Mal's ungiven gift to his son. "I messed up."

"How so?"

"I pried where I shouldn't."

"Ah. Well, you do make a habit of snooping," I murmured, recalling that evening she'd ventured into my greenhouse.

She carefully slid the poppet into the other pocket of her coat before heaving a defeated sigh. "This is different. It's not me being curious or bored. It's me forcing myself on you all. I take and take from everyone in my life. I'm basically a human-shaped parasite."

"You're only just now noticing this? I mean, you are half demon. That is the core part of their nature."

She glared at me. "You have a terrible bedside manner."

It took a second for her ire with me to make sense. All I'd done was state the obvious, but she'd seen it as me being dismissive. Shifting my approach, I added, "I only meant that this is part of who you are. It's nothing to be ashamed of. That would be like telling the flowers not to drink up the rain, or the waves not to lap at the shore. You can't and shouldn't hide that part of yourself."

She looked away from me, her cheeks suddenly a deeper pink than they'd been simply from the cold.

"Don't hide from me. I've witnessed firsthand what you look like when you allow yourself the freedom to let go and be who you were meant to be. There is nothing more sacred on this earth than watching a piece of the Creator's art become what it was designed for. There is true beauty in purpose, even if that purpose is destruction. That's what it means to be part of the natural order."

"You wouldn't say that if you knew the truth."

"Try me," I countered.

Snapping her gaze back to me, she stared into my eyes. "How would you like it if I told you I could crawl into your mind and witness your most hidden memories?"

"I'd tell you that you are not the first with that ability, nor will you be the last."

"Or that I can choose to step into your dreams whenever I want and feed from you without you ever knowing?"

Her emotional confession unlocked a long-forgotten memory from the recesses of my mind. Dreamwalking. It had been so long since her kind had dared to do it, I'd completely forgotten about the possibility. Unexpectedly, the puzzle piece that I'd been searching for slipped into place. She'd just unknowingly provided me with the explanation for the series of dreams the four of us had.

"See? You're speechless. It's horrifying. I've been hurting you all, and I won't continue doing it."

So this was why she'd started to pull away once again.

"You were there in my dream?"

"If I'd known that it was banned, that there were consequences . . ." She bit down on her lip so hard I worried she might draw blood.

"Don't do that," I murmured, freeing her lip.

Merri blinked up at me in surprise. It felt like the moment stretched between us before she returned to herself and took a step back. "It won't happen again."

"What won't?" I asked, too distracted by the feel of her plump lower lip to recall the thread of the conversation.

"I won't take advantage. I'm not going to allow myself to dreamwalk with any of you again."

Well, that just wouldn't do. I could touch her in my dreams. And not just the idea of her, but the piece of her that joined me there. There was no chance in hell I would give that up.

"What if I want you to?"

"See? This is exactly what I'm talking about. You hated my guts when you brought me to your penthouse. Would barely look at me. Now, you're over there with your smoldery eyes and horny words because I've . . . ensnared you."

A soft laugh escaped me because I'd never heard someone manage to be so right and so wrong all at the same time.

"I mean it, Grim," she said, pressing her hands to my shoulders as if to somehow emphasize her next words. "You're a victim. *My* victim. All of this is . . . Stockholm syndrome. You don't really mean it. And maybe you can't understand that, but I do, so it's up to me to be the responsible one."

"You are adorably mistaken, wildflower. We've been giving you the space you need, but there wasn't a single one of us who you hadn't ensnared from day one. I can't speak for the others, but I kept my distance because there is no future for us. All Death can bring is grief."

I could see the war waging in her eyes. She wanted to believe me, but she simply couldn't let go of this narrative she'd created. The one where she'd somehow trapped us into caring about her.

That was our fault.

My fault.

"Ask the others before you decide for them, but I need you to know one thing."

Her brows lifted as she waited for me to continue.

"If there is any world where I can be close to you, even if it's only a dream, I would choose it."

"Grim—"

I stopped her with a press of my finger to her lips. "I mean it, wildflower. Knowing what it was like to touch you. Being able to call you mine . . . it was the greatest gift I've ever been given. No matter the cost."

Her eyes searched mine, and I recognized the look of suspicion in them. She was looking for hints that all of this was false. That her spell was controlling me. Before I could do anything else to ease her fears, she took two steps away from me.

"I . . . I have to go," she murmured, then bolted for the house, leaving me with the weight of my confession as my only company.

CHAPTER TWENTY-FOUR

CHAOS

The sweet scent of my Merri's hair pulled me out of the deepest slumber I'd had in ages. I sighed happily, reaching for her and wrapping one arm around her waist. Soft, warm skin under my fingers had me instinctively pulling her closer, needing her against me.

She shifted and turned around to face me, both of us lying on our sides in my bed, naked but not focused on sex. We were focused on each other.

"Morning," I murmured, my voice raspy with sleep.

"Morning," she whispered, her smile soft but genuine.

"Sleep well?"

"Mmm." Her hum was part agreement, part yawn. With a little giggle, she added, "I don't remember falling asleep."

"I'm pretty sure we exhausted each other until neither of us could keep our eyes open."

Her big blue eyes flicked from mine to my mouth, then back. "It was worth it. Even if I'll be tired today."

I ran my hand down her torso, taking hold of her hip and tugging her closer. "We could just stay in bed."

"Who are you, and what have you done with my moody taskmaster?"

My cock gave a happy twitch. "I'm more than happy to give you orders right here."

Her eyes flared at the hit of lust I'm sure she just picked up on. She pressed a palm to my chest. "I'm sure you would."

"I've never woken up with someone in my arms before," I said, my voice low.

The truth spilling so easily from my lips surprised me.

"What?" She propped her head up with one hand, gaze intent on me as though I'd just unearthed something shocking.

Shaking my head, I reached out and tucked a lock of flame-red hair behind her ear. "It's true. No one has ever stayed long enough to see morning."

"Really? Not even your first love?"

"I've never been in love."

This confession fell from me as easily as the first. It would have been worrisome, except I knew with absolute certainty I could trust her.

"Don't lie to me," she teased. "How could a man like you have never been in love?"

"It's the truth."

"But Sin said—"

She stopped herself and looked away from me. Reaching out, I took her chin between my thumb and forefinger and forced her to return her attention to me.

"Sin said what?"

"That you and he weren't always horsemen. That means you must've had a human life before all . . . this."

"I did."

"So then I don't understand."

"What's so hard to understand?"

"If you were human before, how could you not have a first love? Even six-year-olds fall in love. It's like a rite of passage."

She was genuinely taken aback, and it could not have been more adorable.

"I think you're forgetting that the world I grew up in was not like yours."

"Well, duh, you're like a million years old."

"Not quite a million."

She rolled her eyes. "Fine, but you're old. You look like you could've fought in the Trojan War."

I smirked, raising one brow.

"No!" Her shock had me near laughter.

"It's their own fault for stealing Helen. They had it coming."

"You really lived that long ago?"

"Yes, Red. I lived that long ago. I was a warrior nearly from birth. I grew up with Spartan blood running through my veins and planned to die in battle. War had other plans."

"Okay, fine, but it's not like love was invented in my century. I've read the Greek myths. Those assholes were falling in love left and right. And even Spartan warriors had to get married and make babies. Some of those had to be for love."

"True, but I wasn't one of them."

She stared at me in a mix of something like sadness and awe.

"Why do you look so sad?" I asked, unable to fathom why this creature would care if I ever loved another.

"Because everyone should know love at least once in their life. Even though it can be the most painful thing you've ever experienced."

"Sounds like I didn't miss out on much, then."

She cupped my cheek and brushed her thumb gently over my bottom lip. "No, you misunderstand. Just because it's painful doesn't mean it's not also the most wonderful."

"You've been in love," I stated.

"Yes. Once."

My gut twisted with jealousy. The bastard she'd loved hadn't known how lucky he was. Although he was also very dead, so I supposed he wasn't as fortunate as me.

"How did you know you were in love and not simply lust?"

She traced a fingertip over the ridge of my shoulder, then back to my collarbone as she thought. "Lust is all surface level. It's physical, certainly, but it doesn't go past that ache in your core or the anticipation in your chest. Love is . . . love is all-consuming. But it goes deeper than that. It's the warmth in your heart when you see or think about the person you love. It's that sense of release when you're safe in their arms. It's knowing you'd do anything to make them feel that same safety and security." Her voice wobbled a little, and she had to clear her throat. "It's realizing that you're no longer the axis that your life revolves around. There's another person in the world whose needs matter more to you than your own."

"Motherfucker," I whispered.

She nodded sagely. "And it's even more wonderful when they feel the same about you."

Why did her saying that make me wish I could experience it?

I needed to change the topic before I did something I couldn't take back. So, I grabbed her by the nape and kissed her breathless.

"Guess we're done with the getting-to-know-you stage of the morning," she teased against my lips when I finally let her up for air.

"I'd like to get to know you even better, Red. Thoroughly and for a very, very long time."

She giggled as I buried my face in her neck and bit down hard enough to leave my mark. Then I began kissing my way down her body. The way she moved under me as I rolled her on her back caused her hip to brush my already hard cock, sending even stronger waves of arousal through me. Lust. This was lust. That was all. Even if some of the things she explained about love hit a little too close to home.

Merri was mine for the moment, not forever.

But what was the harm in pretending?

"Spread your legs for me, Merri. Let me in."

She arched her back and whimpered as my mouth found her nipple, and I loved her in the only way I knew how. With my body.

Thighs parted, she waited for me, giving me access to her without reservation. I took my throbbing length in my hand so I could line myself up at her entrance. As I dragged the tip of my cock through her slick folds, she moaned and closed her eyes.

"Eyes on mine, Red. I want to see everything I do to you."

She did as she was told, and as soon as our gazes locked, I slid inside her hot, slick cunt.

Heaven.

That's the only way to describe being inside Merri. I never wanted to leave. "Gods, Merri," I grunted.

She gasped, a panicked look flashing across her face.

I woke with a start, sweaty and alone in my bed, my cock at full attention and desperate for relief.

"You've got to be fucking kidding me."

It had all felt so real. So damn perfect. The thought of anything other than Merri herself helping me find release was unappealing.

With a groan, I rolled over, instinctively grabbing the pillow that I would have sworn she'd just been resting her head on. Instead of smelling her, all I scented was detergent and my own shampoo.

Disappointment hit like a wave. I could have kicked myself for being so upset by something as trivial as a dream, but the truth was, I'd never have a chance at something so intimate with her. And fuck me, I think I actually wanted it.

Why else would I dream about just that?

CHAPTER TWENTY-FIVE

MERRI

"Motherfucker!" I whisper-shouted into my dimly lit bedroom as I slammed my fists down onto the bedding. "Not again."

I'd dreamwalked without even meaning to. There was no way to deny that was what happened. Not once I'd realized I was feeding from him. My talk with Grim must have planted the idea in my mind, and then my slutty subconscious sought out the first available target. Even in my sleep, I was dangerous to them.

The gray light of early morning crept through the crack between my curtains, confirming my decision to toss back the blankets and get my day started. No use attempting to go back to sleep—though it wasn't like I could after the way I'd woken up. The way I was feeling right now, I'd never sleep again.

I shuffled over to the closet and grabbed a fluffy blue robe and some seriously ridiculous bunny slippers I'd found. I had no idea how they'd gotten there or who their original owner was, but they were comfy AF, and that's really all I cared about right now.

Once I was bundled, I made my way down the stairs to the kitchen. Coffee was next on my must-haves list. Who was I kidding?

Coffee was always at the top of my morning list. The promise of a hot cup of liquid caffeine had my mouth watering before I walked into the empty kitchen.

"Annnd go," I muttered, pressing the button to percolate. A few seconds of drumming my fingers and staring at the rich brown liquid dripping into the pot was all it took before I pulled my phone out. I scrolled mindlessly for a minute or two before opening up my messaging app.

ME:

You up?

My time zone math wasn't great, but I figured it was no later than midnight for her, so the odds were in my favor.

ANDI:

What do you think I am? A Golden Girl? Of fucking course I'm up.

ME:

Excuse me, the Golden Girls would be so mad at you for your ageist comment. Those ladies were always up eating cheesecake and talking about sex in the middle of the night, thankyouverymuch.

ANDI:

I stand corrected. I've obviously missed my calling. Let me guilt purchase some kaftans and correct my mistake.

ME:

Thank you

I chuckled, already feeling better. Sometimes you just needed an early morning check-in with your bestie. It wasn't like I could talk to her about my almost sex dreamwalk with Chaos, but I could remind myself there was more to my life than my out-of-control succubus power.

ANDI:

Is the sun even up where you are? Tell me you spent the night partying and are just getting in.

ME:

Not quite. More like trouble sleeping.

ANDI:

Borrring 😭 I'm revoking your Golden Girl card

ME:

Look who's suddenly an expert

ANDI:

as you pointed out, they love two of my most favorite things. I'm clearly an honorary member

ME:

Sex and cheesecake?

ANDI:

Preach 🙏

The coffee pot beeped to indicate my precious was finished brewing. Did I scurry over like Gollum in the cave when he was searching for the lost ring? Yes. No shame here.

My phone chimed again as I brought the steaming mug to my lips.

ANDI:

What time is it for you? You never text me this late.

ME:

It's too early to mention in polite company. You'd be offended.

ANDI:

So, why can't you sleep? Something on your mind?

ANDI:

Let me guess, boy trouble?

"More like horseman trouble," I grumbled.

ME:

It's complicated. Cole got really upset about my live with Sin. He was pretty hurt by it.

Was that really my current issue? No. But it was a partial truth. I was holding onto a lot of guilt over a multitude of things lately.

ANDI:

That's not surprising. It's always a risk, but I'm sure you can soothe his ruffled feathers with some one-on-one time. That usually does the trick.

ME:

Yeah . . . maybe.

ANDI:

Trust me, babes. I've been in the game a lot longer than you. If there's one thing I know, it's men. His ego is a little bruised, that's all. Just make sure he knows he's still your goodest boy and you'll have him purring like a kitten again in no time.

ME:

He said he loves me. Maybe I need to put some space between us.

ANDI:

Of course he loves you. Have you seen you?

ANDI:

Besides, is there really anything so wrong with a man loving you?

ME:

If it blurs the line . . .

ANDI:

You can move the line to wherever it best serves you, sweets.

The sound of someone whistling in the hallway pulled my attention from my messages with Andi. It had to be either Sin or Christian. None of the rest of them would whistle. My money was on the groundskeeper, though. Sin lived the rock star life, and that usually meant staying in bed until at least noon if he could.

ME:

GTG! Talk soon. 

I was blowing on my steaming mug as Christian came around the corner. His attention was on his phone, so it took him a second to notice me.

"Merde! You startled me," he gasped, one hand pressed to his chest, the other pocketing his phone. Then he spotted the coffee in my hand. "Apologies, mademoiselle. I would have started the coffee for you if I'd known you were getting up early."

I held up my mug in a mock salute. "No worries. I'm perfectly capable. Do you want some?"

A smile spread across his face. "You know, I would like that very much. No one ever offers."

"Really?" I blurted, but then I thought about my housemates and shook my head. "Actually, that tracks." I poured him a cup and handed it to him before leaning my ass against the counter. "So, what's new with you?"

Again with the shocked smile. "Do you really want to know? I am not used to guests here caring about my life."

How often did he host guests here? Was Malice running this place like an Airbnb? That didn't seem likely. "Of course I want to know."

He mimicked my posture by leaning against the island. "Well, these are hard times, as you can imagine."

Right. The world was ending. Funny how easy it was to forget that little tidbit when I had things like being a soul-binding hussy to worry about. Was this what perspective felt like? How big were my problems in the scheme of things?

Big.

They were still pretty fucking big. Especially since the hordes of hell were after me to help seal the deal, which was the reason we were hiding out here to begin with.

I sighed. "Yeah. It's . . . a lot." Taking a sip of my coffee, I tried to think of something I could say that wouldn't confuse the human in the room. "Damn, global warming is a real bitch."

Christian gave me an odd look. "That's one way to refer to the apocalypse."

The sip of coffee I'd just taken threatened to come out of my nose. "You know about that?"

"But of course. My family has been protecting this château for centuries. We're in service to Hecate, our goddess. She warned us about the signs long ago."

My eyes widened as realization dawned. "Oh, so you're like a warlock or mage or something? Not just a human."

His answering smile was conspiratorial. "Not just a human."

"Well, that makes things easier. Wait. Do you know what I am?"

"Not at first, I must admit. But I figured it out pretty quickly." His smile widened, and a twinkle filled his eyes as he pulled a simple crystal pendant out from under his sweater. "It's why I fashioned this."

"What is that?" I leaned closer to inspect the small clear stone hanging from a thin leather cord.

"Quartz. It's bespelled to ward off your power."

"I didn't think that was possible. Lilith said no one could resist me, even with magic."

He let out a short bark of laughter. "She was wrong. Typical demon."

I puzzled over that for a moment, confused how Lilith could be wrong about something like that. Unless she'd lied to me, but that didn't feel right either.

"Hecate protects her own. She ensured we would remain safe so long as we are in her service," he explained, likely sensing my confusion.

"Oh, that makes sense."

And it sort of did. If anyone would know how to combat Lilith's allure, it would be a goddess. Lilith might be the first demon, but she wasn't omnipotent. It was possible there were creatures out there who were stronger and more powerful—and more knowledgeable—than her.

I internally flinched at the traitorous thought. If she had been in my head at that moment, she wouldn't have been pleased.

"Mademoiselle? Are you all right?" Christian was staring at me as though I'd been obviously distracted.

"Yes, sorry. I just never knew such a thing existed. It would have come in handy."

Goddammit, I probably could've been handing these things out like candy on Halloween and then just strolled through town like a normal human without worrying about killing people. There had to be a catch. If that was possible, Lilith would've done it for me.

"It takes a great deal of power to keep it active. Of course you wouldn't know."

Right. So no Halloween goodies for me.

Somehow that was comforting. Even though it was an option, it wasn't one that could have actively changed the trajectory my life took.

I waved a hand, wanting to change the subject. "So your family is still out there? Dealing with all the crazy?"

He nodded. "It's just my sisters and me now."

"I'm sorry," I said, feeling my own lack of family.

"It was a long time ago."

"Are your sisters also in France?"

"Non. They are scattered around. Free spirits that travel as the goddess pulls them."

"So you don't talk to them often?"

He walked to the sink and rinsed out his coffee mug before returning his gaze to me. "I have made contact a handful of times since the apocalypse began, but it is always short and difficult. They are safe. That is all I care about. One day we will be reunited."

"Is it really that bad out there?" I shuddered, thinking about what London had looked like before we left.

"Oui. This island has created a—how do you say—bubble of safety. But outside is a great deal of chaos with a few pockets of untouched reality. The more isolated they were to start, the better they seem to be faring."

"I can see that. Especially the places where they are already set up to be sort of self-sufficient."

"Exactement. Which is probably why Monsieur Laurent has me working on expanding our gardens and other enhancements for the property."

"A homestead?"

"Among other things. We are safest here for the time being. If we can grow our own food and sustain ourselves, we will be far better off when the power grid inevitably goes down and the resurgence of the death rattle spreads beyond the few places it has popped up. And with martial law being declared in many countries, it's only a matter of time before the riots that have started in other big cities shift their focus to places like here."

It was shocking to hear how bad things had gotten. Shocking, but not necessarily a surprise. They'd been making movies and video games about the end of the world for decades now. It was basically a road map for how humanity should behave in times like these.

"They declared martial law?"

He nodded. "The US did last night. The UK and Canada this morning."

"What? Really?"

He nodded again.

Why the hell hadn't Andi mentioned any of this? Was I wrong when I assumed she was still in the States? She could be hiding out on a tropical island for all I knew. After what Christian had just revealed, part of me hoped she was laying out on a beach in a bikini, blissfully untouched by the apocalypse.

"If you have people close to you, I would take a moment to reach out and ensure they are safe. It might be your last chance, and Monsieur Laurent won't offer them refuge here, not that most would be able to travel this far anyway, but at least you'll know they are all right."

My thoughts went instantly to Cole. He and Lilith were all I had left. To the best of my knowledge, Andi was safe. And Lilith had forbidden me from contacting her for the time being, which only left him.

My skin crawled as fear took hold. If anything had happened to Cole, I would never forgive myself. I'd left our conversation with him promising not to abandon me, but me cold and distant.

Snatching my phone off the kitchen counter, I shot Christian an apologetic look. "Would you excuse me? I think I'm gonna take your advice."

"Bonne chance, mademoiselle. I hope your loved ones are well."

"Thank you, Christian," I called over my shoulder, already moving out of the kitchen.

Had I realized the state of the world had gotten this bad, I never would have left things the way I did with Cole. I only hoped it wasn't too late to fix it.

CHAPTER TWENTY-SIX

GRIM

"Explain to me why, with over forty rooms in the house, you choose an abandoned cellar *beneath* the property," Malice intoned from his station in the far corner.

"I thought it obvious," I answered, matching his dry delivery with one of my own.

"Pretend it isn't."

"I didn't want this conversation overheard." I glanced at my watch for the second time in less than as many minutes and huffed in annoyance.

Sin burst through the door, breaths heaving. "I'm here! I'm on time. Look at that. A minute to spare." He leaned dramatically against the doorframe. "Commence with the super-secret underground book club meeting." He glanced around, realizing that he wasn't the last to arrive. Then he chuckled and sing-songed, "Uh-oh, someone's in trouble."

A low grumble announced Chaos's arrival before he darkened the doorway. "I'm not in trouble. I arrived precisely when I intended."

"Suuuure, you did. Why is your hair all wet? Did you get into a fight with a tunnel-dwelling swamp monster because they tried to make off with you by dragging you into their underwater lair?"

"If I did, I clearly bested it."

I sighed and shook my head. "Next time, maybe you both could try to remember that if you're not five minutes early, you're late."

"Yes sir, Master Sergeant sir," Sin said, snapping his heels together and offering me a messy salute. He was only able to hold on to his serious expression for a heartbeat before he smirked and winked. "Buuuut it's still probably not gonna happen." Sin leaned close and whispered conspiratorially, "My name really should've been Chaos if you think about it. I'm way more chaotic than he is."

A low tremor ran beneath our feet, sending some bits of dust and rock clattering to the ground.

Sin paled at Chaos's show of power. "Okay fine, you win. You can keep the name."

"We don't have much time. I'll thank you to stop the theatrics." I stepped forward, commanding control of the meeting before Sin started a mutiny. "We need to talk about Merri."

"Of course we do. She's the only thing we talk about these days," Malice complained. "What has she reduced us to?"

My brow raised at the pricklier-than-usual comment. Last I checked, the two of them had been getting on well. Then I recalled the toy Merri had been cradling in the snow. It was pretty easy to figure out what happened from there. She'd clearly stumbled across something Malice hadn't wanted her to see.

"Our little succubus is getting stronger by the day," I said, gaze landing on Mal. "As you all well know."

"And her appetite doesn't seem to be lessening." Sin sighed, running a hand through his hair. "I'm trying to take care of her, fellas. But I'm only one man."

"Her pull is just as powerful as well."

"How is that surprising?" Malice asked.

"She should have more control if she's being fed, but I'm

dreaming of her almost every night, and when I'm awake, I crave her nearness. I can't escape her."

My attention flicked to Chaos as he spoke, the edge to his voice betraying his torment.

Sin made a soft humming sound, his gaze distant as he contemplated Chaos's admission. "It's almost like her power is a beacon calling us to her."

"Is that normal?" Chaos asked.

"For a succubus? Sure, I mean, especially one whose needs aren't being met. But we know that Merri is feeding, so it's strange that her power is reacting basically the opposite of the way it should."

"It almost seems like an addiction," Mal murmured. "Now that she's finally gotten a taste, her body is craving more."

"Well, that's exceedingly unhelpful. We were supposed to be helping her manage her hunger, not causing it to grow," Chaos muttered.

"No, we were supposed to be putting a baby inside her and saving the world." The irritation in my tone was impossible to hide.

"She's a tough one to crack. I tried, and she shot me down."

Sin snorted at Chaos. "It's a real shame. You just aren't a closer, buddy."

"And you are?"

"Pfft. You know I am. You watched the live. I planted my baby batter like a champ."

Malice made a sound of disgust. "Please never refer to your cum as baby batter again."

"Baby gravy?"

"No."

"My special sauce?"

"I'm about to sick myself all over you."

"I believe that's what they refer to as irony. You know, since usually you're the one making people toss their cookies."

I pinched the bridge of my nose and took a long breath before returning my attention to the children in the room. "That's enough.

Sin. You've been unsuccessful in your attempts thus far, but your efforts haven't gone unnoticed. As you just pointed out, Merri's hunger seems to be increasing rather than becoming manageable. That's not something we planned for."

"It wouldn't be a problem if she would just ask for our help. And by our help, I mean your help, since I'm already doing my part," Sin said.

Chaos looked ready to send his fist through the wall, and with it, Sin. "What do you want me to do? I already told you I tried."

"I might have a solution, actually."

"You?" Sin snickered. "How can you help? Did you finally find a solution to the glove condom conundrum?"

"Yes."

Sin's mouth dropped open. "That . . . is not what I expected you to say."

"Dreamwalks."

"Come again?" Malice spluttered.

Sin turned to speak.

"Not you," Malice said, holding up a finger like that would actually stop Sinclair.

"Remember last time how we all admitted to having intense dreams about Merri? Those weren't normal dreams. She was dreamwalking. Visiting us each on the dream plane and feeding."

"It did feel incredibly realistic," Chaos said, mostly to himself.

"That's because it was."

"I don't think I'm following," Malice admitted.

"Succubi and incubi originally fed only in dreams. It was outlawed centuries ago for a number of reasons, most of them political. But the salient point for our purposes is that the dream plane is where succubi are most powerful."

"Incubi were said to leave a female partner pregnant after repeated dream encounters. I've never done it, but I've heard the legends." Sin's brows were furrowed as he continued. "I'm not a true incubus, though, and I honestly thought those were simply stories made up to excuse infidelity."

"Do you think it could work in reverse? Where a succubus could get pregnant via a dreamwalk?" Chaos asked.

I nodded. "I'm certain of it. It's one of the reasons for the ban. The Council didn't want them to overpopulate the rest of the demon masses. They were growing too powerful."

"Then why the fuck didn't you tell us about this weeks ago?"

Chaos was right, of course, but I truly hadn't considered this a possibility because, frankly, I hadn't remembered it was one. "I've amassed a great deal of knowledge in my long existence, and I've forgotten more than most creatures could ever aspire to know. Forgive me if one piece of lore slipped my mind."

"Arguably the most important piece of lore for our current task." Malice's words were snide, and it took everything I had not to hit him.

"Merri still has to initiate the dreamwalks, so it's not exactly like it was a viable option until we knew she was capable of such a thing." I glared at him. "Besides, the skill has become so unused she would have no idea how to do it. Lilith certainly wouldn't dare teach her. And it's not exactly like one of us would have been able to explain it to her."

"So if Merri realized that this was the safest and most satisfying way for her to feed, then why did she stop?" Chaos asked.

The room fell silent as we all searched for an answer.

"I think, maybe, for the same reason that none of us helped her feed until she gave us permission."

"You think this is about consent?" Malice asked.

I shrugged. "We know how important it is to her."

"Do you think she's even aware she's dreamwalking?" Chaos asked the question I was certain they'd all been thinking.

"Yes."

Sin huffed. "And how do you know, Grimsby?"

"She told me herself." They all stared at me as though I'd been holding out on them. "Don't look at me like that. Why the hell do you think I called this bloody meeting?"

Malice had his fingers pressed to his temples and was currently massaging the area. "Okay, fine. So the suggestion here is what, exactly? We give her the green light to feed on us in our dreams, and we cross our fingers and hope that one of you three gets her pregnant?"

"It seems like the best option."

"Why would she be willing to do it in our dreams but not in the real world?" Sin asked.

"Because there are no ill effects on us."

"What do you mean?" Chaos asked.

"Think about it. All four of us dreamt of her, and even though she fed deeply, none of us were rendered unconscious or otherwise harmed. The magic of the dreamwalk must protect us in a way that we can otherwise only experience by sharing the drain." I shrugged again, definitely outside the realm of my expertise. Logically, though, it tracked. So far as I could glean anyway.

"It would remove the largest obstacle if that was the case," Malice agreed.

"Hang on a sec. You said *three* of us. The last time I checked, Chaos and I were the only ones on baby daddy duty. Since when did Daddy Death get added in as a sperm donor?" Sin asked, his brows almost to his perfect hairline.

Malice cut a glance at me. "You already admitted your dream about her was sexual. Did you not touch her?"

"I did. She sucked me off until I saw stars."

"And she didn't drop dead?" Sin blurted.

"Obviously not. Are you thick?"

He smirked. "Only where it counts."

"She's not going to dreamwalk with us again. Not now that she knows it's happening. She made that clear."

Chaos narrowed his gaze at me. "Why?"

"We'll have to make sure she knows we are willing. Convince her it's the best way for her to feed."

Malice looked a little green, but I didn't have time to pander to his issues. The world was falling apart around us, and Lucifer came closer to getting his way with every passing day. If I could take part in our task while also giving in and making Merri mine while doing so, I would. The thought of touching her again, of being able to spend time mapping out her body and cataloging all the ways in which I could make it sing for me was fast becoming my new obsession. It would be all I could do not to beg her to choose me to dreamwalk with next. And perhaps always.

"So what now? Do we need to put our hands together and do a Three Musketeers kind of thing? Or maybe we should do a fertility dance or something to close out this meeting."

Chaos was already pulling the door open, fed up with Sinclair's bullshit. Christian was waiting on the other side, skin pale, hands clenched so tight the bones of his knuckles were nearly showing.

Before I could ask how he'd known where we were, another one of my brothers beat me.

"What is it, Christian?" Malice barked, impatience bleeding from every word. "Can't you see we are in the middle of something?"

"Monsieur, forgive me, but . . . the sky," he sputtered.

"Yes?"

"It is on fire."

OPERATION PFFN SUPER SECRET VIDEO CORRESPONDENCE: #6

Screen blinks to life, revealing a close-up view of Asher's nose and right eye. He takes a couple of steps back, and the image sways as he adjusts the camera. It comes to rest again, focused on his face. He looks like he hasn't slept in days.

<<static>>

Hades: Asher? You done yet? We were sort of in the middle of things.

Asher: Give me a second. I just need to bring everybody up to speed.

<<dog yips and growls>>

Asher: Can you get your dog under control? I'm moving as fast as I can.

Hades: Asshole, come on now. Leave the guy alone. If you're a good boy, I'll let you pee on his shoes later.

Asher: The fuck you will.

Hook: I would make sure you don't leave any out. Just in case. The hound does whatever the fuck he wants.

<<series of dog barks>>

Dahlia: *chuckles* Aw, they didn't mean it, buddy. As far as I'm concerned, you're always a good boy.

Hades: Don't get any ideas, pup. I'm her favorite. If she had to choose between us, it'd be me.

Hook: *cough* bullshit ***cough*** My Wendy bird would never leave me.

Hades: *aggrieved sigh* Not you and I us, him and I us.

<<dog growls>>

Asher: Okay, so to bring you guys up to speed, Hades, Lord of the Underworld, just opened a fucking portal in my living room, and then a fucking ghost appeared to share what she learned on the other side.

Asher makes a few more adjustments to the camera before stepping away to reveal a living room filled with people. A blue and silver portal pulses on the right, a female shape visible in its center.

Alek: (afraid) You didn't tell me there would be ghosts. I don't do ghosts. I've been incredibly clear on this. Is she going to be able to step out of that portal?

Hook: *snickers* Your brother is afraid of ghosts, Tor? What kind of Viking is scared of something that can't even touch him?

Alek: One whose mother is intimately familiar with the process and filled me in on just how malevolent they can be.

Tor: Gods, you're still not over this, Alek?

Dahlia: Would it kill you to show him a little bit of empathy?

Tor: Probably.

Dahlia: Should I remind everybody about your run in with our good friend Kat a couple months ago?

Tor: You promised never to speak of her again, beauty.

Dahlia: Then be nicer to your brother.

Hades: Kiki cannot cross the boundary. Think of the portal like a video call.

Alek visibly shudders, but nods.

Alek: As long as she stays on her side, I'll be fine.

Kiki: Looks like you got the braver of the twins, Dee. Good job.

Alek: He's afraid of dolls. I win.

Tor: That doll was possessed.

Alek: If you want to get technical, it was possessed by a ghost. So really, you're just as chickenshit as I am.

Gavin: Can someone send these two outside or something? We called this meeting to gather information and then paused it so that the information could be recorded and shared. If that's no longer our objective, I have plenty to take care of today and no children of my own I need to parent. I'd like that to remain the case until Roslyn gives birth.

Dahlia: They'll be on their best behavior, won't you?

Dahlia gives Tor and Alek meaningful looks. Tor sighs and crosses his arms. Alek looks away, muttering under his breath.

Tor: *sigh* Yes.

Alek: My terms were clear. She stays on her side, and there won't be a problem.

Kiki: Like I would want to come over there anyway. The underworld is the tits. Plus I've got myself plenty to keep me busy. I'm just here to pass on what I already told Hades.

Asher: I, uh, never thought I'd say this, but I agree with Gavin. Can we get back to what you were telling us?

Kiki: With pleasure. Bear is waiting for me, and I'm just as eager to get this over with. ***clears throat*** It's the horsemen.

<<awkward beat of silence>>

Asher: And?

Kiki: And what?

Hades: What about the horsemen, Keeks?

Kiki: They're at the center of all this.

Gavin: Of course they are. They're instrumental in bringing about the apocalypse. Why wouldn't they be?

Hook: Have you already forgotten our time being experimented on by Lady Death? It wasn't the horse*men* behind that. It was the women.

Kai: Right, but I think what he's saying is that being the other side of that coin, they're every bit as involved.

Kiki: *frustrated groan* No. God, you guys. They are you.

Hook: Darling, no one is me. There's but one Captain—

Hades: So help me if you say your fucking name one more time . . .

Hook: (tauntingly) Hook.

Hades grabs Hook by the back of his neck and shoves him through the portal, where he crashes into Kiki.

<<rustle of fabric>>

Hook: Oof. Watch it!

Kiki: Ow. You're the one who flew into me.

Alek: *shrieks* You said there would be no crossing!

Alek jumps out of his seat and runs out of frame.

<<chair falling to the floor>>
<<footsteps running away>>

Tor: Alek, come back.

Alek: (from off screen) I'm fine right here.

<<sound of muffled pounding>>

Tor: See? It's one-sided. Now Hook is just as stuck as the ghost.

Alek: (from off screen) Nope. All good right here.

<<more muffled pounding>>

Hook: Oi! Let me out. I don't have a visitor's pass. Janine told us all what the side effects were. My poor manhood doesn't deserve that.

Hades: You'll come back over when I'm good and ready, pirate. Not a minute before.

Dahlia: My heart, you know he can't help himself.

Hades looks to Dahlia, the sour expression on his face softening.

Hades: You know I won't hurt him. Just maim him a little until he learns his lesson.

Kai: Goddess knows he could use it.

Gavin: (aside) Do you think they'd let us use that trick on Remi?

Asher: (aside) It's too late to teach that dog any new tricks.

Kiki: Oookay, I'm gonna wrap this up because if I have to spend any more time with Caspian, I'm probably gonna develop scurvy. When I said the horsemen were you, I meant you were all integral parts of the game the horsewomen were playing. They are too. They're the chess pieces this time around.

Gavin: (musingly) They're the mates.

Kiki: Ding ding.

Hades: Those fuckers. They won't answer my calls. I had an inkling something was happening with them, but now I have to talk to them.

Asher: Can you get them to come here?

Alek: (from off screen) I beg your pardon? You want to bring the Four Horsemen here? If they're anything like their counterparts, we'd need some sort of maximum-security holding cell to keep us all safe.

Tor: *snarls* No more cells.

Dahlia: (soothingly) He didn't mean for you. No one is going to lock you up ever again.

Tor: No. More. Cells.

Dahlia strokes Tor's hand and leans over to press a gentle kiss to his cheek. Tor settles at the touch, but his stare grows distant.

Hades: I'll continue trying to meet with them. With the fourth Prince now released, we are on the precipice of the point of no return. They may not know it yet, but the four of them are going to need allies.

Kai: We're sure another Prince was released?

Gavin: What else would you call the aurora appearing as fire-like tears in the sky?

Asher: We're sure, dragon. The aurora is another natural wonder that's been desecrated. That's the Prince's MO. **(adds under his breath)** And again, here I am backing up Count Chocula. The world really is ending. I bet pigs will start flying next.

<<Soft knocking on the portal>>

Kiki: Can I go now? I've shared the thing, and it sounds like you guys know everything else. Pirates of the Caribbean might be my favorite ride at Disney, but like that one pirate who walked into a bar with the wheel on his belt, this one be drivin' me nuts.

Hook: Ha . . . ha . . . ha . . .

Asher stands and moves closer to the camera.

<<clothes rustling>>
<<footsteps coming closer>>

Asher: You can see why I wanted to share that with you. There was no way any of you were going to believe me if you didn't see it with your own eyes. So, to recap, now we know who the missing pieces are. All that's left is to find them. Hopefully Hades is able to connect with them, but if not, maybe one of you will fare better.

Hades: Asshole, fetch.

<<happy dog barks>>

Asher turns away from the screen, revealing the portal just as the small dog jumps through.

Asshole: Come on, Captain Jack. We don't want your dick to fall off before you get topside again, do we?

Kiki: Such a good boy. Taking out the trash for your human.

Hook: Rude. You loved me before, remember?

Kiki: I'm just teasing. Be good to my girl, Cas. Or you'll answer to me.

Asshole: Can I pee on him just a little, boss?

Hook: If I see that leg lift even a centimeter, I will break it. Don't test me, dog. You're adorable, but I know you'll heal.

Asshole: You do remember who you're talking to, right? Cause I've got three fuckin' mouths, and I ain't afraid to use 'em.

Kiki: You sure do, cutie.

Kiki pets Asshole until he's happily panting against her leg.

Asshole: Ah, yeah. Right there. That's the spot. Gods, I love you, toots.

Asher returns to the camera shot, eyes wide.

Asher: Okay, so apparently the dog can talk. Great. I'm gonna sign off now before things get even weirder. If that is even fuckin' possible at this point. Try not to die in the meantime.

<<static>>

End of transmission.

CHAPTER TWENTY-SEVEN

SIN

"Holy shit. You weren't exaggerating when you said the sky was on fire, were you, Chris?" I murmured as we stood outside and stared at the wall of flames streaking across the sky as far as the eye could see. It looked like someone had clawed through the sky like it was a piece of paper and everything on the other side was burning.

"You know what this means, right?" Chaos asked, his eyes also trained upward.

"Uh . . . am I supposed to?"

"The next Prince was released," Malice answered for me.

"That's four. Fucking hell."

"Oh shit, you know it's bad when Grim sounds frustrated." I could feel the heat coming off the trail of fire. It reminded me a bit of that one time I tried tanning. Warm, but not unbearable. Still doing plenty of damage.

"We made it one full cycle without them finding us. That's got to count for something," Malice said.

"Only if it continues to be the case," Chaos replied.

"You think their odds are better now that there are more of them?" Grim asked.

"More Princes means more Knights means a fuck ton more creatures looking for us. That's a lot of ground they can cover."

"The wards are strong," Christian offered. "I set them myself."

"How strong?" Grim wasted no time with platitudes. It was one of the things I liked about him.

"Strong enough they keep strangers from finding this place. No one stumbles upon the château."

A stream of water had begun slipping past us and toward the nearby pond, the seemingly meaningless detail calling my attention to the melting snow. "Hey, would you look at that. I guess no one can deny global warming anymore." I nudged Malice with my elbow.

He glared at me. "Not the time to get political, Sinclair."

"If not now, when?" I shot back.

Shaking his head, Mal returned his attention to Christian. "What do you need in order to strengthen the protection we have? Not allowing us to be accidentally found is well and good, but we need this to be a fortress. The Knights are powerful. The Princes more so. They've no doubt been combing the world looking for us, and it's only a matter of time before they find Merri."

"They aren't the ones I'm worried about," Grim admitted.

Malice shot him a questioning look.

"Lucifer," he answered. "He's been too quiet. He's up to something. Scheming and plotting. There's no way he's leaving the fate of this apocalypse in any hands but his own."

"I will do what I can to shore up the wards, messieurs. You have my word. But . . . if it is Lucifer himself we are hiding from, I can only do so much. He is very powerful." Christian's face had gone deathly pale as he spoke.

Clearly he didn't love the idea of the Prince of Darkness showing up on his doorstep.

Same, buddy.

"Notify me as soon as it is done," Malice ordered before Christian nodded curtly and left us.

"You're bossy," I said.

"Yes."

"Great. Glad we established that. So what the hell are we going to do about this situation? Merri isn't going to like it, and she's not exactly safe here until we know those wards are at full strength."

"So?" Chaos asked, startling me.

"What the fuck do you mean, so?"

"That's been the case since the day we brought her to Grim's penthouse, and it's not going to change no matter what the fuck we do. Lucifer and his pets are hunting her. Period. We can add as many wards as we want, but one day, probably sooner than later, he's going to find her. She's too important to his end goal."

"That's why we have to get her pregnant," Grim said, little tendrils of darkness pooling around his feet and hands, betraying how upset he was. "She's useless to him as soon as that comes to pass."

"I'm just gonna say the thing we've been ignoring, even though you guys aren't going to like it," I blurted.

Malice's gaze swung to me. "What thing?"

"Knocking her up doesn't keep her any safer. It doesn't end when she's got a bun in the oven."

"What do you mean?" Chaos snarled.

"Lucifer is either going to find her and make a baby, or he'll find her and kill her when she's not useful to him. We are going to have to protect her from him until he's dead or locked up."

Chaos loosed a slow breath, his expression hard and eyes trained on the distance the way they usually did when he was contemplating strategy. "The antichrist is only one way that Lucifer wins. He's going to be obsessed with it since it's essentially an automatic victory, but even without Merri to help him make his heir, he can still fight his way to the top. That's the whole reason he's building a fucking army."

"So no matter what happens with Merri, if we want this to truly end, we have to kill him," Grim said.

"Can Lucifer even be killed?" Malice asked.

"If there is a way, I'll find it," he promised darkly.

"We know he's been caged before. So there's that. Could be a way to put things on pause while Grim figures it out," I offered.

The way those shadows coming from Grim darkened told me I had hit a nerve, but I didn't feel the least bit guilty. We all knew the truth. Merri was in danger. She would be for as long as Lucifer walked freely.

Malice's phone began ringing from his pocket, the blare of his ringtone cutting through the tension like a hot knife through butter. He pulled the slim device free and glared down at the screen.

"It's Hades."

All this talk of Lucifer and the possibility that he'd been masquerading as Hades during the last call put all four of us on high alert.

"Answer it," Grim demanded.

"On speaker," Chaos added.

Mal nodded and answered. "Hades, what is it?"

"Do you not know how to return a damn phone call?"

"You seem to think that my schedule revolves around you. Newsflash, it doesn't."

"Maybe you haven't noticed, but the world is fucking ending."

"Yes, I gathered that. I'm pretty well informed on that particular topic."

Hades heaved a very in-character sigh before clearing his throat. "Well, while you were gallivanting all over creation doing God knows what, I've been trying like hell to figure out how to save the damn world from Helene's fucking apocalypse. Think you could put aside your project and help?"

Little did he know our project and his were perfectly aligned.

The four of us exchanged looks. We still couldn't know for sure that this was actually Hades. But if it was Lucifer in disguise, it might be the opportunity we needed to figure out what he was up to and then use that information to keep Merri as far away from him as possible. At this point, I didn't think we really had any other options; we had to follow this lead. And from the resigned set of Grim's shoulders, he agreed.

"Tell us what you know," Grim barked.

"Oh, you put me on fucking speaker, Malice? Nice to hear your voice, Grimsby. Are the rest of your little band of brothers with you?"

None of us answered.

"Get over yourself and give us the information you so clearly have," Grim grumbled.

"Not over the phone. This is a conversation best had in person. As you so clearly demonstrated, you never know who is listening in."

"Fine," Grim growled. "Usual place?"

"I can be there by nightfall."

"Are we even sure that's still possible?" I asked.

Proof that I was yet another secret listener had Hades swearing up a storm.

"Nightfall. Don't be late."

The line went dead, and the four of us stood in heavy silence.

"Are we sure we want to do this?" Malice asked. "It could still be a trap."

"We don't have a choice," Chaos said. "Whether it's a trap or not, this might be our only chance to smoke Lucifer out on our own terms."

Hearing War echo my own thoughts made me feel pretty fucking good about myself. I was so much more than a drop-dead gorgeous face. And body. And dick.

"Someone needs to stay with Merri. We can't just leave her here with Christian as her only protector." Grim glanced over his shoulder at the house, a light blazing in Merri's window making it clear exactly where she was.

It was on the tip of my tongue to volunteer, but Chaos shocked me by beating me to it.

"I will."

"You don't want to run off into the thick of battle?" I asked.

"I'm the best choice to stay behind and play bodyguard. I literally tore that Knight's head off to save her."

He had me there.

Nodding, I conceded to him. "As you were."

"Why don't you stay with him?" Grim said. "Two sets of eyes are better than one."

"Is that safe?" Malice asked.

"You and I are more than capable of dealing with Hades."

"And if it's not Hades?"

"Then Merri still has a chance because out of all of us, Chaos and Sin are the most likely to succeed."

It was a shocking vote of confidence. And mildly terrifying, if I was being honest. I don't think Grim had ever said a kind word about me. But more than that, I don't think I ever heard him admit that he could lose.

And wasn't that the fucking scariest possibility of all?

CHAPTER TWENTY-EIGHT

MALICE

"Goddamn bloody dress codes. I'm a grown man. I'm practically a god. No one should be able to dictate how I dress myself. Especially not a private club in Las Vegas."

Sin leaned in my doorway, arms crossed and a petulant frown curving his lips. "I can't believe you're going to my city without me."

I glanced at his reflection in my mirror. "You're the one who opted to stay behind and help Chaos with Merri. Besides, you're far too recognizable."

"The people love me. What can I say?"

"Well, obviously you can't say anything without drawing attention to yourself. I don't have that problem."

Sin snorted as I pulled a deep plum button-down out of the wardrobe. I glanced between him and the nearly black fabric. "What?"

"Nothing," he said with an absolutely false air of innocence.

I glared at him as I pulled the shirt over my arms. "What?"

"Are you sure that's what you want to wear?"

Halfway through buttoning the shirt, I snapped, "Clearly."

"Okay then."

I knew he was fucking with me on purpose. I knew it, and yet it was still on the tip of my tongue to ask what was wrong with my selection. As I finished with the last button, I turned and faced myself in the long mirror. Dark trousers, sleek shirt, shiny dress shoes that pinched my fucking toes. I looked good. My beard was neatly trimmed, hair slicked back, violet irises brighter than usual because of the shirt.

"Not everyone wants to wear ripped jeans and studded belts, Sinclair."

"I'm just fucking with you, man. You look good. Better than good, actually. I haven't seen you cleaned up like this in at least a century."

"Fuck off."

"I'd say you were trying to impress someone, but Merri's staying here so . . ."

"I said fuck off."

Sin chuckled quietly to himself before sobering. "I need you to be careful. I'm not gonna be there to watch your back, and you and I both know that trusting anyone is usually the wrong decision. This could go badly."

"Could and probably will," I agreed.

"I mean it. At the first sign of funny business, get your ass out of there and back home."

I quirked a brow at the completely uncharacteristic display of concern. "Why, Sinclair. Are you worried about me?"

"Me?" He snorted. "No fucking way, but Merri will be pissed if something happens to you."

"Why would something happen to Malice?"

My gut twisted at the concern in Merri's voice as it filtered into the room from behind Sin. I was angry with her for invading my privacy, but dammit, the way she worried over me softened my ire just a little.

Merri appeared next to Sin in my doorway, her eyes widening in surprise as she took me in. "Where are you going?"

"Out," I said, my voice clipped and not inviting further inquiry.

Not that she heeded the warning.

"Out where? In case you've forgotten, the sky is fucking falling."

"Technically—"

"Not now, Sin," she said.

He mimed locking his lips before eyeing the two of us. "I'm sensing a little tension in here. Maybe I'll just take a walk while you two uh . . . work things out."

The incubus slunk away like the slippery snake he was, leaving me alone with Merri.

"Did you need something?" I snapped, pretending to fuss with my collar just to give me something to do.

"No," she snapped back.

"Then why are you here?"

"No, I mean you don't get to be mad at me. Because *I* am mad at *you*."

That drew my full attention. "How could you possibly be upset with me? I'm not the one who invaded your privacy."

Her eyebrows nearly flew up into her hairline. "Are you kidding me? You've repeatedly done exactly that."

"No. No, Merri, I haven't. We've been working on teaching you how to block would-be attackers. I've never done a damn thing we hadn't agreed upon. I attack, you try to block me. If you fail, I get in. That's how this works. But you"—I heaved a sigh and raked a hand through my hair, mussing the well-styled locks—"you broke into my mind and stole something I wasn't ready or willing to share."

"Malice, no, I didn't. I didn't even know what the hell I was doing. I just sent a little probe, thinking it would bounce off like it always does because you were being weird and just standing there staring off into space, and the next thing I knew, I was stuck in that memory with you. I wasn't snooping. It wasn't intentional. I didn't know how to get myself unstuck until you pushed me back out. It was an accident, and you blew up at me and treated me like I betrayed you or something."

"It was a betrayal!"

"No, it wasn't!" she shouted back at me. "It has to be on purpose to be a betrayal, and as I just fucking said, it was an accident."

She might have had me there, but I was too fired up to be reasonable.

"You never should have tried entering my mind at all."

"You do it to me all the time!"

"To test your barriers. To help you!"

"Well, where the fuck were your barriers, Malice? If you didn't want me in there, why did you let them down?"

Should I tell her my barriers were up and as strong as I could make them? Part of me worried that would terrify her. She was so worried about how powerful she was. The whole reason she'd originally isolated herself had been based on that very thing.

Before I could say anything, she softened her voice and took a tentative step toward me. "I never meant to pry. And I promise you, I will never use what I learned against you in any way. That's your secret, Mal. Your pain. I . . . I just wanted you to know that it's safe with me. You're safe with me."

But I wasn't. Not even fucking close.

If anything, I was in more danger with her than I've ever been in my existence. She'd already experienced parts of me no one else had been privy to. Both willingly and without my consent. The way she'd taken my pain from me the first time I fed her wasn't something I'd soon forget.

Fuck.

I couldn't continue letting her in. She would ruin me.

I'd barely survived Odette. But there was no way I would come back from Merri.

Odette had strung me up by my balls and broken my heart. Merri would consume my soul.

"I have to go."

"Malice—"

I brushed past her, not stopping even though I could hear the pain I was causing in the shattered way she said my name.

All I allowed myself was a brief moment to close my eyes. Then I pushed forward, shoving all these unwanted feelings down as deep as they would go.

I had a devil to deal with.

The scents of unwashed human, stale alcohol, marijuana, and hot garbage permeated the air as we materialized in the dark alley on the edge of the Las Vegas strip. The mortals would have you believe everything was business as usual, despite the notable destruction of some of the most iconic hotels. The Stratosphere was broken in half. The Sphere looked like a ruined disco ball, with only a few of the panels still able to flash their various images. The hot-air balloon at Paris had shattered, and the tower was little more than scaffolding. But people still came and went as though nothing was wrong.

At least those who could afford to bury their heads beneath the sand. The truth was in the alleyways. That's where the transients found shelter and the drugs they'd resort to in order to block out the terrors around them. Not much made me wary, but the sheer number of humans who were stood around staring blankly at things I couldn't see gave me the willies.

"It's a shame to see them like this," Grim said as we moved through the alley. "They're either numb to it all or ignoring it until the bitter end."

"You could help them on their way," I pointed out. "Wouldn't take much for you to reap them."

Grim gave a brief shake of his head. "It's not their time."

"Since when has that ever stopped you?"

"More often than you could know."

A man in a hood came ambling toward us, his steps slow and shuffling. Grim was careful to keep his hands in his pockets when it became clear that the guy had no intention of moving out of our way. We both did our best to shift to the right, but he still managed to fall into me. I caught him and carefully helped him upright.

Brilliant blue eyes captured mine as wholly as the hand fisted into the fabric of my shirt. "Stop wasting time."

"Pardon me?"

But apparently that was all he had to say on the matter, because he was already on his way once more.

"Bloody crazy," I muttered, brushing off my shirt.

"Let's get inside. I don't like the way it feels out here." Grim knocked on the nondescript door and waited for the bouncer to answer.

A small window on the door slid open, and Grim simply said, "Manhattan."

Without any fanfare, the door clicked open, and light spilled out into the alleyway.

"After you," Grim said, pulling it open so I could walk in.

Calling this place a club was a bit of a misnomer. There was no music, no crowds, no scantily clad servers offering drinks or other delicacies. Just a simple hallway leading the few who knew of this place's existence to a series of private rooms. I had little doubt that all manner of deals had been struck behind these walls. The kind of deals where world leaders found themselves assassinated or wealthy men mysteriously ended up dead in their hotel room due to an 'overdose.'

I didn't need anyone to tell me which door to open. Hades always used the same one, and I expected nothing had changed.

"Took you long enough," the man himself said as Grim and I stepped into the room. "Shut the damn door and let's get this over with. There's too much going on for me to be away for long."

Grim eyed the space carefully, but it was only the size of an average living room. And there were no hidden doors, meaning there was nowhere for anyone else to hide. "Just you tonight?" he asked.

A furry white head popped up in Hades's lap, followed by a loud bark.

"Just me and Asshole."

"Is that . . ." I started.

Hades jerked his chin in a nod. "Grab a seat."

"He's so cute and fluffy. It's a very different look for you, Cerberus."

The dog growled and snapped at me, even though there was no way he'd reach me. "Careful, now. He's likely to come over there and piss on your leg if you keep picking on him."

Grim took a seat at the round table, and I joined him. "What is this all about, Hades?"

The man in question steepled his fingers and leveled his gaze on us. "You four are the key to stopping this apocalypse."

"Tell us something we don't know," I muttered.

Hades's focus narrowed on me. "Is that so?"

I waved a hand. "Why don't you keep on with this big speech you've so clearly prepared, and I'll let you know when you get to something new."

"Well, I'd hate to simply repeat old news. How 'bout you tell me what you know, and I'll chime in when it's something I don't."

Grim sighed. "Why am I constantly surrounded by children?"

"The world is ending, the Princes are being released, and Lucifer is amassing an army. If he doesn't get his antichrist, then it will be a war to end all wars." I gave him the shortened version because I didn't want to bring Merri into this until it was absolutely necessary. This was definitely Hades, but he could still be on Lucifer's side.

Hades leaned forward in his chair. "The antichrist?"

"Yes," Grim added. "He's got two ways to win this thing. One, fight. Two, breed. The latter ensures him an instant victory."

Hades let out a low whistle and sat back in his chair, one hand rubbing his jaw. "Why does it always come down to procreation?"

"What are you talking about?"

"The horsewomen. It was the same for them."

When neither Grim nor I responded, Hades blinked and sat forward again, this time resting his forearms against the table and clasping his hands. "Seems like we got to one of those parts you don't know. Which is surprising, seeing as how you were instrumental in one of their games."

"Continue," I drawled, attempting nonchalance while my insides were squirming.

"Do you remember when we saved you four from Hel?" Hades asked.

Grim nodded.

"That woman who was with you? She's mine."

"Persephone?" Grim asked, his surprise palpable.

"Reincarnated," he confirmed. "Her name is Dahlia. She's Hel's daughter. The other men with me that night are also hers. We're actually the third such group brought together because of the horsewomen's games. All three groups have a child of one of the horsewomen at the center. And I've come to learn that you all are the fourth. So if you haven't found your partner, you need to be on the lookout for her."

Grim and I were careful not to give anything away, neither of us so much as looking at each other.

"So . . . you're telling us Death had a child?" I asked, heart in my throat.

"Yes. And so did War. Pestilence . . ." Hades flicked his eyes to me.

"Yes." I hated how tight my voice was.

"She had two."

I swayed in my seat, realizing that this was what she'd referred to when she said she had plans for our son. "Pan is part of this?"

Hades nodded. "From the way they tell the story, he's one of the only reasons they succeeded. He sacrificed his horns to save the others. Gabriel rewarded him with a second chance."

I didn't know what to do with that information. It was all I could do to breathe around the two-hundred-ton weight sitting atop my chest.

"And you think we're destined to find whom? Famine's daughter?" Grim asked.

I stiffened and pulled away from my thoughts of Pan as understanding dawned. That was why Merri was so powerful. She wasn't only a succubus. She was the daughter of Famine.

"That's the conclusion we've come to. You need to find her and keep her safe. Since Famine technically never got her round, your group may not find its way together as naturally as the rest of us did. It's really hard to know, but one thing we're certain of is that all four groups are going to need to come together if we want to stop this thing. Our army against his."

"So the rest of you are all working together?" Grim's tone was dubious at best. Hades didn't work with anyone. It was why he'd been sent to manage the underworld.

"Yes. My wife is pregnant. I can't afford to let my ego get in the way of ensuring our child has a world to grow up in."

I recognized his confession for what it actually was, a way of establishing trust. He was trusting us with something crucial, hoping we would do the same.

Too bad for him I wasn't about to risk Merri's safety. Not even for the one person we might call friend.

"And you want us to join your merry little band, is that it?" The temptation to do so, if only to come face-to-face with Pan, was enormous. From everything Hades had said, I could only assume Odette no longer needed him for some nefarious purpose. But that also meant that she had no reason to protect him, so my interference might even be more damning now than it would have been in the past. The possibility was enough to stop temptation in its tracks. I couldn't be the reason his life was robbed from him after he'd fought so hard for it. I would not be the reason she killed him.

"Well, yeah. You're in this whether you want to be or not. Fate hand selected you."

"Fate or Famine?" I asked.

"Aren't they one and the same at this point?"

Grim stood, his expression stoic and unreadable. "I'd say it was good to see you, but I don't like to lie. Hades, best of luck. We will be in touch."

He jerked his chin at me, a silent order to come with him. Part of me wanted to stay and pump Hades for information about Pan, but I also knew we needed to go. This was even bigger than we'd thought, and the implications from all we'd learned only made everything more complex.

We didn't simply need to breed Merri. If Hades was right, we might just be destined for her.

As we stepped out of the room, leaving Hades behind, I pulled out my phone, desperate to ensure Pan's safety. I typed out six words in a message to the lord of the underworld. Six words that crushed my sad excuse for a heart but I knew were necessary.

ME:

Don't tell Pan who I am.

A message came back almost instantly.

HADES:

You have my word.

CHAPTER TWENTY-NINE

CHAOS

It had been a long time since I'd cared what a woman thought of my appearance, but I really fucking cared now that Merri was in my life. I just needed her to want me a fraction as much as I wanted her. She'd been a constant presence in my mind since I woke up from that dream this morning. And the ache I'd felt for her had only grown since Grim's news. I had to hear it from her lips. I needed to know if she'd been there with me. If what had happened in that dream might not have just been my subconscious wishing for something.

Fuck, I could still feel her as I slid inside right before I so cruelly woke up.

The soft murmur of voices from down the hall turned my head and had me following in search of the woman I craved. She was with Sin, spending time with him, opening up to him, and I needed to be part of it. If I was going to claim my spot in her bed, I sure as hell couldn't do it from another room.

Her voice reached me first. "When's the last time you fed?"

"I'm fine," Sin assured her.

"Uh-huh. Liar."

"I'm not lying."

"I might believe you if I was blind. But I can see the dark circles under your eyes and the tension around your mouth. You're hungry."

"Merri, I am just fine. I fed not long ago, remember? You were there." Sin's voice turned playful at the end, and she let out a soft giggle in response.

"Then why don't you look it? Also, I've fed since then. If it's possible, I think I'm hungrier than ever."

By now I was just outside the door of the library, able to clearly make both of them out. They were facing each other, Merri with her hands on her hips, Sin with his head cocked as he studied her.

"I've noticed that too," he admitted. "Your appetite seems to grow the more often you feed. Malice said it could be a pseudo addiction after so many years of essentially starving your succubus."

"I didn't starve her," she protested.

"You were living off fumes, kitten. Basically eating a cube of cheese every time you felt like you might pass out. Like that one chick in *The Devil Wears Prada*."

Stepping inside the room, I cleared my throat to let them know I was there. "He's right, Red."

Sin preened from where he was standing next to her. "I'm sorry, I don't think I heard you. Can you say that again?"

I rolled my eyes. "She's right too. You look like shit."

"Rude."

"Just stating facts."

"Careful, I can do that too," he taunted.

"But I don't look like shit."

"No, but you're wearing cologne." Sin sniffed. "Trying to impress someone, Chaos? Got a big date lined up for this evening?"

The back of my neck warmed at his taunt, but I ignored it. The truth was, yes, I had a very important date. Merri just didn't know about it yet.

"You look great, Chaos. That shirt is really working for you," Merri said, her eyes drinking me in. "Are you going somewhere?"

Was that a little disappointment in her voice?

"I'm exactly where I'm meant to be."

Sin gave me a knowing look, mouthing, "Cockblocker," at me.

I might be, but Sin didn't realize that he and Merri had given me the ammunition I needed in order to do it. Merri might deny her own needs, but she wouldn't ignore Sin's.

I smirked. "The way I see it, seems like the both of you are in need of my services."

"What are you—ooooh. Oh my God, Chaos. Are you saying you're going to feed me?" The shock in Sin's voice would've made me laugh if his choice of words wasn't so annoying.

"You're not a baby bird, Sinclair. Shut your fucking mouth. And I'm not doing it for you. That's just a bonus, I guess."

"What did you have in mind?" Merri asked, eyeing me warily.

"You and me, Red. Sin can watch and take notes."

Sin scoffed. "Notes? *Notes*? I do not take notes. I give them. In fact, this is a great idea. A little role-play. Especially since we both know you're not ready for a threesome yet, big guy."

I didn't rise to his bait. Instead, I looked to Merri, whose eyes were bright with interest. "Role-play, huh?" I asked her. "You like that?"

Her cheeks went pink. "It sounds fun. I could use some fun."

Sin's smile grew. "Any limits to this fun, kitten?"

She bit down on her lip, eyes bouncing between the two of us before she shook her head. "No. No limits."

Hook, line, and sinker. Just like I'd thought. Merri hadn't wanted to take me up on my offer to help her out the other day, but now that Sin's needs were involved, she was able to do the mental gymnastics required to allow herself to give in. I so loved a loophole. They were key to all winning strategies.

He rubbed his hands together. "Excellent."

"So how does this role-play thing work?" I asked, stepping closer to Merri, my dick already half hard at the thought of getting to touch her.

"Well, let me put my director hat on. I have to think about this. Three of us, a nice big house . . . This is clearly screaming for a forbidden affair scenario."

I couldn't help but raise a brow. "How do you figure?"

"Well, if you won't let me participate, that takes out some of the biggies, like stepbrother and his best friend, or hot twins."

"But we aren't twins."

"It's called role-play, Chaos. It's all about imagination and timing. Which leads me back to the forbidden affair. If there's three of us, but only two getting their hands and other parts dirty"—he winked at Merri—"then it's gotta be the two lovers trying not to get caught, oooor, maybe a cuckold situation."

The way Sin was looking at Merri said all he needed was her permission.

She grinned, her gaze flicking to the chair nearby. "That seat is perfect for some observation."

"Yessss." Sin strode to the chair in question and adjusted it so it was near the fireplace with a solid view of most of the room. "Okay, so Chaos, you're the pool boy, and Merri, you're my sexy-as-fuck trophy wife."

I frowned. "Pool boy?"

"Milkman?" he tried again.

Merri made a face.

"Next-door neighbor? Business associate? Bodyguard?"

There was no missing the way Merri's cheeks went pink at the last suggestion. Or the pulse of arousal that emanated from her.

Sin snickered. "Looks like we found our winner. Bodyguard it is."

I had to admit, I liked hearing she saw me that way. Her protector. It wasn't that far off from reality, but up until recently, I'd only ever heard her refer to the four of us as her captors.

"I'm your husband, a famous Hollywood actor—obviously—and I've been away shooting on location. You're a star in your own right, and you've got a stalker. Chaos has been here protecting you for weeks, and the two of you have refused to act on your desire for each other, but I'm coming home, and you can't hold back any longer. Annnnd, go."

"Just like that?" I asked when Merri and I both remained awkwardly where we were.

"What more do you need? Fucking cue cards?" Sin jumped out of his seat and grabbed me. I gave him a healthy dose of side eye when he tried to manhandle me into position.

"What the fuck do you think you're doing?"

"Helping you. Now move. You can't fuck her from across the room."

While Sin had been giving me the weirdest pep talk I'd ever heard, Merri's arousal filled the space, the magic radiating from her igniting my own desire. She'd wandered to the bookshelves and was making a show of searching for something to read.

"Get over there, *bodyguard*. I'll come in when it's time. Just let the tension take over. We both know it's already there."

I wasn't much of an actor, and trying to come up with lines felt about as natural as plucking a cat. But I didn't need to pretend when it came to what I felt for Merri, and with the evidence of her arousal pressing against me, I didn't overthink it.

I moved until I was standing right behind her, my breath causing her hair to stir.

"He's on his way home. I'll have to leave you tonight," I whispered.

She stiffened, reaching back and pulling her hair over one shoulder to expose her nape. Fuck, the bite mark I'd given her in my dream was right there, staring me in the face. Breaking character for a second, I leaned forward and brushed my lips over the reddened skin. "I know about the dreamwalks."

The hand holding the book trembled, and she set it down hastily. "I-I'm sorry," she whispered, making to turn around.

I caught her by the hips and held her in place. "I'm only sorry we weren't able to finish what we started."

This time her gasp turned into a moan as I bit the same area again, deepening the mark I'd already left.

"Oh God." She leaned into me, her ass pressing against my hard cock. "One time. If you're leaving, I need to have you at least once."

Oh, so we were back in character now? I could work with that.

"How do you want me?" I rasped in her ear. Almost instantly, I realized it was the wrong question to ask. She was distracted by all the possibilities, and I didn't want her thinking. I wanted her lost in this moment with me.

It was then that I realized what a gift Sin had given me. His scenario gave me the opportunity to capitalize on the urgency I was already feeling.

"That's his car," I whispered, picking her up and carrying her over to the little desk a few feet away. It had some books and a lamp on it, but I sent them crashing to the floor with my arm.

"You'll have to hurry. He's going to find us."

I spread her legs and fitted myself between them before gripping her by the nape of the neck and forcing her to look into my eyes. "The next time you see your husband, I want my cum dripping down your thighs. I want you smelling like me. Full of me. Carrying me inside you."

"Fuck," she whispered.

"Exactly. You'll never forget me after tonight."

Merri's pupils were blown, her face and chest covered in a pretty flush. She was wearing a cropped V-neck workout shirt and some skintight black leggings. Reaching down, I let my knuckles caress her center, feeling the heat against my skin. She rocked against the barely there touch, demanding more. Taking a bit of fabric in each of my hands, I tugged. Hard. Her leggings split at the seam, baring her slick center to me.

"Look at how wet I make you, Red. You're already dripping for me, and I've barely touched you."

"I've been wet since the moment you walked into my life."

I couldn't tell if she was acting or not, but damn, I hoped for the latter.

Bending my knees, I lowered myself so I could bury my face in her pussy and make her come on my tongue, but she stopped me with her hands in my hair.

"No. We don't have time. Didn't you hear the front door? He'll be here any minute. Fuck me like you're never going to see me again."

I didn't have time to unpack the protest her words sent crashing through me.

"Then you better hold on to something, Red."

She obediently gripped the wood on either side of her thighs, spreading her legs wider for me as she did.

"Such a good fucking girl. I'm going to ruin you for him. You know that, right?"

"You'd better get to work proving it. My husband knows how to fuck me."

Jealousy burned in my blood at her challenge. My hands went to the fly of my jeans, and in moments, my bare cock was there, nudging at her hot, slick entrance.

She gasped as I pushed in just an inch, then she whispered, "It was real. The dream."

"I know."

"How?"

I reached up, palming the back of her neck and the bruise I'd left there. "You're wearing my mark."

Then I drove myself deep inside her until she cried out. Her body was made to accept mine. There was no other explanation for the way she made me feel. The lust coming off her in waves only added to my own, and soon she was holding onto me for dear life as I fucked her hard and fast.

Merri gasped and stiffened, causing me to falter for just a second. Her eyes weren't on me but trained on something over my shoulder.

"Don't stop on my account," Sin drawled.

I swear to the gods, if this motherfucker tries to stop me, I will impale him on something and leave him for dead.

I cupped her chin between my thumb and forefinger. “You better look at me and only me while I’m fucking you, Red.” Her big blue eyes snapped to mine, a moan breaking free as I continued pistoning my hips. “I want you to come for us now. I want you to show your husband how good I’m making you feel.”

“Fuuuck,” she whined, her pussy clenching around my dick.

I put my thumb in my mouth and sucked on it before reaching between us. Using the pad of my thumb, I rolled her clit and gave her that extra push she needed to fall over the edge. When she came the lights flickered and my knees went weak. I threw my head back and let my orgasm take me, a harsh bark of pleasure filling the room as my cum flooded her.

Being with her was even better than I’d imagined. More satisfying even than victory on the battlefield, which was saying something for me because, until this moment, that was what I’d lived for.

I started to pull back, both of us moaning as I slid out of her. I drank in the sight of her, primal pride filling me at the proof of her enjoyment. Those blue eyes were hooded, her chest rising and falling with rapid breaths. Her skin was luminous, her hair vibrant in a way that almost hurt to look at, alerting me to the fact that she’d fed.

“Damn, you guys are really fucking good at that. I didn’t even need to tell you what to do.” Sin’s voice was full of satisfaction and a little breathy.

I glanced at him over my shoulder. He sat in the chair Merri had assigned him, legs spread, dick still in his hand, cum splattered on his now bare chest. He looked just as healthy as Merri did.

“Glad we could help,” I muttered.

“One of the best meals I’ve had. Next time, I’m going to have to participate too. Can’t let you have all the fun.” He got up and winked at us. “Guess it’s time for another shower.”

I turned back to Merri as he left, wanting to return to our conversation about the dream, but whatever opening there'd been had passed.

She jumped off the desk, practically running as she followed Sin. "Yeah, me too."

After she was gone, I knelt down and picked up the tattered remnants of her leggings, balling them up in my fist. Merri might think she could avoid talking to me, that I wouldn't push for more between us now that I knew the truth. But she was wrong.

She could run, but she couldn't hide.

I'd find her. And when I did, there was no way I wouldn't make her mine.

CHAPTER
THIRTY
LUCIFER

You know, there was just something about an isolated tower in the middle of nowhere that did it for me. Call it melodramatic or even theatrical, but the image of a crumbling turret with the backdrop of a flaming sky and the crashing waves as the soundtrack set the mood for my apocalypse perfectly.

"Darling, I'm home," I sing-songed as I pushed open the door to my guest of honor's cell.

My lips curved in delight as I took in the sight of him on his knees, arms bound above his head.

"My, my, I can see now why leather isn't the go-to choice for prison attire. It really doesn't breathe at all, does it?"

Gabriel's head lifted, the matted blond hair that had been hiding his face falling to the side and revealing my brother's fury-filled eyes.

"Release me."

I laughed, my pleasure at having him at my mercy absolutely delicious. "No, I don't think I will."

"You cannot keep me here."

"Can't I? I seem to be doing a bang-up job of it so far." Holding up a finger, I started ticking off my achievements one by one. "Firstly, no one knows you're missing, so they aren't looking for you. Secondly, this tower is warded, so even once they figure it out, they won't be able to find you. Third, well, no need to give all my secrets away, are there? I'm not one of those silly villains who monologues all the good stuff. Show, don't tell, am I right?"

Gabriel took a shuddering breath and rolled his gaze up to the tiny barred window.

"How many are left?" he asked.

"Princes? Only three now, I'm afraid. You're going to lose. You know that as well as I. Why don't you join my side now and avoid all the messy fighting and torture, hm?"

"My answer to you now is the same as it was the last time."

I tsked, not needing to fake my disappointment. "Gabriel, Gabriel, Gabriel. What am I going to do with you? I have your wings, you know. Just say the word, and they can be yours again. Wouldn't you like to be returned to your full angelic glory?"

"Not if it means joining you."

So stubborn. My brothers always had been. Michael was even worse. But I did have one ace up my sleeve. The ultimate carrot I could dangle. Because truth be told, Gabriel was powerful, and having him on my side would be a boon.

"And what if I told you your Ruby was on the table? That the two of you could be together, and you'd have to sacrifice nothing to have her? I can give you that. All you have to do is say yes, brother."

Pure, unadulterated rage flashed in his eyes. "She is not yours to barter with."

"Really?" I laughed. "Because from where I'm standing, my reign is a foregone conclusion, which means everything and everyone that walks this realm belongs to me. Your soulmate included."

Gabriel shuddered, his head tipping up as though he were beseeching our father.

"He won't help you. And it's only a matter of time before you see things my way. I do have one question for you. How can you put your faith in a father who has done this to you?"

"What do you mean?"

"I am willing to give you everything you've ever wanted. I won't take your grace from you, I'll return your wings, I'll let you have your soulmate. All I ask is for you to stand at my side. *He* showed you your other half and then told you there was no way you could keep her unless you wanted to be disgraced. Unless you fell."

"God works in mysterious ways."

I smashed my fist into one of the stone walls, a loud snarl ripping through me at his obstinance. "You are such a fool, Gabriel. You are blinded by your faith."

"Better to serve in heaven than rule in hell."

My eye twitched at his butchering of my line. "I'm pretty sure that's not how the saying goes."

He stared hard at me, jaw set. "I pray one day you'll understand how easy it is to be selfless when you have something worth fighting for."

I snorted. "Pathetic, as always." Then I opened the cell door and began to walk away. "I do hope you'll take the time I give you to reconsider my offer, brother. Eternity in shackles is a long time."

He didn't answer me, but truthfully, he didn't need to. One way or another, I'd break him, and the Messenger of God would be mine to command.

CHAPTER THIRTY-ONE

MERRI

My boots made a squishing sound as I walked along the path that bordered the château. The earth was weirdly cracked and dry in some places, while other areas were thick with what could only be described as muck. The grass, or what was left of it, was flattened and brown, creating an endless sea of bleck in every direction. And the trees . . . They were stick-like sentinels, their brittle branches naked except for a few silent birds.

This was no spring awakening. It was something else, both sinister and unnatural.

As I drew in a long breath, my lungs protested the hot, dry air, the sensation reminding me of holding a blow dryer in front of my face and trying to breathe. It stung and burned, my chest tightening as though refusing the air. This place shouldn't feel like the desert. There was nothing remotely desert-like about it, especially not in the dead of winter. But here I was in nothing but a t-shirt and yoga pants, a bead of sweat running down the back of my neck as I wandered the property.

Out of all the catastrophes that had struck the earth since the start of this apocalypse, this was the first one that truly made me believe our days here were numbered. I could only imagine the havoc this fiery sky would create if it remained for much longer. I doubted it would be long before the oceans ran dry and it was no longer possible for us to do things like grow our own food or, you know, hydrate.

That thought sent panic buzzing through my veins. We'd all die slowly and painfully. And those of us creatures who were truly immortal would be destined for an existence of torture. The picture unfolding in my mind was absolutely terrifying.

As I rounded the corner, Christian came into view. He was standing on a small step stool near one of the windows while he ran his hand over the stone facade. Red liquid dripped from his palm, and I gasped as I realized he must be hurt.

"What are you doing? You're bleeding!"

Christian spared me a glance over his shoulder. "I'm strengthening the wards, mademoiselle Merri. Nothing to worry about."

I immediately felt foolish. Cheeks burning, I attempted to save face. "Oh, haha, right. I thought you might have cut yourself on a rusty nail or something. The last thing we need is you to get tetanus."

He smiled at me, gentle as always. "It warms my heart to know you would worry about me. But do not trouble yourself. I am just fine." He returned to what I assumed had to be delicate work, leaving the two of us in companionable silence.

I didn't have much—okay, any—experience with wards. Unless you counted the ones that kept me hostage at Blackwood. What little I did know was the equivalent of vampires like blood. Are you ready for this chestnut? Witches created and maintained wards. The end. So as you can imagine, watching Christian work was the apocalyptic equivalent of Netflix.

I was riveted.

"What do you need the blood for?" I asked.

He cocked one brow and looked at me like I might've asked the dumbest question ever asked. "The magic."

"Does any blood work or just yours?"

"Any blood will suffice, but mine is more powerful, and this ward requires a great deal of power."

"And do you just swipe it all over? Like that stuff you can put on cars to make the rain bead up on it?"

I could tell Christian was trying not to laugh at me. "Non. It is quite precise work, actually. I must place my blood in key spots to keep the ward intact. Think of it like a web. Everywhere the strands intersect must be strengthened."

This property was huge. That had to take ages.

He noticed my expression and chuckled. "It is a big job, but one I work on regularly. I have a schedule so that it is easy to maintain. What I am doing now is reinforcing the key wardlines. Specifically the ones that run parallel to the ley lines deep in the earth."

He was officially speaking Greek as far as my comprehension went. "Sounds hard."

Christian's grin told me everything I needed to know. He might as well have patted my head and told me I was pretty.

"How long is it going to take you?"

"The better part of a week. Unfortunately for me, no one else on this property is capable enough to weave magic of this kind."

"Not even Mal?"

"Not even him. Although don't tell him I said that."

"Don't tell Mal what?"

Both of us turned to face Sin as he sauntered toward us from around the corner.

"Nothing," I said with a cheeky grin.

"Oooh, keeping secrets, huh? Bet I know how to get you to talk," he said with a suggestive lift of his brows. "What are you doing out here, anyway? It's about as comfortable as a naked walk through the Sahara."

"Know that for a fact do you?"

"I never say no to a dare," he quipped with a flirty grin.

I left Christian's side and closed the distance between me and

Sin, giving him a light shove on the chest. "I wouldn't know anything about naked desert walks, but I couldn't stay indoors any longer. I spent a long time hiding in my room in *Iniquity*. The outside air is something I can't give up. Not yet."

His expression went soft and lost all of its playfulness. Well, shit. I hadn't been looking for pity.

"Come on, I want to show you something. It isn't outside because I'm not the biggest fan of hanging out in hell on earth, but I think you'll like it." He held out his hand for me and I took it without consciously deciding to.

Somewhere between my vow to keep my distance from these men and partnering with Chaos to feed Sin the other night, I'd completely given in. It was too hard to maintain walls between us when they were actively showing me that they cared about me and my well-being. Even if the only reason they cared was because of the accidental link I'd formed between us with my dreamwalks, it was still my catnip. As a person who'd spent so much of her life starved for affection, both physical and emotional, I had zero resistance against it.

His thumb rubbed the back of my hand as we walked. It was a simple gesture, but everything about it felt right. Fuck, my head was a jumbled mess of emotions. I wanted this kind of intimacy, and if I was being honest, I wanted it with him. With all four of them. Which meant I'd royally fucked up.

Christian might have woven a web to protect us all, but I'd trapped myself and the horsemen in one of my own making. One I hadn't even realized I was creating.

I still couldn't believe that I'd accidentally drifted into Chaos's dream. Or that he knew about it. He'd all but said he wished I'd stayed there. But that had to be because he didn't understand the danger my presence there posed to him.

"Hey," Sin called softly, giving my hand a tug and pulling me out of my thoughts. "You okay?"

"Yeah, sorry. The apocalypse has been on my mind a lot." I

gestured to the bleak landscape around us. "It's not as easy to ignore anymore."

He tilted my face toward him and smiled at me before dropping a light kiss to my forehead. "Well, let's see what we can do to get your mind off it, huh?"

Sin

Man, I hoped she liked what I'd set up for her. It was a gamble. This date thing. I'd never done something like this before, but I'd been studying romantic comedies for the last little while, and I learned that if you wanted to build something real with your girl, you had to make it about more than sex. I'd like both. Real and sex. It was fucking terrifying.

And not just because we weren't supposed to keep her.

But that was future Sin's problem. Right now, I was just focused on connecting with her in a way that made her hopefully want to fall into bed with me for no other reason than because she wanted to. Currently, the only way we ended up in Pound Town was when one or both of us needed to feed, but I wanted to be more than her go-to bangburger. I wanted to be her man. One of her men. Whatever.

Which meant I had to rely on more than my sexual prowess to get her to be with me. I had to woo her if I was going to become one of the men she wanted to keep. The fact that I even had to plot for something like that was absurd, but here we were. A little voice in my head crooned, *That's the difference between lust and caring about someone.*

If Hades was right and the four of us were destined to be hers, that meant our connection had to be a lot stronger than Lilith had indicated. Anyone could be a sperm donor. Not just anyone can be what Hades suggested. And sure, maybe the four of us might be the only beings in existence that were equipped to face off against

Lucifer, but that couldn't be the only reason fate had thrown us in Merri's path.

And we weren't even going to talk about the fact that Merri was probably Famine's daughter. I couldn't touch that one just yet because all it did was make me more convinced that she was made for me. It definitely explained why I was so drawn to her when I hadn't ever been drawn to anyone else. She was more like me than I'd known. Part horseperson, part sex demon. Aside from my counterpart, who had taken her succubus powers and warped them into something malicious, Merri was the only other person like me in existence. That couldn't be a coincidence.

"What in the world did you do, Sin?" Merri asked, her voice dragging me from my maelstrom of thoughts.

"I thought we could have a little sip and dip."

"A what?"

"You know, a date night. Where we sip"—I pointed to the champagne chilling in an icy bucket—"and dip." This time I pointed to the two tabletop easels I'd found and the array of old painting supplies. When Merri didn't immediately say anything, I rubbed at the back of my neck. "I did some research. It's supposed to be pretty popular. But if you think it's stupid—"

"No. No, Sin, I don't think it's stupid. You set this up for me?"

"For us."

The wonder on her face was reward enough. If she could just look at me like that all the time, I'd be happy. Wow, was this what dating felt like? I understood why people did it now.

"Where did you find this stuff?" she asked, moving over to the little stations I'd set up for us.

"Chaos's room."

She stumbled, turning around so fast the end of her ponytail whipped her in the face. "Excuse me?"

"Oh, didn't he mention his recreational activity of choice? He said he found it meditative. He's a big fan of that one dude. Mr.

Rogers, no. That wasn't it. The guy with the afro and the baby squirrel."

"Bob Ross?"

I snapped my fingers and pointed at her. "That's the one."

"You're telling me that Chaos, the horseman War, is a fan of Bob Ross."

"Yeah, big time."

Her eyes were as wide as saucers. "I . . . I have no words."

I smirked. "You should see his face when you mention happy little trees."

She beamed at me as she picked up a paintbrush. "So where do we start?"

Striding to the champagne, I picked up the bottle and popped the cork before pouring us each a glass. "First we sip."

She took hers and clinked the crystal with mine, bringing the flute to her lips and taking a taste. "Oh, that's really nice."

"Don't tell Mal. I found it in the back of his wine cellar, so I'm sure it's some super rare snooty vintage."

She giggled as she set her flute down. "What are we painting?"

"Each other."

She stared at me for a second before laughing. "I think you've wildly overestimated my artistic abilities. You're lucky if a stick figure comes out with the right number of limbs."

Laughing, I took up my place across from her and began squirting each color of paint out onto the makeshift palettes I'd fashioned from two paper plates. "You'll be fine."

"I'm really more of a paint-by-numbers girl."

"We'll call it abstract. Feel free to embrace your Picasso era."

She huffed out another laugh as I added some red and yellow to the plates. "Oh, I can pretty much promise that."

"I'm sure whatever you come up with is going to be perfect, kitten."

She shook her head at me, and I couldn't help but notice that she hadn't stopped smiling. Painting had totally been the right choice.

"So we just stare at each other and paint?"

I shot her my best smoldering look, which just made her giggle again.

"If you're really worried this won't work, we can always go to my backup plan."

"And what's that?"

"We can get naked, paint each other's bodies, and roll around on a sheet."

Desire flashed in her eyes—and in the air between us—but she pulled herself together before taking another sip from her glass. "Maybe next time."

Oh, definitely next time.

I wanted a commemorative canvas. I'd mount it above my bed so I could look at what we'd made together whenever I wanted. And now my dick was hard. No. This wasn't about sex. This was about romance.

We were wooing.

Woo-ing.

Not fucking.

Yet.

Nearly an hour later, we'd finished the bottle of champagne, and Merri was deep in concentration on her art. I'd completed my portrait ten minutes before but was perfectly content just watching her work. She had this adorable habit of sticking the tip of her tongue out every time she brought her brush back to the canvas.

"Let me see what you've got so far, kitten," I murmured as I came around the table to sneak a peek.

She gasped and spun around, blocking the artwork with her body. "No! It's not ready yet."

"Oh, come on. I just want to have a look."

I couldn't resist touching her, so I slipped my fingers around her waist and tickled the sliver of skin exposed by her shirt. She squealed and squirmed in my arms, bringing us face-to-face.

"You have a little paint on your face," I murmured.

"I do not!"

"Do too. Riiiight there." Before she could move, I swiped my index finger in what was left of her green paint and drew a line down her cheek.

"Sin!" she protested with a laugh.

I couldn't help myself. She was so fucking beautiful, and all that squirming she was doing had her rubbing up against me. I leaned down and kissed her until she was still and breathless.

Then, glancing over her head, I said, "Looks good. Best stick figure I've ever seen."

She huffed and shoved me back, but she was smiling.

As I returned to my place, I began humming a melody I couldn't get out of my head. It had been haunting me the past couple weeks. This happened sometimes; a song would come to me in fragments, sometimes just a few chords or maybe only some lyrics. I knew better than to chase it too hard. It would come to me when it was ready.

I didn't clock the change in Merri until I was back at my station. She'd gone pale, her eyes locked on to me, fingers clenched so hard around her brush they'd turned white. "Wh-where'd you hear that?" she asked.

"Hear what? Oh, the melody?" I shrugged. "It's just something that's been stuck in my head. I think it might be the beginning of a new song."

"Oh. Uh, okay." She seemed flustered as she hastily put her brushes away and glanced at the watch she wasn't wearing. "I have to go. I'm late for a session with Chaos. This was nice. Thank you."

Before I could protest, she rushed out of the room and left me with the taste of her lie in the air. I knew she didn't have any sessions this afternoon because I'd checked with both Chaos and Malice before planning my surprise.

So what the fuck was that about?

CHAPTER
THIRTY-TWO
MALICE

I moved through the house without really seeing my surroundings. Christian's update had been positive, though that was expected. His work with the wards was vital to our remaining here undetected, and the reinforcements he was fortifying would ensure that continued to be the case. It was reassuring to know that he only had a couple more days of work ahead of him.

Maybe once he was finished, I would start breathing easy again.

Liar.

I scowled at the little voice in my mind. The one that knew the conflicted way I was feeling had nothing to do with wards. I'd been out of sorts since Hades's revelations. Longer, if I was being honest, but who wanted to do that?

Merri's importance to the state of the world wasn't new information, but to know Hades considered us a crucial piece to this puzzle beyond simply breeding her was too much to take. He'd said we'd find our partner. That she was, like the other three before her, the key to stopping this with us at her side. I didn't want to be some lovelorn fool like him. Love made you weak. I was not weak.

As if the universe was listening to my thoughts and wanted to prove me wrong, I came to a dead stop outside of my room, my eyes drawn to the delicious redhead standing on her tiptoes as she attempted to place something onto the shelf above my desk.

For one long heartbeat, I gave into the temptation to drink in the sight of her in my space. Noting how right she looked amongst my most prized possessions.

"What are you doing?" I snapped, pushing back the *feelings* I didn't want to hold space for.

She let out a little squeak of surprise and flinched before spinning around to face me, her cheeks pink. "The door was open."

"So you think you can just walk right in?"

"I thought you might like to have that back. It's important to you."

My gaze went to the poppet she'd returned to its rightful place. I was such a raging arse.

Her eyes dropped to the floor, and she fidgeted. She looked so innocent standing there in her pajamas, a damp spot blooming over the fabric beneath her braid. She must have just finished showering and getting ready for bed. The thought of her naked and dripping in suds took over my mind, and I grumbled in disgust. Not with the image, but with my weakness. Here I was, acting exactly like the thing I most despised.

"I found it in the snow. I was going to give it back sooner, but . . . well, the sky is on fire and you hate me."

She sounded so miserable I had to intervene.

"I don't hate you."

"Yes you do."

"No, Merri. I don't hate you. Not for lack of trying on my part."

She tilted her head like an inquisitive little bird. "You wanted to hate me?"

"I don't think it should come as any surprise that I didn't want anything to do with you. But that wasn't exactly up to me, and despite my best efforts, you wormed your way beneath my skin anyway."

"This is a very strange conversation. If you're trying to convince me that you like me, I'm not sure it's working. Especially not after the way you've been avoiding me the last few days."

How did I admit to her that I was avoiding her because I liked her? Because the way she made me feel was the most unsettling thing I'd experienced in my long existence? She barreled through my walls like they weren't even there. No one should have been able to do that.

"I'm sorry I invaded your mind the way I did. I wish you understood that it wasn't on purpose. I will never intentionally do something that might violate your privacy again."

Fucking hell, I needed to fix this. She was taking the blame for something she couldn't help. I had caused it by pushing her and by opening her up to mind work.

"I suppose it's not the worst of my secrets for you to have stumbled across."

She blinked at me in surprise. "What?"

I moved closer, needing her to read the sincerity in my expression. Taking her by the hand, I admitted. "I might have, you know, overreacted." It was harder than it should have been to force the words from my mouth. I wasn't exactly an expert at apologies. In fact, I could hardly remember the last time I attempted one.

"I'm sorry, what?"

"Don't make me say it again."

She grinned. "Maybe just once more?"

"I'm sorry, hellcat."

The way her entire body relaxed and her face softened told me that perhaps I was better at this than I'd previously thought.

"Thank you for bringing it back to me," I murmured. "It does mean a great deal to me, even if the memory is painful."

She stepped close enough that I could smell her body wash, then lifted onto her toes to brush a sweet kiss on my cheek. "You're welcome."

She started to drop back and step away, but I couldn't bear the thought of distance between us. Grabbing her by the braid, I tugged, pulling her face back to mine. She stared at me in wonder, her eyes searching mine for some explanation for my completely uncharacteristic reaction. But there wasn't any I had to give. I was acting purely on instinct at the moment.

"Just once more," I whispered before my lips claimed hers and I gave myself what I really wanted.

Merri melted into me, her hands threading through my hair and her body pressed flush against mine. She felt fucking divine. Like she belonged there.

Just as quickly as it began, the kiss ended. I had to stop it, or I'd never stop. I'd lose myself in her.

It took a second for her eyes to flutter open and then another for clarity to take hold. Her fingers went to her swollen lips, and she took a hurried step back. "I . . . I have to go."

She was at the door before I'd even come back to myself.

"Merri, wait," I called.

Turning to face me, expression expectant, she waited as I'd asked. There was a stiffness to her, though. A guardedness I recognized as clearly as if I were looking into a mirror.

"Sessions resume as normal tomorrow."

She relaxed at the return of my gruff formality, and with a curt nod, she left.

Pinching the bridge of my nose, I did the only thing I could. I let out a heartfelt, "Fuck."

CHAPTER THIRTY-THREE

CHAOS

The musty scent of this underground lair we'd claimed for our secret meetings infiltrated my senses, making my lip curl in disgust. It reminded me far too much of my past life. Times when we'd been captured and held underground. When I'd been forced to fight my way out and leave my men behind.

My arms were crossed and face set in a scowl long before Grim ever deigned to show himself.

He appeared in the doorway and immediately clocked my expression. "What?"

"What happened to 'if you're not five minutes early, you're late'? Or does that only apply to us?" I snapped, gesturing to the other two horsemen who'd already joined me.

Grim's unaffected reaction told me everything I needed to know. That was exactly the case. He adjusted the cuffs of his shirt and leaned against the doorframe, gaze trained on me. "Well?"

"You're not even going to come inside?"

Sin chuckled. "I told you this would happen. Grim thinks the only secret meetings that matter are the ones he sets up."

"He's usually the only one who has something worthwhile to say," Malice offered.

I shot him a withering scowl. "Traitor."

"I'm simply honest. Grim is the oldest. He's the most patient. Death will wait out anything because he knows he will win."

Flinging my arm in Grim's direction, I asked, "Does that look patient to you?"

"Actually, yeah," Sin said, giving Grim a cursory once-over. "Definitely doesn't seem like he's got anywhere else to be."

I turned my attention to Malice, who was nodding along with Sin. "Pretty much the definition of patience."

"Fuck all of you." A pulse of power ran through me, causing the ground beneath our feet to quake.

"Chaos, are you quite finished with your little temper tantrum?" Grim rumbled as he inspected his fingernails.

It was all I could do not to throw something at him. "We think Merri needs to know the truth."

Grim arched a brow. "The truth?"

"Yes."

"And who is . . . we?"

"Jerry and Todd," I deadpanned before rolling my eyes. "Who the hell do you think I'm talking about?"

"So I'm to assume this is a decision the three of you have come to together?" Grim asked.

"Don't lump me into it. I'm still on the fence," Malice said.

The three of us turned to Sin, who stuffed his hands in his pockets and shrugged. "It doesn't feel right keeping it from her anymore. It was one thing before we knew her and cared about her." He sort of mumbled that last bit, almost like he was embarrassed by the admission. "Now it just sort of feels shady. I don't like lying to her."

"You're not lying to her. You're just not telling her the whole truth," Malice offered.

"I'm far from the morality police, but I'm pretty sure that's lying."

"A lie of omission is still a lie," I said.

"That's a stretch. We are keeping something from her for a very specific reason." Grim finally pushed off the doorframe and entered the room, leaving the door open.

"Shoe on the other foot, would you feel the same if it was Merri keeping something from us?" I asked. "What if she was using us to try and get knocked up? Would you be okay with that?"

Malice couldn't control his reaction to that, his lip curling in disgust and his eyes flashing with rage.

I knew exactly what I'd done with that one. Malice had intimate knowledge of what that exact scenario felt like. He'd be much more sympathetic to our request if I could make him see the similarities. Surely a three-to-one vote would go in our favor.

"But she's not," Grim said simply, as if that magically canceled out the point I'd just made.

"Grimsby, you cannot possibly imagine this ending well if she finds out we've been scheming behind her back this entire time."

Grim's expression remained stoic, his eyes meeting mine briefly before he shrugged. "Then she hates us. It doesn't matter at that point, does it?"

"I've been working so hard to get her to like me. I don't want Merri hating me when she finds out. None of you can say you don't care if she hates your guts. You all like her just as much as I do."

I shifted uncomfortably where I stood, finding myself in the uncommon position of agreeing with Sin. Now that I'd gotten a taste of what it could be like to have Merri, I didn't have any intention of letting her go. He was right. I did like her.

Malice looked uncertain, which didn't surprise me, but Grim's reaction did. It was so rare to see any tangible emotion on his face, and right now, he was pissed.

"And this is the exact reason we cannot tell her. Why are you incapable of seeing that?"

As he finished speaking, his face flickered, revealing something I hadn't seen in centuries. His true face. Sin blinked, taking an unconscious step away from the angry horseman. I didn't blame him. No one wanted to be present when Grim let that side of himself out to play.

"What do you mean?" Sin asked.

"We cannot afford for Merri to be upset with us and thereby isolate herself. We must accomplish our goal. Don't you get it? The feelings of one do not outweigh the lives of millions. We have to succeed. We have to impregnate her. If we don't, we may as well just hand her over to Lucifer right now because what the fuck are we doing here if we aren't serious about putting a stop to this?" Grim's shadows spread across the floor, betraying his irritation. "We can't risk her falling in love with any of us either."

"Why not?" I asked before I could stop myself.

"Because we have already seen her loyalty. She'd choose staying with us over saving the world. We can't allow that to happen."

"How are those mutually exclusive?" I asked, for once not being able to follow the logical path he was setting.

"Because we will always be who we are. Our purpose will not change simply because we averted this apocalypse. It will still fall to us to begin another, which means we can never give her back the same. We will never be free to choose her over the destiny set before us."

My gaze swung to Mal, who'd gone painfully quiet during Grim's outburst. "Do you agree?"

"How can I not? We are who we are, Chaos. It is unchangeable."

I knew that any hope Sin and I had of swaying Malice to our side was gone. Grim had made an excellent point. No matter what happened with this apocalypse, we were still the horsemen. We didn't exist for things like love and companionship. That future was not available to us, and it never would be. Merri deserved better.

She deserved a life that had the potential to include some kind of happily ever after, not some bastardized version of whatever relationship the four of us might offer.

"Fuck," I whispered, more upset now than I'd been before this meeting started. It had been so long since I'd known hope I'd forgotten the hole it left when it was torn away.

"I can tell you finally are starting to understand our situation," Grim said, not unkindly.

"You know what? Don't invite me next time," Sin said, shoving away from the wall and striding toward the door. "I fucking hate book club."

CHAPTER
THIRTY-FOUR
MERRI

Warm beams of sunlight spilled through the window in my favorite room of the house. I was perched on the window seat with my bare toes resting on the small end table I'd commandeered while I meticulously painted each nail. I didn't even want to think about how old that piece of furniture was, but I was certain if Malice caught me, he'd have strong opinions about what I was doing. Nothing jazzed up antique lacquered wood like a little *Bastille My Heart* dripped along the surface.

At the thought of Malice, my heart gave a flutter in my chest, bringing to mind everything I'd been trying so hard to forget. Not because that kiss he'd laid on me hadn't been amazing. It had. Easily one of the top five kisses I'd experienced in my life. Okay, top three. Each one had been given to me by men in this very house.

Men I'd obviously tricked into caring about me.

And *that* was why I couldn't dwell on the kiss. Or Sin's date. Or the brush of Grim's leather-clad finger over my lips. Or the way Chaos had felt while he was inside me.

Fuck.

Perhaps I'd tricked myself into caring about them as well. The bond worked both ways, didn't it? I'd manufactured feelings and shot myself in the foot while doing so.

I let out a frustrated breath, hating the position I'd found myself in. I wish Lilith had never told me about the bonds. Then, at least, I could pretend that there was a future for me and the men I was lusting after.

Footsteps behind me yanked me out of my pity party, and I snapped my head toward the sound. Christian stood a few feet away, a feather duster in his hand.

"Oh, mademoiselle, forgive me. I didn't realize anyone was in here."

"It's no problem. I just really like the light in here. It's perfect for painting my toenails."

He glanced at said toes and gave an approving nod. "The color suits you."

"Thanks. Don't tell Mal I used his table, okay? I have a feeling he might have some issues with that."

Christian's lips quirked in a barely there smile. "I might know where a few replacements are stored in case of a casualty." But then his smile faltered, and he glanced over his shoulder as if uncertain if he should stay or go. That hint of uncertainty from him raised an internal alarm.

"Everything okay?" I asked.

"I . . ." He gave another cursory check around the room. "Mademoiselle, forgive me if this is over the line, but there is something I need to share with you."

"Okay," I said, my gut churning at the seriousness in his tone. I capped the nail polish and straightened, giving the groundskeeper my full attention.

"I have been debating whether or not I should tell you this. I am and always have been loyal to Monsieur Laurent. But you have been so kind to me, and I can see you have a gentle and loving soul. I would hate for you to be taken advantage of."

Taken advantage of?

"Christian, what are you getting at?"

"I overheard the four of them yesterday when I was assessing the dry goods we keep on hand. We have been trying to build our stock in case of emergency."

"Overheard who?"

It was a stupid question, but I needed to hear him say it. That was the only way to make it real.

"Monsieur Laurent and his three guests. There is no other way to say this . . . They are racing to impregnate you with one of their children."

A ball of ice settled in my stomach. "What? Impregnate me? But . . . why?"

He shrugged. "I do not know. It seems as though they are in competition with each other. Why do men do any of what we do?"

I shook my head, unable to form words in the wake of the truth grenade he'd just lobbed at me.

"One thing that was clear, mademoiselle, was they had no intention of letting you know about their plans."

I couldn't believe what he was saying. It was unthinkable. I had no idea why they would want such a thing, but also no reason to doubt Christian. As he'd just pointed out, he was loyal to Malice. There was no upside to him telling me what he'd overheard, just a lot of risk.

The horsemen might have seemed human to me lately, but the truth was, they were far from it. They were powerful, god-like, and didn't play on the same field as most creatures. To them, creating a life might have been the ultimate test of their prowess.

But why me? Why were they playing with me and my emotions? Because they were stuck with me? Because I was convenient? Because I'd all but begged them to fuck me so I could feed?

I knew I was being a little dramatic. If anything, they'd been the ones begging me, but that was because of the stupid bond I'd accidentally created.

Wait. Could that be the reason?

Had I unwittingly made them want this? Knowing what I did about Malice's son, the thought made me sick to my stomach. He seemed like the last being in existence who'd want another child, given the trauma he had around his firstborn.

Another thought swam to the surface. Sin had been trying to get in my pants from day one. I'd resisted both him and Chaos.

The words Chaos had growled in my ear about wanting to breed me echoed in my mind. I'd stuck to my guns and turned him down that time, but then I'd accidentally dreamwalked with him again.

Had the bond only made me more compliant?

"Please take care, mademoiselle. I do not wish to see you hurt. If you decide this place is no longer safe for you, all you must do is tell me. I will help."

"Why? If they found out, they'd make you pay." It seemed a funny detail to worry about, given everything else swimming through my mind, but it also felt like the only question I might actually get an answer to.

"Because you cared for me when no one else did. And you remind me of my sisters. I would risk the same for them. And I would wish that if they found themselves in your position, there would be someone like me there to look out for them."

"Thank you, Christian."

He held my gaze, his sincerity and concern boring into me. "I will leave you to your painting. You know where to find me if you need me."

I nodded, mutely watching as he left the room.

The sun that had only minutes earlier felt so warm and cheerful no longer felt like a safe haven.

How could I have been so careless and forgotten who the horsemen were?

They were the quintessential bad guys. Of fucking course they would be up to some shady shit, even if they did catch magically induced feelings. I was such a trusting fool, blinded by a set of handsome faces and a few sweet words.

God, what was wrong with me?

But the more important question was, what on earth was I going to do now?

CHAPTER

THIRTY-FIVE

GRIM

"This is bloody ridiculous. We've been over it more than once," I grumbled under my breath as I stormed down the hall toward Merri's quarters. "You say you can take care of yourself, but I don't see any evidence of that. And if you act like a child, I'm going to treat you like one."

I stood outside of her door, glaring at the wood as if it had personally offended me. She'd been hiding from us for days. At first, I'd thought Chaos had gone against my wishes and spoken to her, but he, along with the others, had sworn she was avoiding them as well. It had gone so far that she actively left a room if one of us walked in.

Death was not one to be ignored.

I did the ignoring until the time was right. That didn't change, no matter how pretty the subject might have been.

With an annoyed huff, I reached for the knob, pausing before I turned it. She could be in the middle of filming. If she was feeding, I didn't want to interrupt her. The last glimpse I'd gotten of her had revealed deep purple smudges beneath her eyes and formerly vibrant ruby hair that had lost its luster. The time she was able to safely go between her feedings had dropped significantly. None of us understood exactly why her window of power was closing rather than getting wider, but there was no denying our little succubus was starving. She was on the verge of collapse once more. I'd seen it firsthand in my penthouse and had promised myself I'd never let her get this way again. But here I was, breaking that promise.

"Wildflower? Are you in here?" I called as I knocked. My heart ratcheted up when there was no answer. "Merri?"

Still nothing.

I flung the door open, suddenly terrified I'd find her slumped over her desk or in a limp pile on the floor.

"Merri. Where are you?"

Apprehension danced across my skin as the weight of silence filled her room. My gaze raked across every corner, and when I didn't find her, I rushed into the attached bathroom, expecting to find her unconscious in the tub.

Nothing.

She wasn't there.

"Where the fuck are you?"

Dangerously close to spiraling completely out of control, I reached for the hairbrush resting on the basin. Before giving into my panic, I needed to assure myself whether there was true need for it. Plucking one long strand of hair from its bristles, I sent a little tendril of my power to it, testing it for advanced signs of decay. In other words, I was checking for evidence that death was waiting in the wings. If anyone would sense it, it would be me.

Reassured, I left the bathroom and began making my way out of her boudoir, but a flash of red from the window caught my eye, and I stopped in my tracks. It was her, outside in the maze with the fucking groundskeeper. If he wasn't careful, she'd drain him dry at this rate.

It had been too long since I'd last got to look my fill of her. Even in her current state, she was stunning. Though her cheeks were far too hollow and I could make out the rise of her collarbones beneath her thin shirt. Merri needed to feed. Why was she punishing herself?

Why is she punishing us?

Because she's a stubborn brat who needs to be taught a lesson.

Knowing that the dreamwalk was real. That she'd been there with me, on her knees, calling me Daddy while all but choking on my dick had done something to my brain. Clearly, she didn't know what was good for her, or if she did, she was ignoring the truth. But I knew. I knew exactly what she needed: Her Daddy to make damn sure she got everything she required.

It looked like I was going to have to force the issue.

Keeping one eye on her, I absently reached for a scarf she'd slung on her desk. Lifting it to my nose, I breathed deeply of her unique scent. My body reacted instantly, my dick coming to life behind my fly. All it took for my body to react was a fleeting thought of her these days, but that fragrance was like a lightning bolt of lust.

Again I took a deep breath, needing another hit of her. The result was the same. My balls were now aching for release.

"Fuuuck, baby girl. If you would let me feed you, I'd be the best meal you ever had," I rasped as I opened my belt and began to work my zipper down.

My fucking cock was a throbbing length of steel, and it needed attention. Lucky for me, I had Merri's perfume scented scarf at the ready. A little bit of her to help ease the ache. I'd only just wrapped my hand around the base of my shaft when it happened. Merri smiled at that rodent.

Absolutely fucking not, wildflower.

Your smiles are for us.

I cast a glance at her bed, so soft and inviting, just like her. She needed a reminder of who she had at the ready, just waiting to give her sustenance. Four of the most powerful men in history. Not a sniveling little Frenchman who didn't know his arse from a hole in the ground.

Shoving my trousers and boxer briefs down my hips in one rough move, I set my sights on a new task. I wouldn't only use her scarf to find release for myself; I'd leave my pheromones all over her bed. The succubus in her wouldn't be able to resist such a strong echo of sexual energy. She'd have to give in and feed.

If she insisted on running from us, fine. I'd chase her. There was no escaping from Death. Not once he set you in his sights.

Tossing the scarf on the bed, I crawled across the duvet, taking extra time to rub my face along the blanket as I made my way up to the pillows. Her pillows. Fuck, this whole bed smelled like her.

I rolled my pelvis into the fabric, the image of Merri spreading her sweet thighs for me filling my mind. The subtle friction had me biting back a groan, my hand grabbing for one of her pillows as I did it again. God, this was as much for me as it was her. It had been too long since I'd found my pleasure because I'd been waiting, saving it, for her.

"Oh fuck."

The thought of Merri coming back to her room, of finding the present I was leaving her, spurred me on.

"What are you going to do when you smell me all over your sheets, wildflower? Will you touch yourself and think of me?"

My words were just a harsh whisper as I rolled on my back and brought the pillow to my mouth. Reaching down, I stroked my cock, precum spreading over the head and down the shaft as my arousal grew to near-painful heights.

I thrust into my hand, pretending it was her tight cunt as my climax loomed ever closer. This wasn't going to last much longer, but it didn't need to. In fact, it would probably be for the best if I was able to flee the scene of the crime as soon as possible.

"God, Merri. Do you taste as good as you smell? I need to fucking know."

With another tortured groan, I rolled back onto my hands and knees, bracing myself just above her duvet. The scarf was close enough to my face that it was catching the soft pants of my breath. I bit down, taking it into my mouth and nearly suffocating myself in her scent, pretending that it was her I was drinking in.

Once again the hit of her scent had me near feral. I continued to roll my hips into the pillow that was now lodged firmly beneath me.

I could hear her moans and whimpers as though they were real. The sound of my Merri making herself feel good was something I could never forget and something I'd always be able to conjure at will.

"Fuck, you're such a bad girl, teasing me by flirting with that other man." I thrust hard, balls tightening at the thought of spanking her into submission. "You'll take your punishment, wildflower. You'll take every fucking thing I have to give."

Her voice from my dream flashed into my mind, the words sending me over the edge. *"Am I forgiven, Daddy?"*

I came with a ragged groan, hips pistoning into her bedding as jets of cum shot across the fabric, rubbing into my skin and soaking the pillowcase. She would know I'd been here. There was no way to hide it. But I didn't fucking want to. My girl was hungry, and I'd just rung the dinner bell.

"Come and get it, wildflower."

CHAPTER THIRTY-SIX

MERRI

I stood in my doorway, my entire body coiled tighter than a spring. One second I'd been intent on taking a shower to remove the sweat and grime from my walk in the labyrinth, the next I'd frozen like a cat who'd just caught sight of its prey. Grim had been in my room. I could fucking smell him even if he hadn't left clear evidence on my bed.

"What did you do, Daddy?"

Saliva pooled in my mouth as a low throb of arousal pulsed in my belly. I'd been hungry before, starving even, but not like this. The bed called to me like a beacon, beckoning me as though it was the only port in a dangerous storm.

The last three days had been hard. I was no closer to having an answer about what to do with the information Christian had given me, so I'd done the only thing I could. I hid—from all of them. Escape wasn't an option. Not only did I have nowhere to go, but a starving succubus wouldn't last long without causing chaos, and the last thing I needed was to basically toss a flare over my location for the ones hunting me.

My bedding was rumpled, the duvet askew and blanket out of

place, but the thing I homed in on was my crumpled scarf that lay next to a pillow I certainly hadn't put in the middle of the mattress.

I was kneeling on the bed before I even made a conscious thought to do so, my baser urges now firmly in the driver's seat. Fuck, he smelled delicious. I needed more of him. Face pressed to the duvet, I inhaled as I ran my nose over the places he'd been. Lust permeated the fabric, a teasing phantom promise of what he could give me if I would only ask.

A strong pulse of arousal ran through me, making me uncomfortably slick between my legs. Now I was hungry and turned on. I couldn't think beyond those two pressing needs. Closing my eyes, I imagined what Grim would have to do to make such a mess of my bedding, my hand gliding down my leggings as I did.

The white pillowcase edged in delicate lace with a pretty blue floral print had a suspicious wet spot in the center. He hadn't. Had he? Reaching out, I ran my fingertips over the damp patch before bringing them to my nose.

Oh, he most certainly had.

I'm sure most women would probably have been horrified by the discovery, but a horny succubus? For me, it was the most delicious gift.

"Daddy's been naughty," I whispered, smiling to myself. "Defiling my pillow."

I ran my fingers over the wetness again before bringing them to my lips and sucking them clean. His flavor burst on my tongue, just like it had when I'd sucked him off in our dreamwalk. Closing my eyes, I fed. It wasn't near enough, but it took the edge off.

The flood of him through my system, both in my mouth and via my power, was enough to bring me right to the edge of climax. Grim had done his job well. He'd known I would be helpless to resist such an offering in my current state.

I couldn't find it in myself to be upset with him for his heavy-handed approach. I was too moved by the reason behind it. He'd wanted to take care of me in the only way I'd allow.

Goddamn him.

There was so much he didn't know. So much I'd done wrong.

And I couldn't forget the little detail of their competition to knock me up. They'd kept plenty from me. I should still be angry.

Instead, I was touched and turned on.

I could only do something about one of those things. Which was why I focused on the pressure of my fingers circling over my clit, my face turned towards what would for now and forever be known as Grim's pillow.

I came in less than a minute, a quiet but powerful orgasm that had my toes curling and his name escaping me on a whimper. I hoped he was listening.

Apparently the combination of finally feeding plus the release was enough to send me straight to sleep. Or maybe that was just the safety I felt being surrounded by the scent of one of the only men who'd ever tried to take care of me.

I knew this hadn't changed anything. I was still pissed, and if and when I confronted him, there was a lot he had to answer for. But nothing was going to be resolved tonight, so there was no use worrying about it.

Instead I was going to bask in my afterglow.

An afterglow that turned into a beautiful dream I hadn't expected. Soft, warm sand, a perpetually setting sun, the calm lapping of waves, and strong hands rubbing my back and working out the tension I hadn't even known was there.

"Oh, keep making those noises, darling, and I'll have to break my promise to remain a gentleman."

"I'm pretty sure you never made one of those," I murmured, sleepy and content.

Luc's laughter was warm against the back of my neck as he leaned down to press a kiss there. "Of course I did."

"That feels so good," I moaned when he dug his thumb into a particularly stubborn knot.

"What has you so tense, my beautiful girl? You're here in

paradise with your dream lover. What could make you strung so tightly?"

I sighed and rolled over, sitting up on my elbows so I could face him. He was still one of the most beautiful men I'd ever seen. My brain was a real hot guy factory.

"My life is a shit sandwich."

Luc frowned, his eyes seeming to sparkle in the sunlight. "How so?"

I scrunched my nose and shook my head. "I'd rather not talk about it. The whole goal of this place is to forget the real world."

He studied me intently. "Maybe your subconscious knows you need something else."

"Like what?"

"To unburden yourself."

Rolling my eyes, I huffed out a laugh. "You don't want to hear this."

"Try me."

"The men who are supposed to keep me safe are secretly trying to get me pregnant. How's that?"

His eyes widened, and a flash of anger lit their depths. "What?"

"Yeah. It's a whole contest. Who can knock up the succubus fastest."

He reached out for me, his hand curling protectively around my ankle. "You need to get away from them."

"And go where? The world is ending, and I also have the legions of hell after me. Apparently."

"Don't you have somewhere you can run to? Someone who'll take you in?"

My thoughts immediately went to Lilith. "Not anymore. It's not safe for me to go back home."

"Not home. Somewhere else. Somewhere no one would know to look for you."

Andi's offer came to mind, but just like I had in real life, I'd dismissed it. Malice knew about Andi from his snooping in my phone. I wouldn't be safe with her for long, and the last thing I wanted to do was bring four angry horsemen to her doorstep.

"Merri, you can't stay with these men. They aren't putting your best interest ahead of their devious desires. You're so lovely and kind. There has to be more than one option. Who else do you know?"

His name was on the tip of my tongue like it had been summoned there. "Cole."

"Who is that? Is he safe?"

"He says he loves me."

"That doesn't make him safe."

"Doesn't it?"

Luc smiled. "I suppose it might. Go to him. Run from these men who want to use you as their broodmare."

"I'm not strong enough."

He reached out and stroked my cheek with the back of his hand. "You know what you need to do to remedy that."

"But you're not real."

His knuckles brushed over my cheek again, their warmth causing me to curl into them. "Aren't I? I can touch you. That seems pretty real to me."

"You're just a figment of my imagination."

"So you should probably listen to me, then, since it's really you telling yourself what you need."

Something about that logic turned my brain into a pretzel. "I guess."

He leaned forward and feathered his lips over mine. "Let me give this to you, Merri. You need it."

"Yes," I whispered, so fucking hungry it hurt. My skin was hot and tight, breasts heavy, thighs rubbing together uncomfortably as I searched for friction I couldn't find. I needed him to give me some relief.

Luc smiled before closing the distance between us fully and kissing me, his tongue pressing between my lips and his body lining up with mine. I wrapped my arms around him, urging him closer.

There was a yawning ache inside of me, begging to be filled.

"Please."

"Oh, it will be my pleasure to give you everything you could ever wish for, darling. And maybe even something you wouldn't dare think of."

He ground his pelvis against me, the hot, thick length of him everything my body craved. But before I could move my panties aside and welcome him into my body, a terrible, twisting ache collected in my belly. Pain unlike anything I'd ever known radiated from deep within me, making my back arch and my eyes well with tears.

I screamed, skin on fire, gnawing agony burning in my gut.

Oh God. Was I dying?

No longer writhing beneath a sexy man on a beach, I was back in my bed, trapped in a nightmare created by my body. Pain was rolling through me in waves, making it hard to breathe, let alone think clearly.

Another scream tore from my throat, and Sin burst through the door, chest heaving, eyes wild.

"Merri? What—Oh fuck."

Before he could even reach me, every muscle in my body seized, and my eyes rolled back in my head. Darkness took me then. Blissful nothingness that pulled me deep, deep, deep down where I was safe and nothing could ever hurt me again.

CHAPTER
THIRTY-SEVEN
LILITH

My footsteps echoed in the corridor as Drystan and I walked toward my office. I knew what needed to happen, the calls I had to make, but I didn't have to like it. Those horsemen had thus far let me down, and it was time to take matters into my own hands. I hated getting my hands dirty.

Okay, lies. I loved meddling. I just preferred utilizing others to do the heavy lifting for me.

"Lilypad, you look tense. What's the matter?"

Drystan ran his fingers over the chain connecting us before he finally reached my wrist. I fought a shiver of desire, not wanting to let him know he'd elicited a response so easily.

"I think we need to reinstate the Council."

He sneered. "Does that mean I'm going to have to tolerate more of my brethren running around?"

I rolled my eyes. "I don't know what it is you have against Jensen and Finbar."

"They dare to believe their Shadow Court holds a candle to the realm of nightmares."

I gave our chain a tug. "It's not your realm anymore, pet. You belong to me now."

"It will always be my realm. An exiled king is still a king," he muttered, pouting.

"You were never crowned, darling. You're a prince at best, a fugitive at worst. The Wild Hunt considers you an enemy for a reason."

"Not a legitimate one."

"Does it really matter?"

"Not to them," he said with a shudder and a haunted look in his eyes.

He'd only spoken about the horrors he'd experienced at their hands once, the night he'd come to me to strike a deal. My protection in exchange for his loyalty and servitude. Since then, I'd hidden him in plain sight, the chain between us muting his power and making him impossible for The Hunt to find. I was the only thing standing between him and annihilation. Sort of like Merri and this fucking apocalypse.

The migraine I'd only just managed to stave off came roaring back, and I whimpered, lifting a hand so I could squeeze the bridge of my nose.

"Dearest," he murmured, his concern evident. Crombie wore his mask of petulant prince so perfectly no one but me knew the truth. He was far kinder and more compassionate than anyone would ever suspect.

"It's just a headache. I will be fine."

"Come, let's get behind closed doors, and I will take care of you."

I let out a disbelieving laugh. "How exactly will you do that?"

A waggle of his eyebrows piqued my interest. An orgasm just might do the trick, at least temporarily. I had a sneaking suspicion this headache had a great deal more to do with the state of the world rather than a lack of endorphins.

"Well, you can certainly try," I murmured, allowing him to pull me into his body as he pushed open my office door.

The light was off, so the room was bathed in darkness when he pressed me up against the wall, mouth feverishly working the length of my neck.

"Mmm, that's a nice start, pet, but you know there's a better use for that tongue."

He let out a dark chuckle before nipping my collarbone. "I'm working up to it. Patience isn't your strong suit."

If we'd been in a scene, I would have punished him for that reply, but there were times I loved it when he took control. Even craved it, perhaps, though they were few and far between.

Just as my Drystan cupped one large palm between my thighs, the lights blazed to life, followed by a voice that sent ice through my veins.

"Oops, sorry. Did I interrupt?"

My eyes snapped over Drystan's shoulder to my desk, where none other than the Prince of Darkness sat. He was playfully perched atop it, a wicked smile curling his lips.

"You've looked better, Lilith. I must say, you're honestly looking a little tired. Aren't you getting your beauty sleep?"

My belly churned with unease as Drystan turned around to face the only creature I truly feared. Lucifer Morningstar had once been my everything until the day he cast me aside. That was when I learned the truth of what had been between us. He'd never loved me. I was simply a means to an end. A demon created by his promises of eternal love and power but used for something far different. My link to Adam's second wife. Eve.

"What are you doing here, Lucifer? We had a deal." I crossed my arms, if only to hide the trembling in my fingers.

"A deal? That's not how I remember it. If I recall correctly, you stole something from me and ran off into the night. I simply chose not to give chase . . . *wife.*"

Drystan visibly flinched before reaching for the chain between us and tugging with a strength I had never seen from him.

"Drystan, no!" I shouted, terror crystalizing within me as the delicate golden links broke.

Power rushed through the room, the scent of ozone filling the air, electricity crackling around us.

"What did you do?" In one foolish move, he'd just thrown away the only thing protecting him from The Wild Hunt's pursuit. As soon as they caught wind of his return, they'd come for him.

Lucifer laughed and clapped his hands.

"I suggest you choose your next words with care," Drystan snarled. "She is mine."

"Oh, this is delicious," Lucifer crooned. "Look at you and your little boyfriend. Good for you, darling. I wasn't faithful either, in case you were curious."

"We were never married," I ground out, losing what little hold I still had on my temper.

He waved a hand. "Practicalities. We would have been if such a thing existed in those days."

Drystan was vibrating with barely contained fury, and I could feel his power coiling around the room like a gathering storm. The more power he used, the easier it would be for his enemies to find him. I had to put an end to this before everything I'd worked so hard for fell apart in a single fell swoop.

"Lucifer, enough with this nonsense. Why are you here?"

"Very well. If you insist on foregoing the pleasantries, we can get straight to business." He sighed and playfully rolled his eyes before pinning me with his gaze once more. This time there was no cruel smirk on his lips, just the promise of violence. "If you want to leave this room alive, you will tell me everything there is to know about one Meredith Deveraux."

The Mate Games: Apocalypse continues with Malice, coming soon. You can pre-order your copy here but we also have something to make the wait a little more bearable.

You can download your copy of Chaos's bonus scene at www.themategames.com/ChaosBonus or you can download it on audio and listen to it at www.themategames.com/ChaosAudioBonus

THE MATE GAMES UNIVERSE
BY K. LORAINE & MEG ANNE

WAR

OBSESSION

REJECTION

POSSESSION

TEMPTATION

DEVOTION

PESTILENCE

PROMISED TO THE NIGHT (PREQUEL NOVELLA)

DEAL WITH THE DEMON

CLAIMED BY THE SHIFTERS

CAPTIVE OF THE NIGHT

LOST TO THE MOON

DEATH

HAUNTING BEAUTY

HUNTED BEAST

HATEFUL PRINCE

HEARTLESS VILLAIN

Apocalypse

Sin

Chaos

Malice

Grim

Lucifer

More by Meg & Kim

<u>Twisted Cross Ranch</u>

A dark contemporary cowboy reverse harem

Sinner's Secret

Corruptor's Claim

Deadly Debt

Also by Meg Anne

Brotherhood of the Guardians/Novasgard Vikings

Undercover Magic *(Nord & Lina)*

A Sexy & Suspenseful Fated Mates PNR

Hint of Danger

Face of Danger

World of Danger

Promise of Danger

Call of Danger

Bound by Danger (Quinn & Finley)

The Chosen Universe

The Chosen

A Fated Mates High Fantasy Romance

Mother Of Shadows

Reign Of Ash

Crown Of Embers

Queen Of Light

The Chosen Boxset #1

The Chosen Boxset #2

The Keepers

A Guardian/Ward High Fantasy Romance

The Dreamer (A Keeper's Prequel)

The Keepers Legacy

The Keepers Retribution

The Keepers Vow

The Keepers Boxset

The Forsaken

A Rejected Mates/Enemies-To-Lovers Romantasy

Prisoner of Steel & Shadow

Queen of Whispers & Mist

Court of Death & Dreams

Standalones

My Soul To Take: A Forbidden Love Meets Fated Mates PNR

ALSO BY K. LORAINE

The Blackthorne Vampires

THE BLOOD TRILOGY

(Cashel & Olivia)

Blood Captive

Blood Traitor

Blood Heir

BLACKTHORNE BLOODLINES

(Lucas & Briar)

Midnight Prince

Midnight Hunger

~

THE WATCHER SERIES

Waking the Watcher

Denying the Watcher

Releasing the Watcher

~

THE SIREN COVEN

Eternal Desire (Shifter reluctant mates)

Cursed Heart (Hate to Lovers)

Broken Sword (MMF menage Arthurian)

~

STANDALONES

Cursed (MFM Sleeping Beauty Retelling)

REVERSE HAREM STANDALONES

Their Vampire Princess (A Reverse Harem Romance)

All the Queen's Men (A Fae Reverse Harem Romance)

About Meg Anne

USA Today and international bestselling paranormal and fantasy romance author Meg Anne has always had stories running on a loop in her head. They started off as daydreams about how the evil queen (aka Mom) had her slaving away doing chores, and more recently shifted into creating backgrounds about the people stuck beside her during rush hour. The stories have always been there; they were just waiting for her to tell them.

Like any true SoCal native, Meg enjoys staying inside curled up with a good book and her fur babies . . . or maybe that's just her. You can convince Meg to buy just about anything if it's covered in glitter or rhinestones, or make her laugh by sharing your favorite bad joke. She also accepts bribes in the form of baked goods and Mexican food.

Meg is best known for her leading men #MenbyMeg, her inevitable cliffhangers, and making her readers laugh out loud, all of which started with the bestselling Chosen series.